Also by Steven Key Meyers:

Novels

That's My Story

Save the Max Man!

Family Romance

The Wedding on Big Bone Hill

Queer's Progress

Springtime in Siena

All That Money

Good People

Nonfiction

The Man in the Balloon:
Harvey Joiner's Wondrous 1877

Plays

A Journal of the Plague Year,
and Other Plays and Adaptations

My Mad Russian

Three Tales

Steven Key Meyers

My Mad Russian: Three Tales

**SMASH
& GRAB** press

CARAMOOR *is the estate in Bedford, New York (Katonah post office, fifty miles north of Times Square) famous for its house museum, year-round concerts and summer music festival. Starting in the late 1920s and through the 1930s, Walter Tower Rosen and Lucie Bigelow Rosen, his wife, built Caramoor as their weekend and summer retreat, incorporating in a large Mediterranean villa eight or ten period rooms pried from European manors and palaces, and filling the place with art and furniture collected over many years. A cultured lawyer, Mr. Rosen was managing partner of the investment bank Ladenburg Thalmann & Co. The equally cultured Mrs. Rosen — descended from the Phelps and Dodge families of copper-fortune fame — toured North America and Europe performing on the first electronic instrument, the Theremin.*

What follows are two novels and a memoir inspired by my first job, working — a callow, somewhat callous youth — at Caramoor as its teen-aged underbutler from 1970 through 1972.

My Mad Russian *is a fictional retelling of the story of the Rosens' relationship with Dr. Léon Theremin, the Russian inventor of the world's first electronic musical instrument, the Theremin.*

Another's Fool *is my fictional treatment of the Caramoor Music Festival's early days, in the 1950s.*

And I Remember Caramoor *is a memoir of my time there.*

My Mad Russian

for my bosses at Caramoor,
Michael Sweeley, Renée d'Arcy,
Hilton Bailey, Martha Coyle Clark and Robert Clark,
with gratitude

Society passed up and down Fifth Avenue in its automobiles, and was there a furrow of anxiety on Society's brow? — None.

P.G. Wodehouse
Psmith Journalist (1915)

Prologue

MY DETECTIVE, BOB ARGENT, left word with my butler in Katonah on Friday evening past 11:00. Our guests, including the distinguished cellist who played after dinner, were retiring, and Dora and I were thinking of bed, too. Argent couldn't stay on the line, but Franz promptly found me, and I had William bring the Cadillac around at once. In the country the November air felt raw.

"Fill 'er up, Mr. Berlin?" William asked as I got in the limousine's rear. Normally he gassed up at our own pump at the end of the weekend.

"We'll do that on the Taconic," I snapped. "No time now."

That put the proper spirit into him. To Dora I'd explained that the office needed me. In not quite 20 years of marriage, the office never before had needed me on a Friday night, but she said simply, "Hurry back, dear. Or will you stay in town?"

"William, of course drive carefully," I now directed, "but please with as much speed as you can."

Tilting his cap backwards, he said into the mirror, "Yes, sir, Mr. Berlin," and thanks to the 16 cylinders of the Cadillac's engine, I was flung against the leather and the trees began to flash past amidst screeches of rubber as we rounded the curves. It was a 1930 model that I bought one week before the 1929 Crash; four years later, I was finally glad that I had. Grabbing a strap, I hung on, nauseous.

Without further instruction William pulled into the service area on the Taconic State Parkway, a cottage group in glazed terra-cotta suggestive of an alpine village. Arc lights blanched the attendants' faces as they filled the gas tank. We were off again within minutes.

"The house, Mr. Berlin?" William asked when decisions loomed at Hawthorne Circle.

"Yes, please, the house," I affirmed.

My limestone Beaux-Arts house on West 54th Street, on the north side of the block anchored at Fifth Avenue by the University Club and at Sixth by the Warwick Hotel.

But Argent's summons came because of what he observed, not at my house, but a few steps to its west, a brownstone six stories tall, also my property.

For years I'd rented it to gentry for whom a good address was desirable, but such had vanished with the Depression, or my tenant had, anyway. After the house stood vacant for two years, I turned it over for a peppercorn rent—$1 a year—to a young genius, Piotyr Alexandreyevitch Primov. The mad Russian had fitted it out as an electrical laboratory, where he conducted research on his Shado-Rays and assembled for sale models of his *Primover*, the electric musical instrument powered by Shado-Rays whose eerie caterwauling made me absolutely weary of life. My wife, however, was devoted to the *Primover*, studied with its inventor, and was fast becoming an expert player.

Though the *Primover* was something new under the sun, it was Primov's mastery of Shado-Rays in the astonishing form he called *Shadio* that was to serve as the basis for the large investment I was preparing.

Shadio held the promise of being an advertising and decorating gold mine. It would transform the American streetscape: Anyone walking past a store window rigged with *Shadio* would unwittingly animate it. Bulbs and neon tubes would spark alive, flashing slogans and patterns in lights across the glass, designs, colors and rhythms varying with the personal silhouettes and individual gaits of passersby. More mundane devices might also operate at *Shadio*'s command, lifting items, revolving them, making the window dance.

And in the home, *Shadio* would vary the lighting, open or close curtains, turn radios on or off as one moved from room to room, as well as function (so Primov assured me) as a burglar alarm. All in all, *Shadio* represented the most enticing financial opportunity of my life, and the first of any appeal to come my way since the Crash.

On 54th Street, I told William to pull up. He nosed to the curb in front of the bar of the Dorset Hotel, some yards west of my house. Thus ended our mad dash into the city from Katonah, 50 miles in just over one hour.

We sat behind the car's smoked glass. All was quiet. Aside from an occasional taxi, a man or two walking down the street, nothing moved. My house was dark, but from every floor of Primov's house next door light leaked from the edges of shades and curtains.

The bar's brass revolving door whooshed a breath, my door opened and Bob Argent, removing his hat, shoved into the backseat next to me.

"Evening, Mr. Berlin," he said. "Sorry to disturb you so late."

"Hello, Bob. What's—*uh*—going on?" Though I tend to fall into it when with him, I don't think his argot suits me.

"Not quite sure, sir. No one's gone in or out since I called your house. Telephoned after a Ford dropped off four guys who ran up Primov's steps and forced the door with crowbars. Set off a god-awful racket—some kind of alarm. One of them might have been your friend Col. Dead Eyes.

"The Ford drove off, but see that van?" He pointed to a one-ton delivery truck, of the kind used by department stores, idling 20 yards ahead of us. I saw the flare of a match in the driver's side mirror. "Pulled up five minutes ago. Seems to be waiting."

"What for, Bob?"

"Won't know until that door opens."

Argent is an outstanding private detective who does occasional work for my firm, though usually of a financial nature. A World War veteran, and veteran, too, of several years with the New York City Police Department, he holds degrees earned at night in accounting and law. In addition to being smart and capable, he is of intimidating size. Weeks earlier I had asked him to keep watch on Primov for me.

We sat for some time. I sorely wanted to go in my house and put the whole thing out of my mind, pull the covers over my head and go to sleep. Instead we sat. William ran the engine to keep the heater going.

Finally, starting with the top floor, every light in Primov's house went off and its double front doors opened. A short figure in a shapeless overcoat peered up and down the street, leaned over to set the door stops, then straightened up to allow three men to maneuver past him a sizable packing case on a hand truck. The men carefully bumped it onto the stoop.

The short one—who indeed looked to be the man I called *Col. Dead Eyes*—closed the door and wiped down the doorknobs with a cloth he shoved in his pocket as once more he looked up the street. A limousine was no unusual sight on that block.

"Bob, you're right," I said. "The one in gabardine? That's Col. Dead Eyes."

"Christ," said Argent. He knew that I believed Col. Dead Eyes to be an operative of the secret Soviet security apparatus, the NKVD.

Meanwhile the men were bumping the packing case down the steps to the sidewalk. It measured some three feet wide and three feet deep by four feet tall, and obviously was heavy. I imagined that it must contain the newest *Primover*, retail price $2,000, for the instrument's dimensions were about the same when its two protruding antennae were detached. But to make it howl required plugging it into an accompanying trunkful of tubes and speakers; did the thieves not know this?

The men eased the hand truck across the street, to the rear of the delivery van. Opening its back doors, they lifted out and positioned a ramp, then effortfully pushed the packing case up and aboard the truck.

"So Stalin has a hankering for electric music?" I remarked. "Wants a *Primover* of his own, for those long Moscow nights?"

And welcome to it, I was thinking.

"Mr. Berlin, I think they're making off with the original," Argent murmured. "With the man himself."

This jolted me. "Good God! Can he breathe?"

"They won't kill him. Not in transit."

The truck's rear doors slammed shut. Two men apparently remaining in back, the other two piled into the cab and, with a grinding of gears and gasps of exhaust, the vehicle did a U-turn and made for Sixth Avenue, passing within ten feet of us. The name of a Grand Street furniture store adorned its side.

Argent prompting William, we turned around and followed past the El. I expected the truck to take us to the waterfront regions of piers and warehouses that I visited only when embarking on a Cunarder.

But at Seventh Avenue it turned. The stoplight delayed us, but we were able to make up the distance in the gaudiness of Times Square, catching up as it passed the gilded front of the Paramount Building. Our car felt dangerously conspicuous as we followed.

"Any guesses, Bob?"

"Headed for the docks, Mr. Berlin—maybe in Jersey. At any rate, I'm guessing some pier used by Finnish ships."

But not Jersey; just short of the Holland Tunnel, at Charles Street, the truck turned onto Pier 46 and was admitted through sliding gates of chain-link. We hung back across West Street, beneath the elevated highway, and watched it approach a gangway slanting off a freighter tied up at the wharf. On the ship's bow was painted some long Scandinavian name. The Hudson River gleamed like metal.

The truck's rear doors were thrown open, the ramp flung down and—men massing to arrest its slide—the case guided to the ground. Working the hand truck beneath it, they wheeled it towards the gangway.

"OK, Mr. Berlin, we call the cops now, we get 'em on New York soil," Argent said. "'Cause, though Shorty don't know it, they're going to have to winch that thing aboard, and that takes time."

"Let me think about this, Bob."

The packing case proved too wide for the gangway. The men turned it. It almost fit; almost, but not quite.

"If we wait, Mr. Berlin, it becomes Federal. Once it's on board? Customs, Coast Guard, F.B.I."

"Bob, I understand. But there are considerations."

Among them the fact that only that afternoon— November 17, 1933—President Roosevelt had announced that, after 15 years of shunning the Soviet Union, the United States was granting it recognition and posting Mr. Bullitt as Ambassador. That presented the possibility that the packing case in effect was a diplomatic pouch—that Primov was already beyond our reach. The thought gave me a sick feeling in the pit of my stomach.

At the gangway, caps came off and heads were scratched. Col. Dead Eyes furiously shook his fist at the gunwales—he was positively jumping up and down—and there ensued much shouting back and forth. Displeased, he crossed his arms and began slapping his bicep in a Cossack tattoo. The men put themselves into attitudes of waiting.

"Mr. Berlin, there's a phone just back there." Argent gestured at a lunch counter aglow beneath the highway. "Shall I? Call the cops?"

"Not just yet, Bob." I nibbled at the carved ash wood handle of my walking stick. "Let me think."

1.

I ATTENDED the famous Armory Show of 1913 on its first Saturday.

It was a miserably cold and gray February day. I would have preferred to go during the week, when it was less crowded, but that wasn't feasible. Also I would have preferred to walk — my flat was in Murray Hill, across from Morgan's house — but the sidewalks were slippery, so I took a taxi the dozen blocks downtown. The streets were slick, too, and my cab nearly hit a horse hauling a coal wagon.

The Armory, a brick structure with stone dressings and an arched roof, stands on Lexington Avenue at 26th Street. I stepped inside, paid admission, from the program familiarized myself with the layout of the various "galleries" laid across the floor — arranged by country of origin — and plunged into the worst. I knew I wouldn't like it. I went because one had to.

I work as a banker, but live for art. Isn't art everything? But art, to my understanding, is the emotive representation of reality expressed through techniques developed over the centuries within historical context in any number of highly developed genres. What lay before me in the Armory was not *art*. It was broken crockery thrown on the floor in tantrums of aggression and dementia.

Is mine too severe a theory? It accounts for the art I love; for Chopin and Rembrandt, Michelangelo and Titian, Goya and Giotto, Palladio and Beethoven. What I beheld, mockingly installed in that misleadingly martial space, gave me no esthetic pleasure—only chills of foreboding.

Nor was I alone in feeling thus. To the contrary; the Armory buzzed with shock and disapproval, and also with a species of fear. People edged past the "art," keeping as far away from it as possible, tracing serpentine routes with the care of Hansel and Gretel threading their way through the forest.

Every generation faces the challenge—and responsibility— of pushing the traditions of art a little bit forward. I admit mine—I was born in 1875—has had difficulty doing so. After all, Delacroix achieved a kind of perfection; no one can dispute that. But to give up and leap into the cesspool? The graces and values of accurate drawing and observation, of emotional weight, *gone*? The Impressionists, whose blurred glitter was, in its day, so confounding, have themselves been shoved aside by the even more uncouth crew that, embracing chaos and abstraction, created the disassembled, disintegrated, decaying works that at the Armory surrounded me.

When I reached Galleries H and I—*French Paintings and Sculpture*—I had penetrated to what New Yorkers were already calling the *Chamber of Horrors*, for there lurked the dread *Cubists* and *Fauvists*. Awful, but I could at least discern method, albeit a madman's, to the Cubist ambition of rendering three dimensions on a surface of two, method dependent on geometry and exact analysis. However hideous the work, I could hear Giotto whispering *at last! at last!*

Hung between simpleminded puddles by one Matisse was the show's *pièce de resistance*, M. Duchamp's *Nude Descending a Staircase*—a bird's nest of lines and angles in thin brown pigments, an abstract rendering *sans* modeling of body mechanics. Spectators sidled past in repulsion, regarding her — *it* — as they might a horse dying in the street.

But to my eye even more flagrant were the bleeding daubs of a picture near by called *Woman with Mustard Pot*. Really, *Woman with Mustard Pot?* It depicted a female with a scooped-out face melting in blue and orange. She was disfigured; diseased; poxed; boiled alive; opened up on the operating table; ready for the embalmer, or fresh from him; dug up from the grave and anatomized by Dr. Burke. Monstrous, outrageous, a canvas with not a tittle of beauty to it! Every verity lacking!

Yet somehow it presented, and with gorgeous tactility, a personality complete.

It was the work of somebody with the unlikely name of Pablo Picasso. He worried me. If he were not so obviously a charlatan, he could be a master. There was a kind of logic to his picture's curling drips and patches of color; even (my stomach rebelled) a kind of music. A step beyond Piero della Francesca? Surely not. But as to skill? Skill was not lacking to M. Picasso.

This is what upset me, standing there, as others went past, shunning Miss Mustard Pot as they might a deformed beggar. Not an inviting work of art; not a Delacroix around which a crowd could safely gather for enjoyment and edification (there was an excellent Delacroix across the way). No, seeing this woman lean her head on her arm and confidently invite our scrutiny was like watching the burning fuse of a stick of dynamite, and I appreciated that she'd been painted with just that insane, anarchistic desire to blow us all up!

One year later, at Sarajevo, everything did blow — to smithereens — and it's not put back together yet, nor shall it be, not in my time, if ever. And courtesy of MM. Picasso and

Duchamp, a glimpse of the fractured future was given me.

I snorted, thinking thus direly, even as a young lady stepped in front of the picture and peered at its expert impasto. A statuesque beauty in the pre-War mode—the corset at (literally) its last gasp—she resembled a bouquet of flowers; ruffles spilled forth at her breast, and her hat burst into bloom above her flower-like face.

Inclining her head, she remarked to me, "She wants bicarbonate of soda."

"Or a nice dark tomb in which to rot undisturbed," I answered.

She laughed, this girl, and I came to myself.

"Beg your pardon, Miss. I didn't mean to speak with such vehemence."

"I don't see the harm. She's not to your taste?"

"No," I declared. "But she disturbs me because in fact she's telling me that my taste isn't up to understanding her. A most sophisticated work, and see how *beautifully* painted. She thinks herself a masterpiece! So it won't do to sneer. No, with the assurance of a Leonardo this picture *insists* on engaging me— assumes I'm prepared to come to grips with it."

And the young lady paid me the compliment of looking again at the mess, trying to penetrate it. This while spectators wound past Indian file, careful not to get close lest they catch its germs.

"Is it, then, great art?" she asked.

"If great, it's a greatness that brings no comfort."

"Cold comfort, then, without padding against the pain of life? But is that padding what we should most value in art?"

It was this remarkable speech that caused me to forget M. Picasso's pigment debauch and really look at her. Not only was this young lady tall, she was lovely; pale, with excellent features, blue eyes, and a high and delicate voice. She was exquisite, in fact, but possessed definite personality. The oldest verity expressed in new form.

"Indeed," I answered, "but when one's face is shoved into a dung pile—"

"*There* you are, Dora," rasped a harsh voice whose accompanying bright eyes lit into me fiercely.

I recognized the older woman who swept in to claim the girl: Mrs. Jenny Brase, the *Honourable* Mrs. Jenny Brase, wife of the Hon. Lionel Brase, former wife of the copper magnate Jed Jessup, and herself the daughter of Fred Sweet, newspaper publisher and Lincoln's Minister to France. An illustrious figure, encased in the gray-haired frame of a woman only some ten years older than myself.

"Yes, Mother," said the young lady—giving me a shock as great as Picasso's.

I hastened to introduce myself. The mother reared back dismissively, but Miss Dora Jessup grasped my fingers warmly.

I understood Mrs. Brase's behavior—that of the mother of a most eligible young woman. Her daughter was a great heiress, and known to be a handful. Two years earlier, she had fled her family, then sojourning in London at Halliwith House, the Hon. Mr. Brase's father's Mayfair residence—his father, formerly the richest commoner in England, having been elevated to Viscount Halliwith—and weeks later been discovered (by an excited popular press) living in a theatrical boarding house, and in fact to be playing a part in the suburban revival of a Pinero play. I remembered the headlines.

Mrs. Brase reached to pull her daughter safely past the next monstrosity, a chromium combination of, I believe, *breast* and *chair* by one Brancusi; what one might expect to come across in the ruins of a burned-out hardware store.

"Miss Jessup, may I see you again?" I called.

"We're at home on Thursday," she said before Mama could yank her away.

2.

THAT THURSDAY I left the office early and went uptown, walking so as get oxygen in me, for I was nervous.

The Brases lived, in town, in Mrs. Brase's late father's old mansion on the south side of Gramercy Park. The neighborhood was a generation out of date for Society, but that was all right, for the Hon. Mrs. Brase was unconventional.

The calculus of unconventionality is difficult for me to parse, being rather foreign to my character. I imagined that it could not have been entirely convenient to stay in Gramercy Park when fashion had swept far uptown. But essential to Mrs. Brase, I understood, was the pleasure of proclaiming herself socially secure in the New York waters so treacherous to mere mortals, and therefore to do something different, something *unconventional* — staking a place, not in the avant-garde, certainly, but within view of the avant-garde's rear guard. Thus she maintained her old-fashioned mansion in a neighborhood fashion was passing by.

Socially secure she was, of course; aside from the Dutch families who still own so much of the ground underlying the city, no one more so than the daughter of Fred Sweet; ex-wife of Jed Jessup; spouse of a Viscount's son. Though some of her childhood friends were now *Lady This* or *Lady That*, the mere *Hon.* suited Mrs. Brase; her lack of a title was itself a kind of boast that in herself she possessed such a superabundance of prestige that she could do anything she liked, even live in Gramercy Park. That she was even given to rubbing people's noses in it was attested by her scandalous later career lecturing on *Galvanic Union*.

The Brases' summer residence, considerably grander, was a château on the St. Lawrence River in Quebec. They also passed much time in England, in London and at Halliwith Hall in Hampshire, Viscount Halliwith's great new house built to the best 16th-century models, and at their own manor on the Sussex coast. It was universally agreed that, though a divorcee, the Hon. Mrs. Brase was blameless, and also that she had wrung from her errant first husband the full price of his wronging her.

I rang, and the butler admitted me along with two glistening children who arrived at the same moment. Lustrous youths, their unformed features were suffused with humidity—eyes wet, lips moist and red—and their flesh gave off a rank nursery odor.

Mrs. Brase's drawing room looked onto the square, which was itself overlooked by the Metropolitan Life tower lately erected several blocks to the north. Large paintings of the Hudson River school made the room gloomy; one depicted her father's place at Highland Falls (next door to Morgan's). A Steinway grand piano stood near the windows, and a child at its keyboard was tinkling some fragile popular tune.

Some six or eight other children—*boys*—infested the room. They were Dora's age, 20 or 22. For all that persons that age move constantly and fast, their locomotion is a species of somnambulism: They are not awake. The process of waking up to life is painful, and one our civilization feels it best to postpone, and which children themselves are happy to push off as long as they can. So although the young people strewn about Mrs. Brase's drawing room might have been on the verge of yawning, propping themselves up on their elbows and looking around, to find out how life in actuality bears the same relation to their slumbrous upbringing that fairy tales do to newspaper headlines, they were not there yet. They napped still, entirely taken by themselves, even as, snickering, they tapped their feet to the music's jerky rhythms or looked longingly at Dora as she poured tea, with equal longing at the cakes piled up in front of her. Clearly they were there to woo her. The dreaming youths wished to wake up affianced to Miss Dora Jessup!

Dora! Striking, tall even as she sat, Dora was torn from another page entirely—fully awake. Although one saw her the pastmistress of New York's every haughty tribal custom—expert at the tea table, for instance, in Society at that period involving a ritual more elaborate than that of the Japanese Imperial Court's—clearly she had surpassed that world, found somewhere a more accurate consciousness of life than any taught her at the Brearley School or McGill University. I found her fascinating.

"Mr. Berlin!" said Mrs. Brase. "You came!"

There was no joy in that voice. I pressed her fingers, smiled at Dora—Dora's answering smile, I must admit, a mere convention—and went to the piano.

"May I?" I murmured to the child at the keyboard and, when he craned helplessly up at me, sat down and shoved him off the bench with my hip. My fingers hovered over the keys and played. . . yes, *Chopin*. My fingers chose Chopin.

Too early for a nocturne, so the *Fantasie Impromptu*, in C Sharp minor, Opus 66. Taxicab clarions punctuated the more intense passages. Though seldom given credit for it, Chopin is purposeful. People prefer to imagine his music dreamlike and evanescent, product of the fairy culture that so enamored 19th-century Europe. But Chopin has a spine of steel. His is music fully, tragically awake, gleaning its beauty from life's real circumstances.

I paid no mind to the room as I played; never can. I must watch my fingers range up and down the keyboard, participating in this life to which I have so little conscious entrée. But as the last notes died away, and my hands lifted from the keys, my foot from the pedals, I was aware of a hush.

Looking up, I saw the blank faces of boys astonished into muteness, and Mrs. Brase's features a cauldron of dawning apprehensiveness, and Dora, still and composed, looking at me steadily. Only now did I notice the Hon. Lionel Brase, sitting in a chair near by, knitting, the needles clicking steadily.

Mrs. Brase led ironical applause and said, accusingly, "You *play*, Mr. Berlin."

"I try, Mrs. Brase."

"You play beautifully," Dora said. "So *beautifully!*"

"Thank you."

"But you are not an artist?"

"Alas, no, Miss Jessup. As a boy I hoped to be, but Mr. Paderewski one day kindly permitted me to play for him, and even more kindly advised me to view music as a private joy, and to enter the law, or some such."

"So you —?"

"Entered the law."

Mrs. Brase put in, "Are you not on the Street, Mr. Berlin?"

"Yes, ma'am. I'm at Dillinger Muenster — my mother was a Muenster, you understand. But I started in the law."

"Tea?" asked Dora with beautiful simplicity.

"Yes, please."

Her mama asked, "Mr. Berlin, where were you educated?"

"Here in New York, ma'am, privately, until at 16 I entered Harvard College and, later, New York Law School."

"And what is your position at Dillinger Muenster?"

"Senior partner, ma'am."

"What do you *do?*" asked Dora.

"I try to make myself useful, Miss Jessup. You know corporations come to the Street to find capital. We make it available to those with solid prospects for growth. I serve on the boards of some half dozen. Also we underwrite bond offerings, making rather a specialty of railway bonds, and provide banking services. Of course, we own a seat on the Exchange as well."

Mrs. Brase blushed, her features hardening. "If it's not too personal a question, Mr. Berlin, what faith do you follow?"

"I'm Episcopalian, ma'am, a parishioner of St. George's Church, on Stuyvesant Square. In fact, I'm an usher there."

"We attend Calvary," said Dora.

"Such a beautiful church!"

Mrs. Brase persevered. "Were you *born* into the Episcopal Church?"

"My mother was. I was baptized at the age of seven, ma'am, the year after my family arrived from Germany. Jesus Christ is my savior, Mrs. Brase."

"Ah," she remarked, with no note of satisfaction. But, balked, unable to brand me, as she clearly wished to, a Jew, she receded.

The boys began to take their leave, disappointment heavy in their faces, for Dora, combining money and beauty, was the catch of that season, or any other. But they would live.

Meanwhile, as her mother watched with lips pressed flat, Dora turned to me and said, "Mr. Berlin."

"Yes, Miss Jessup?"

"Would you care to attend a concert with me? Or perhaps

see a play? You see, we're in town only until May. If we wish to improve our acquaintance, we must set about doing so."

We improved our acquaintance.

Thus it was from a mess of broken pottery—the 1913 Armory Show—that I came away with the substance of my whole life since.

Merci, M. Picasso!

3.

ONE DAY IN March 1914 the New York *Times* published a characteristic photograph of Dora—eyes half-closed, lips parted, hair an aureole flowing behind her like a sort of shifting halo—next to an announcement:

Miss Dora Jessup
To Wed Max Berlin
Friends Surprised

Well, no, they weren't. I had undergone so extensive a round of teas and dances, dinners and country weekends that our engagement could *surprise* no one. What the *Times* conveyed was Society's dismay at seeing its nightmare come true—a Semitic polluter claiming one of its own.

Dora didn't give a hoot. I had proposed—shrewdly, I believe—in the conservatory of her father's house on Fifth Avenue, when for one evening he allowed the full splendor of his wealth to shine forth. I forget in whose honor the ball was held, but we found ourselves sitting on a silken settee beneath panes of glass being pelted by fat wet snowflakes, away from the crowd, the orchestra's strings slicing through the palms.

Being in her father's house made Dora excited, if also upset; their contacts, unfortunately, were few, her feelings for him strong but mixed; she endured a kind of perpetual grief for him. I took her in my embrace and offered her the solid arm of an older man who undertook safeguarding her welfare as his life's task. She consented to marry me.

Friends Surprised? Of course I resented it. Society kept watch on me as though a keen eye would detect my nose hooking like Fagin's. Oh, it peeped at me with big scared eyes. It hadn't before met, or at any rate mixed with, one of the tribe of Berlin; this it wished me to know. Thus over our nuptial galas hovered elegiac clouds; the end of something had arrived, and the beginning of something else, in a set receptive to nothing new except, by perpetual necessity, money.

But to any remonstrance I might have made concerning *Friends Surprised* (naturally, I made none), the answer would have been, "Oh, no, Mr. Berlin, the surprise is that a girl so young would marry a man of 37 or 38 four inches shorter than herself and whose resources, however substantial, are not comparable to hers as heiress to a fortune of the first water."

However, Dora could never have been satisfied with any conventional scion of good family, any dutiful offspring of wealth, any grind of the counting house or law office, or any rich loafer, either. The same inner impulsion that caused her flight to the theatre prevented it.

Our wedding occurred in June 1914, at Calvary Church, a splendid affair amply attended by Society.

We honeymooned in Europe—as it turned out, our last opportunity to travel there for years. We sailed aboard the *Mauretania,* my chauffeur William (whom I filched from the Astors after the *Titanic* disaster) in third class, and landed a week later at Cherbourg. Awaiting us was my new Minerva automobile.

The voyage, our fellow passengers agreed, had been tranquil and uneventful, but it was our honeymoon so, naturally, for us memorable. I found Dora entirely trusting; touchingly satisfied to place herself in my hands. Ludicrous in one so well born, beautiful and wealthy, but my bride proved magnetic to pain. Her sensitiveness offered endless hostages to fortune—another with every breath. It was my job, 24 hours a day, to stave off and ameliorate pain; a charge I took on willingly.

Traveling across the Continent in those days was hardly less effortful than for Horace Walpole making his Grand Tour in the 18th century. We set out every morning and pioneered cross country to our destination. Roads were rough, blowouts frequent, supplies of gasoline uncertain.

In the front compartment, Dora's lady's maid, specially engaged for the trip, sat next to William. His wife was her usual maid, but Martha, caring for their infant, with another on the way, stayed home, so by arrangement with a London agency we hired an Italian lady's maid (we did not need to know that she was in her own right a decayed countess, but she was; competent in her duties, also).

William turned his considerable rough charm on Serena. To start, they had not two words in common, but within days it was apparent that off in the far recesses of the inns and hotels we put up at they were bedding together. Bliss radiated from the front compartment; as from the rear, Dora's fingers interlaced with mine.

We were leisurely following the Loire when news came, on June 28, of Archduke Franz Ferdinand's assassination. I can only plead the distractions of a honeymoon for my obtuseness in sticking to our itinerary even as ultimata began to fly. We traversed Lombardy without haste and passed a week at the Hotel Danieli in Venice, my favorite city despite its summertime heat, and there I introduced Dora to my dealer, Mr. Shell.

For I was a collector of art and the decorative arts; collecting was my favorite activity and relaxation. Dora entered into it. I told her (only now!) that the dream of my life was to build a house in the country, a Renaissance court unto itself, a palace where everything that met the eye would be beautiful and where life could be lived as it should be. It was for its sake that I collected. She entered into that dream, too!

Mr. Shell had many prizes for us that summer. Our favorite purchase was the *Juliet* gate, a carved pink marble garden gate (weighing ten tons) from the Verona palazzo of the Cappelletti family that inspired the story of Shakespeare's play. At the other extreme, inches high, was a Florentine ivory of the early 15th century showing a nude and confident youth wooing his veiled lady love sitting at the window above. In addition, there were majolica platters painted by Orazio Fontana, 16th-century bronzes, and—quite apropos—some rich peasant bride's 18th-century dowry of painted furniture, sophisticated in its pretended naïveté, voluptuous with *S* curves.

Mr. Shell also put us on the traces of a lovely room of gilded *boiserie* and painted panels dating to 1700—a faint reflection of Versailles, a charming production. We saw the "Loggia Room" *in situ* in a villa near Padua, bought it, and Mr. Shell dispatched a crew to prise it out of the walls and eventually bring it to New York, where it would repose in my warehouse in The Bronx until we were finally ready to build.

From Padua we headed for the Brenner Pass. En route I woke up to reality. High time; it was the end of July 1914. The atmosphere in the Tyrolean village where we stopped for lunch was fraught. I ordered a stein of excellent local beer and with its help was given, almost too late, some small glimpse into the future. Easy, really—in the street a mob of German speakers pursued two Italians past where we sat. I perceived that Europe's ancient inner rot was manifesting itself, pushing up as in a Mannerist *Last Judgment,* where long-buried skeletons and bodies half-decomposed are reanimated to claw to the surface of a wrecked and smoldering Earth.

I told Dora we must go home immediately — turn west, avoid Austria and Prussia, drive for the French ports as fast as we could go.

"Oh, Max, no!"

"I'm sorry, dear."

"Max, really! Cut short our *honeymoon?*"

She pouted, but I told William of the change in plan, he turned the Minerva around, and we drove until the last sliver of daylight.

We drove hard for three days. A train would have been more comfortable, but might have made us vulnerable to official action. Crossing into France near Mentone, we were delayed while an ambitious border guard telephoned his commander regarding my passport's disclosure that I was born in Prussia. But Dora transformed herself into an American madwoman! She raved unstoppably in perfect French (albeit with a Québécois accent), and to shut her up, they waved us past the barrier. Lucky; some foreign nationals surprised by war's outbreak were detained for five years.

At Marseilles we were fortunate to find a freighter with a few passenger cabins embarking that evening for Baltimore, even more fortunate, after negotiation, to be allowed to board (although it cost me the Minerva!). We had barely reached the Atlantic before the radio-telephone brought news of armies on the march. Our summer purchases meanwhile were forwarded to Mr. Shell; they languished in Venice for the next five years; nor were his storage rates cheap.

Dora was upset that our trip ended without a sojourn in

England, where she had the entrée of the great houses. I, too, was disappointed not to add her dukes and earls to my store of acquaintance, or to savor the last of the long Victorian peace. But we escaped Europe by the skin of our teeth. Our ship being French, I was afraid it might be impounded before it landed us in America; but we got home, safe, even as war erupted.

4.

Curious how the happiest times compress themselves in memory, how quickly they are told. For 15 years our lives followed a satisfying and untroubled course.

On our return from Europe we moved into the house on West 54th Street, a wedding gift from Dora's father; he had the goodness to put the deed in my name. Plastering and painting were still going on — obviously, we were in it weeks early — and never actually stopped, for we were constantly installing antique architectural elements or ancient wallpapers or paneling, even incorporating whole rooms imported from Europe into the house's fabric.

The side street between avenues suited us. It made an attractive enclave. The Lehmans had their houses there, and John D. Rockefeller's city residence, and the enormous mansion his son built, were just across from ours. Not far away, on the other side of Sixth Avenue, were mews for the cars. So well did I think of the neighborhood that I quietly bought up the brownstones flanking mine, as well as four behind, on West 55th.

We were blessed in 1915 with a son; our daughter was born two years later. He was a lively and attractive lad, she (my special joy) strong-minded from the start.

Dora flourished in her demanding role, so central to sustaining our lives. Every morning, she met with Cook and housekeeper to discuss menus, authorize purchases, keep abreast of everything going on in the household. There were the constant fittings that maintained her status among New York's best-dressed (she made Fortuny pleats famous!), the requisite attention to exercise, hair and nails. Entertaining being integral to my business life, we frequently gave dinners and parties, and our musicales attained some small fame, she doing the lion's share of devising programs and guest lists.

Sir John Lavery captured my little family in the picture from 1921, painted in creams and greens, that hangs in our sitting room: Dora, addressing a card at her Pompeian bronze desk, interrupted by the children pushing up to her, our boy brandishing his toy airplane. Somewhat later *Harper's Bazaar* photographed her with the children in a dreamy portfolio of idealized motherhood.

Except for a few years of adjustment immediately after the War, America prospered, Dora and myself along with it, and we could ignore the world's problems. Her dividends, which during the War were enormous—simply enormous—from about 1921 grew again to sums that left us agog. And my enterprises thrived. My firm prospered, and the companies on whose boards I served tocketed profitably along.

My work made up a large part of my happiness, as it must for any man. Dillinger Muenster is located in the clouds above Broad Street. It's a peculiarity of New York that so influential a firm should have no more physical presence than a lobby plaque. Walk past the door of 25 Broad Street, you have no idea of it. No, it is that modern thing, a mental construction, leaving traces in the financial press, to be sure, but having no factories of its own, no plants, nothing but six floors in a skyscraper.

We are, in the first instance, a private bank. If your wealth is sufficient, you may bank with us, and we will make it convenient for you to do so. We are also what some have taken to calling investment bankers. We have capital available, and though we invest only where we can exert a continuing influence, where we do invest, we tend to do well. And then there is the bond business. In the "tombstone" the *Wall Street Journal* prints after a deal closes, you will generally find our name halfway down the page. Not lower; not higher; halfway down the page. That is as we wish it.

Visit us, and you step off the elevator into a reception room richly appointed, but that displays no sign, gives nothing away. I do not believe in giving anything away. Our Mrs. Pritchard will greet you, and may direct you behind the door. Make any sort of fuss, however, and our Mr. Callahan will lumber up from his lair to escort you out.

But say that Mrs. Pritchard admits you. You enter our bright, utilitarian, buzzing workplace. The offices are staffed by the smartest people we can find. My large office, paneled in walnut, holds a southeast corner—I find the morning sun pleasant, whereas the western sun can be too much. The finest Tabriz I ever saw covers the floor, and Renaissance bronze figurines and inkwells stand about. On the walls hang pictures on the martial theme that predominates on Wall Street. My desk is the 18th-century table at which Austria and Prussia concluded their little war of 1866; I care less for that association than for its handsome marquetry. Behind my castered chair are ranged stock tickers, a teletype and three telephones that connect me to the world. In the corner is a more conversational grouping, and there I spend much time.

For my job requires solitary thinking, which makes for some of my happiest hours. I sit down with a cup of coffee and think; look across New York harbor and cogitate about what I have read or heard or observed. Perhaps also I confer with one or two of my partners. I have a knack for seeing just a little ways into the future—sometimes an hour, sometimes a week, a season, more rarely the trend of years—and this talent (if talent it be) contributes to my prosperity.

Of course, my prosperity depends also on that of the men I know and those I employ. So, too, the social parts assist—chatting over the phone, mixing at my lunch clubs or after-work clubs. But the heart of what I do is to sit at my window and watch ships dragging their chevrons across the harbor, or the cars going up and down Broad Street, or the people the size of ants crossing it, and trying to peer ahead.

Not that my days are dreamy or without pressure. When thought clarifies, I take action—get on the telephone or dictate to Mr. Gresham, my secretary.

5.

SOMEWHERE, AS THE Twenties wore happily away, I heard a distant rumor that Leningrad's Hermitage Museum might be persuaded, if approached with sufficient discretion (and cash), to sell pictures from its stupendous collection.

Of course the possibility made my mouth water. Through a route I hoped would be just serpentine, just direct enough — using the good offices of Averill Harriman, who knows the most astonishing people — I put out a feeler.

I came to know the Hermitage in the summer of 1909. Almost as a lark I sailed with a friend from Danzig and spent two weeks in St. Petersburg in the season of white nights. I recall carriage drives past vast, astonishingly beautiful old palaces arising out of seas of wooden shanties; but spent most of my time in the Hermitage.

I visited the first day, and returned every day thereafter. The thing about masterpieces is that you cannot step in front of one and tell yourself, *Oh, it's a masterpiece,* and move on. No, it claims you — detains you for long minutes of hard work *looking.* I saw hundreds of pictures, most of them unpublished, *masterpieces* without end: Rembrandts, Titians, Raphaels, Caravaggios spilling from the walls! Consequently, it was with a greedy heart that I followed the drama of the Bolshevik Revolution and the Czar's fall, heard the rumor and extended my feeler.

Months later came its lone little upshot. My secretary one morning hastily announced, "Sir Joseph Duveen" even as that personage swept into my office *en prince*, trailing him a little man with dead eyes.

"Mr. Berlin, *do* forgive the intrusion," Sir Joseph said, filling my hand with his. "So pleased to meet you at last!"

"To what do I owe the pleasure, Sir Joseph?"

Duveen was an international art dealer in a class of his own. Though I'd never met him, I'd long felt at no great remove; when I was at Harvard, Mrs. Jack Gardner was good to me, and of course she was Bernard Berenson's patroness, and Berenson now served as Duveen's authenticator.

Evading my query, and neglecting to introduce his companion, Sir Joseph perfunctorily admired my view of the harbor. He was more interested in some of the objects in my office, particularly a tempera by Paolo Uccello depicting some Renaissance kerfuffle or other—it bristled with pikes and broadswords, headless bodies littering the foreground. Appropriate, even typical, decoration for a Wall Street office; one of my partners actually likes to distribute bullets for staff to display on their desks.

"Where did you find *this?*" Sir Joseph asked.

I murmured, "Mr. Shell has sold me many—"

"Oh, yes: Mr. *Shell.*" He sounded like a man picking up a dead mouse by the tail.

We sat down at the windows, and over coffee he told me what he came to say, suavely lamenting that, alas, the Soviets had granted his arch-rival Knoedler's the exclusive license to offer works—*could I imagine it?*—from the Hermitage!

It was clear to me that if Duveen were inserting himself

into Hermitage sales, even if only to disclaim involvement, not only had Knoedler's better watch out, but my pocketbook wouldn't be up to the task; I like a bargain, and Duveen allowed none. Amusing, though, that my feeler should elicit so grand a response as a personal visit from Sir Joseph Duveen!

I thanked him, we shook hands, I moved towards my outer door, expecting them to follow, and the little man with dead eyes flinched — evinced a definite disinclination to pass through our foyer again.

"Have you a back way, Mr. Berlin?" Sir Joseph asked. "My friend. . ."

He swung towards his companion. The man was very small (even I loomed over him), and his eyes washed over one like erasers. It was easy to gather that in regards to Hermitage sales, he served as Duveen's (or Knoedler's) Soviet handler. An agent of the NKVD, I thought even then. *Col. Dead Eyes*, I dubbed him.

"Of course. This way, please."

I escorted them into Dillinger Muenster's rear regions, to a hallway leading past washrooms and lunchrooms where, atop a plinth, is mounted a Gatling gun. The lethal thing shines bright as a carnival ride; Mr. Callahan polishes its brass every morning. Salvaged from a Philippine battlefield by one of my partners, it was placed there as encouragement to the youngsters; of a piece with Wall Street culture.

And the Russian was a boy again! On Christmas morning!

Burbling with laughter, Col. Dead Eyes capered up to the Gatling and, blissfully caressing it, grabbed its handles and aimed it down the hallway, scattering panicked clerks with his abrupt *"R-r-r-r-r-r-r! R-r-r-r-r-r-r! R-r-r-r-r-r-r!"* His eyes took life and flared up — but so unpleasantly one wished they would revert to lifelessness.

6.

I LONG COURTED MR. C.H.P. Gilbert to design my dream house. Architect of New York's grandest structures, from Fifth Avenue mansions to block-fronts along Riverside Drive, he also raised numerous palaces across Long Island's North Shore. No one, I thought, could better help me carry out my ambition than the master of every style.

But Mr. Gilbert wished to retire. As early as 1919, he told me he couldn't help me. Still, I persisted in occasionally taking him to lunch and describing to him the latest additions to my warehouse from our summertime tours of Europe.

One day in 1925 he shuffled into my office, mailing tube in hand, and from it unrolled a gorgeous chalk rendering labeled *Music Room for Dora and Max Berlin*. Against a sky of electric blue, it depicted a squared-off stucco mass beneath a hipped red-tile roof, five great rose windows punctuating a wall rising over an arcade: a room 100 feet long, 46 feet wide, with a ceiling 32 feet high.

Precisely what I wanted: Simple, capacious, perfectly proportioned.

He stated that he could do nothing more. When I expressed dismay, he introduced me to his companion, Mr. Rittenhouse.

Mr. Rittenhouse, an architecture graduate of Columbia University fresh from post-graduate studies in Europe, was very young but, in the event, we hired him and, over time, came to see him as the right architect for our house. Accurately archeological in his designs, he proved adept at the idioms we enjoy.

For we knew what we wanted, Dora and I: something like the ducal palace of Urbino. Beginning as a castle in the Apennines, Urbino evolved into a center of art and culture epitomized by the duke's serene, graceful, gigantic palace. Dora adored its great outlines massed against the sky, its enchanting courtyard, its irregular and rambling quality. We intended to assemble the European prizes we stored in The Bronx—porticos and ceilings, doorways, altarpieces, tapestries, suites of furniture, *cassoni*, pictures, sculptures, rugs, plus some 15 exquisite rooms wrenched entire from chateaus and castles—into a palace of verities. (In California Mr. Hearst was building along similar lines, but of course with West Coast vulgarity.)

Every few weeks we visited Rittenhouse's studio off Union Square to check on his progress. He had the sky-lighted top floor of a building designed by himself that featured arched windows between protruding piers. There, on top of a table, stood the model of our villa with our latest ideas realized. Lights artfully played upon it, and interior renderings were tacked to the walls.

Though made of cardboard and balsa wood, the model enchanted us. Its parts broke away: roofs could be lifted off, walls pulled out. We crouched and crept, adding chimneys, shifting wings. After an hour lost in dreams, when it was time to go, Rittenhouse went around turning off his green-shaded lamps, the city obtruding with the sounds of traffic, and Dora and I, coming to ourselves, would sweep him off to dine.

I also kept an eye on what came to market in New York, paging through the catalogues, pencil in hand. In the Twenties the older men were letting go their collections or, dying, found it done for them. Auctions at the Anderson Art Galleries and Parke-Bernet yielded occasional prizes. One had to be careful about provenance, of course, for mistakes—not to say deceptions—were made. But what I bought at auction nicely supplemented our summertime loot.

By 1928, however hesitant we were to commit to so large a project, the time had come for Dora and me to build. I am by nature conservative, but I had to admit that money was rather piling up; it seemed even prudent to invest some of it in a country house. Of course the timing turned out to be unfortunate.

The immediate impulsion was Dora's hearing that her cousin wished to sell her place in Katonah (Katonah post office, but nearer Bedford Village). Dora suggested that we drive out to take a look.

It's a sweet countryside—at that time, sweeter still, as being less populated and more rural; dairy country until land prices started to rise after the War. It was well served by railroad, the New York Central's Katonah station stop but two miles away, and already the Saw Mill River and Taconic State Parkways were being planned.

Dora's cousin had built 40 years earlier. Her 120 acres extended over the tallest hill around, Mount Aspetong, which we climbed through the bare late-winter woods and from whose top we could espy Chief Justice John Jay's upright old farmhouse a mile to the west, to the southeast a distant band of Long Island Sound.

Finding that the tract would suit our needs, I bought it. The old mansion would have to go, of course, though its numerous outbuildings could be preserved for servants and tenants. We were left with the question of where to position our new one. To Dora's sorrow, the hilltop wouldn't do; I had no wish to poke up a monument to myself visible for miles around. It's a flaw of Mr. Rockefeller's place at Pocantico, otherwise perfect, that one can drive up the Taconic and at a certain juncture see it plain.

No, as Rittenhouse pointed out, a better site lay along the slope's lower reaches, nearer the stables and barns. He adjusted his plans to the topography and began letting contracts. Our house would rise a quarter mile away from the hill, massed in suave counterpoint to it. We would build the Music Room first, then in stages enclose a large courtyard with wings even more gigantic.

The first spadeful of earth was turned on Monday, April 9, 1929, after an annoying wait for the airplane I hired to photograph the scene. But finally, uncertain as a moth, a biplane hove into view and circled; the kids dug heartily into the ground while the construction crew looked on indulgently. As the plane was buffeted away again, the crew stepped over strings strung from stakes and started up their steam excavators.

That spring and summer were noisy, smelly and exciting. We came out every weekend and camped out in the largest of the old cottages with Cook's picnic basket. Progress was amazingly fast. Hammering and sawing went on to a late hour. Concrete was poured and girders hoisted up over the trees and framework clad with the architecture of Renaissance Italy! It excited me to the bowels to have to raise my eyes from the blueprints in order to see my house. The Music Room's vast cellar held boilers, laundry and storage rooms, plus a six-car garage with gasoline pump and mechanics pit. Upstairs, we laid teak flooring, flagged the courtyard and sorted our collection of Tuscan columns into the cloister surrounding it.

Soon it was time for the Tessellata family to move in — they occupied two cottages for twelve months — and begin plastering; three generations of the most artful plasterers in the world imported from Cassino on Mr. Shell's recommendation. The Tessellata technique makes plaster resemble travertine, with an open, shell-patterned texture.

We loved romping through the enormous, echoing, half-finished Music Room. The outer side had projecting bays and a sizable alcove (its fireplace big enough to stable an ox); French doors and a magnificent Florentine portico of oak (ca. 1490) looked onto the courtyard. At one end Solomonic columns of porphyry framed the stage; from high up the opposite end peered a musicians gallery. The ceiling, of carved walnut, was taken entire from a cathedral in Sicily. E.F. Caldwell fashioned the enormous chandeliers and standing lamps for us.

While the Music Room was being finished, we threw up a servants' wing off one corner, off the other a roomy caretaker's cottage, and were happily planning the West and East wings, working out the pleasurable puzzles of how best to install the rooms and treasures stored in The Bronx, fruit of more than 20 years' collecting at an expenditure that, in the final reckoning, far exceeded *one million dollars*.

We anticipated moving into Ca'Dora (what else could I name it?) the following year. To facilitate journeys between Manhattan and Westchester, I purchased a Cadillac V-16 limousine.

7.

THE STOCK MARKET crashed on *Black Thursday*, October 24, 1929. *Black Monday* bumped it down further; on *Black Tuesday* it collapsed utterly. Trading on those days was so heavy the ticker ran all night long; it chattered nonstop with news that, however bad, was only the beginning. Over the next three years, the stocks of the Dow Jones Industrial Average lost *90%* of their value.

Everybody saw it coming; everybody, apparently, but me. Astute as people thought me and, frankly, as I thought myself, feeling the floor fall away beneath my feet—again and again— came as a sickening shock. Ever since, I have frequently run into men who tell me thank God *they* saw it coming and got out in time; "Thank God!" they repeat, then ask to borrow $10.

The Twenties had been hectic and heated. The American farm sector early went wrong, with a serious decline in land values, and certainly Europe showed signs of instability. But that things were so completely unbalanced? That stocks, factory orders, employment, banks, *everything* would crash in a lethal daisy chain? Collapse so completely as to leave no patch of solid ground from which to stage a recovery?

Late on Black Tuesday, tickers extruding endless loops of

ribbon, I took stock of my personal position. I received no margin calls, for I never bought stock on credit; so much to the good. But my shares? My other assets? My wife's? Their value was ruthlessly washed away.

Dora's holdings were concentrated in her inherited stock in Jessup-Spence Copper. The bluest of blue chips, with enormous reserves and modern facilities around the world, Jessup-Spence reeled as demand for copper *vanished*. It had to mothball whole mines and whole fleets of ore carriers, lay off tens of thousands—put itself into hibernation, as it were. Dividends were cancelled; that stream of income dried up.

Through the end of 1929, and the whole of 1930—*and* 1931, *and* 1932—business at Dillinger Muenster in effect ceased. Stocks and bonds could not be sold; underwriting of every kind stopped. No one had the money to do anything.

Mr. Hoover had my confidence. As the world's leading mining engineer, he was well known to the Jessup-Spence interests, and I personally knew him to be a serious, cultured, brainy person, and humane besides. A good man, I thought, to happen to have as President when the boom went bust! Without flinching, he took the requisite painful steps of cutting expenses, reducing spending and raising taxes; he wasn't going to compound the harm with budget deficits!

But to my surprise (and his), this did not improve things. Instead things got worse—much worse. Capital vanished. Day by day, in seeking to shore up our assets, and those of my firm's clients, I felt like a man trying to scoop up water with his fingers, and so did everyone. The business techniques that made the country rich no longer worked. The old verities proved out of date, ineffective, useless.

And naturally I had made the single worst money mistake of my life. For 30 years the dream of building a country house had motivated me to put money by steadily. Cash on hand bought the costly acreage in Katonah and paid the enormous cost of building the Music Room—the rump Ca'Dora, as I feared it might remain. If in 1928 or 1929 I'd instead sold *stocks*, then at their peak, to raise the sums necessary, and thus preserved our cash, we would have been easier for years, and might even have been able to complete our building program.

The challenges following the Crash were huge but unappealing—they didn't involve making money, striking out on new enterprises, bringing mind and ability to bear on opportunities. No, it was cutting losses—wintry retreat, retrenchment, a game of survival; no fun at all. I was reminded of perpetual winter at Valley Forge.

Nor did I foresee how every known mechanism of recovery would prove so useless, leaving us, even these ten years on, like forest creatures caught in quicksand. A solid bottom has eluded us, though I expect the coming war will place things on a sound footing at last (if at unthinkable cost).

Of course, work on Ca'Dora had to stop. But we couldn't leave our life's dream a ruin in a meadow. Rittenhouse helped us cobble together, on the fly, a kind of completion. Instead of throwing up three more wings, each massy as the Music Room and rising skyward—pennants flying from the tallest point!—then artfully descending to the surrounding gardens, with rooms opening off both sides of broad corridors, we enclosed the courtyard with wings but two stories high, one room deep, and could install only eight of our imported rooms.

Then we moved in. Throughout June of 1930 moving vans disgorged their contents and Rittenhouse arranged the furniture, hung the pictures, provided the final touches. We slept there on the 4th of July—after shooting off rockets in the courtyard—and spent the rest of the summer there. Most weekends throughout the year we go out.

It's a fine house, spacious and certainly comfortable; only

painfully smaller than what we'd dreamed of—in square footage not half what we set out to build. As originally planned, Ca'Dora would have been the largest place in Westchester County; as finished, I believe some four or five are bigger.

Our bed tells the story. Mr. Shell helped us acquire it in the wash of the War directly out of the Barberini Palace in Rome. Gianlorenzo Bernini designed it for his patron Pope Urban VIII in the style of his *baldacchino* over St. Peter's altar: Helical columns slathered with gilt and studded with Barberini bees and laurel leaves spiral up to a canopy gilded with a radiant sun and hung with red velvet embroidered in gold. The headboard resembles an altarpiece. The whole is nine feet long, eight feet broad, twelve feet high.

But to fit it into our bedroom as built we had to cut it down. We took the capitals off their columns and the columns off their plinths and stood them about the room; stored the canopy and hangings in a barn. It's the best we could do, but every time we go to bed, I remember how Fate cut us down.

8.

HOW BAD DID things get? Looking out from our city bedroom one night in 1930, I noticed that Mr. Rockefeller's house was dark. I assumed that his lights had fused, that in ten minutes all would be well. But his house remained dark, and eventually I learned that he'd ordered that the lights be turned off when he was not in residence. Why? To save money — *pennies*. The richest man in history feared destitution!

If *Rockefeller* could see himself a raggedy old man shuffling along the bread line, hoping for a crust or swallow of soup before they ran out, what hope for the rest of us?

And the Great Depression, I sometimes worried, was become Dora's Depression. Running our houses gave her a great deal to do, and she did it consummately well, but naturally she found it somewhat constraining — somewhat routine, even dull. So would I have, I'm sure. She did sometimes assist with Calvary Church's Ladies Auxiliary soup kitchen, but that depressed her, too, as a reminder of how her world had changed.

Our lives never were the high-society round they might have been. That Society is a game for children is a view we share. But with her name and wealth, Dora was irretrievably a part of it. In that sphere she reigned; but if that sphere vanished, who in fact was she? In a sense (and I don't mean to be frivolous), the Depression was worse for her than for others, as being an attack on an heiress's *raison d'être*, her very identity. More and more frequently Dora appeared preoccupied. Once I went in her dressing room and found her staring so pensively into the mirror that she was unaware of my presence for minutes. A restlessness, a new turbulence, arose within her. Her eyes would rest on me but not focus, unless with surprise; sometimes with dismay.

Part of the problem was that our children were growing up. Little Max was on his way to being six feet tall. With his and Elyse's adolescence there came into the atmosphere a palpable chemical wash of hormones, something excited, high-strung, furtive. Sex entered the house.

In the summer of 1931, hoping to divert her, I carried Dora off to Europe. Not with the intention of buying anything, however; we had to economize. But we stopped in Venice to visit our friend Mr. Shell, and such treasures did Mr. Shell have on hand! Europe was even poorer than we, and ancient families that had held on to amazing things forever were now wild to get rid of them; they had to eat, after all.

I tried to resist, but didn't entirely succeed. It was on that trip that we bought the exquisite doors from Ca' Rezzonico painted by Tiepolo, and the lacquered *chinoiserie* anteroom prised out of Versailles itself in some revolution or another. Tearing ourselves away, we proceeded to Berlin, so as to check up on my father's two sisters.

At one time the old ladies had been so well fixed they made a game of spurning suitors. But the War and its aftermath did for them, and it was my remittances that saw them through the Twenties. Germany's hyper-inflation—a loaf of bread costing a wheelbarrow of currency—threw the economy back to barter. Not starving meant scrambling out to the fields for food, carrying such articles of modern life as could be traded. My remittances necessarily of late reduced, I was determined to carry my aunts off to the States.

The sisters still made a go of it in my grandfather's house on Tiergartenstrasse but, as Tante Agathe whispered to us, Tante Aline now accepted a follower, a man who lived on his farm not far away; he stocked their larder with meat and vegetables, in return for some certain amount of— handholding.

One day we accompanied Agathe by train to visit my grandparents' graves in Potsdam. As we returned to the station in early evening, a troop of black-shirted men came marching up and assembled in front of it. Standing in ranks, they shouted in unison something which at first I couldn't catch and, after I did catch it, couldn't credit: They were throwing out their right arms and yelling *"Heil Hitler!"* They reminded me of Ku Kluxers back home, loud-mouthed bullies too stupid to realize their intellectual inadequacy, but ready to beat up anyone their illogic failed to persuade. In a word, dangerous.

Their hysteria became extreme as, torches flaring, an open Mercedes drove up and in the back a man with Charlie Chaplin's mustache languidly stood up to return their salute: Herr Hitler himself!

He addressed the ranks without microphone or text, but no need of either. As he faced those bulging guts and moist eyes something inhabited him—an afflatus took hold, for 20 minutes a screed emerged. His screed blamed the Jews for Germany's troubles and sentenced them to death! Not for an instant did he slacken—he filled that square with death to the Jews, and it was meat and drink to the men in black shirts; filled their bellies, left grateful foam on their upper lips.

My aunt made no move except to let down her veil. Fortunately, Dora does not understand German.

For me it was an epoch — it raised the curtain on the future a little ways, let me see how far Hitler's talent of instilling madness into the mob (especially given Germany's predisposition to hysteria) might carry him.

Riding back to Berlin, I suggested to Tante Agathe that she and her sister come live with us in New York. Plenty of room; I would bear all expenses; they would find many old friends there. Dora pressed her as well.

My aunt bent on us rather a pitying look and stated that neither she nor her sister would ever leave their father's house.

Before leaving Germany, we visited Munich and bought from another client of Mr. Shell's in near-by Dachau a cunningly wrought barrel-vaulted oaken chamber dating to gothic times. Today it's my dressing room at Ca'Dora.

9.

AS WE SAILED HOME — aboard our beloved *Mauretania*, of honeymoon memory — Dora accused me of brooding.

Guilty. I spent the first days of our August crossing in a deck chair looking into gray waters, meditating Depression, a coming conflagration, an entire world not making sense according to anything I knew. West of Ireland I turned 56. *I'm 56*, I thought, *and I know less and less.*

Dora surprised me with a birthday present, secretly procured for her by Mr. Shell: an exquisite little Cellini given up by the princely family whose Rome palazzo it graced for 400 years. A male nude in bronze, 14 inches high, it's the most beautiful object I own.

Unfortunately, though priceless in any real sense, its cash price also was great, as inevitably I found out. Dora's good intentions notwithstanding, her purchase rather impoverished us. We had to tighten our belts.

Be that as it may, I set Cellini's nude before me on my stateroom desk, and in my abstraction noticed how the light every moment flecked him differently, dripped down his sides in patterns that reminded me of nothing so much as the patches of color in Picasso's *Woman with Mustard Pot.*

It threw me back to the Armory Show, where with outrage I'd seen old verities undermined and knocked down. But the art under attack at that time, I belatedly realized, depicted too safe, too settled a world; rather a fairy-tale world. The Armory art, messy though it was, was more *alive*, more true to life, than the old stuff.

I'd left the Armory miffed and angry, sure those "artists" were throwing away 3,000 years of patient progress in depicting beauty, indulging themselves in presenting their violent and disarranged views of the world.

Now I realized theirs was not the world of 1500, or 1700, or even 1860, but a world on the verge of catastrophe — theirs an all too accurate prophecy of 1914 and 1931. Perhaps "beauty" is not even the point of art; is a distraction; perhaps art's job is not to show the surface of things, but to explore what lies *behind?* I could see now that the outrageous new forms were supported by the old humane values — that Picasso was, as it were, a gloss on Cellini, and that each for his era was valid.

So, yes, I brooded.

But brooding bore fruit. Calling for the ship stenographer, I dictated, then cut and edited on his typed flimsies. It might be futile, might already be too late, but I tried to think through the darkest single issue overhanging Europe: the reparations the Great War's victors were still wringing from Germany.

Conventional wisdom has it that demanding reparations gives notice to aggressors of the costs to be paid, thus deterring them and preserving peace. But in fact requiring Germany to send money out of the country when she desperately needed to rebuild helped to feed her chaos. Year by year, an economy thrown out of whack by defeat was grinding and slapping along ever more asymmetrically, doing ever more damage and giving Hitler greater appeal to the masses.

Landed in New York, I circulated copies of my 20 pages, and on the advice of my friend Walter Lippmann read them out at a dinner for bankers at the University Club:

> Was our German reparations scheme devised by Lewis Carroll? For only by means of the *Alice-in-Wonderland* expedient of borrowing <u>from</u> us has Germany been able to pay <u>to</u> us such sums as she has paid.
>
> Twice have the Allies reduced her debt. But what is the point of <u>reduction</u> when she cannot afford to pay <u>anything</u>? Moreover, the Allies insist on cash, but from fear of competition restrict German trade. How then can Germany earn the cash to repay us?
>
> The time has come to dissolve this punitive, humiliating, illogical arrangement; time to forgive Germany's debts. Yes, she will benefit—but <u>so</u> <u>will</u> <u>we</u>!

My hope? To pull the rug out from under Herr Hitler — defuse his issue, damage his appeal — *before* he acquired statutory power; plucking from her side altogether the sword the Allies so loved to twist might, I hoped, bring Germany back to the brotherhood of nations and scuttle Hitler altogether.

The usual photograph memorialized my speech. It shows an assemblage of penguins, a hundred men in correct evening dress crammed in at tables and thoughtfully handling brandy snifters, diminutive me at the far end, nervously trying to make my points.

But the men I addressed were owed money, a lot of it, and wanted every *pfennig*. As I spoke, they heaved restlessly, tossing napkins aside and muttering at my radicalism. I was speaking sincerely, I hoped with wisdom learned from 35 years in business, but they weren't having it. The *Times* and *Wall Street Journal* reported on my talk, and I distributed a thousand printed copies of it to men of influence. I was doing what I could.

Well, I tried.

Mr. Hoover ran for re-election in 1932, and Mr. Hoover lost. My friends were aghast. We needed, they thought, a President who could disregard the people's starvation, tear down the "Hoovervilles" that sheltered so many, cut the budget still more — needed someone who, hunching over the tiller, would steer us deeper into the storm.

I supported Mr. Roosevelt. Reality had nullified every move Mr. Hoover made. The old verities of economics were not holding — the traditional tools were powerless to help.

Roosevelt was on to something, I felt, when he embraced Keynes's topsy-turvy theories, blithely pledging to go into debt if necessary to stimulate things. After all, we were in the bewildering state of being as energetic, well educated and able as before, but more than a quarter of us were out of work, many more on reduced hours, nothing was going on anywhere, and Dora and I hanging on I couldn't say how.

10.

THAT WINTER WAS animated only by the shuffling bread lines of the hungry unemployed. But Mr. Roosevelt took firm hold from the day of his inauguration. His closing the banks would have startled me, except it was what I'd have done myself.

It was a new world. Roosevelt's edicts and proposals were as shocking as, in her day, M. Duchamp's strutting *Nude*, but unlike Mr. Hoover's budget-cutting met the actual needs of the moment. One had, at last, a premonition of turnaround.

And that was before Dora's mother came to town!

Mrs. Brase and her Hon. lived much as they always had, though from time to time cutting back, bewailing having to face life without a second-under-kitchen-maid in Quebec or assistant-under-gardener in Sussex. But with global depression, Jenny Brase girded up her loins and, as she had during the Great War, brought to the world her happy doctrine of *Galvanic Union*.

Galvanic Union? Don't ask. Went back years, to her supposed liaison (after divorcing Jessup, before marrying the Hon.) with Nikola Tesla. Whatever their relations amounted to, Tesla's name remained potent for her. Mentioning him put her into a state like Elsa Lanchester's in *The Bride of Frankenstein;* breathing hard, she would begin to move angularly, shake out her hair and hold strands of it out to its surprising length.

Although Tesla may have been an electrical genius on the order of Edison, he was by no means his business equivalent. Almost off-handedly, Edison founded enormous industrial concerns—General Electric! Consolidated Edison! Tesla fathered nothing you can buy. Still, he was famous, and Jenny Brase knew how to capitalize on his fame.

During the War she toured with a troupe of bare-legged dancers and a stock of curtains and veils, footlights, spotlights, lenses and coils, bringing Tesla's vibratory phenomena to a battle-weary world. Now she was at it again. Engaging Town Hall for half a dozen "lectures," she slathered the city with posters that showed lightning bolts shooting out of her head like snakes from Medusa's. In jagged characters was written *TESLA* with, just smaller, *Galvanic Union* and *The Honourable Mrs. Jenny Sweet Jessup Brase.*

She actually sold enough tickets to fill her six Town Halls, mostly with women of a certain age, plus a few husbands. At the appointed hour, the curtains opened on darkness and the foreboding rumblings of an organ. Amidst a battery of flashing lights, the fluttering of veils, out would step my mother-in-law outlandishly garbed in red-orange chain-mail. She advanced shouting, *"Tesla!"* A shocked silence. Raising her arms, she would repeat, *"Tesla! Tesla! Tesla!"* and from the three Tesla coils onstage would arc tendrils and branches of purplish-blue lightning! Arms out, she stood unmoved, safe in the midst of sizzling lightning bolts and smoky blasts of thunder even as the reek of ozone filled the house!

As they say, you had to be there. She'd go through her paces, dropping hints and shouting reminiscences, veils veiling, curtains revealing, dancers expressing the rest in bare limbs that flashed in the lights while the organ rumbled and electricity arced. At intervals she would retail her (utterly ordinary) memories of meeting Tesla at his Long Island and Manhattan laboratories in 1903 or 1906 or whenever: What a warm, ardent man, she remembered, absolutely vibrating with genius and advocating with all his force

> *Galvanic u-ni-on!*
> *Sole hope of man and wo-mi-an!*

Now we were come to the heart of the excitement. *Galvanic Union!* What on *earth*—?

And trust me, we never found out. It sounded shocking, and certainly the terms *direct current* and *alternating current* figured in it (the former condemned, the latter—Tesla's own invention!—spoken of *ecstatically*). Amidst an ever more fevered waving of veils, higher kicks by the dancers, the organ's mad runs up and down scales, speeches incomprehensible to mere men, the lights would shine brighter, lightning crack faster, moans, gasps and cries arise from the audience. After her last ecstatic, orgasmic gasp of *"Galvanic U-ni-on!"* the house would go dark. *Finis.*

When the lights came on again, halfway, the ladies in the audience were seen putting themselves together, assuring each other that it was *marvelous,* just *marvelous,* and casting accusatory glances at any males who might happen to be scattered amongst them.

Meanwhile, through it all, the Hon. Lionel Brase sat backstage knitting. His specialty was scarves; never went beyond scarves, but expert at them. He was so placid, I sometimes had the impulse to plug his finger into an electric outlet.

This being New York, the papers sent critics to Town Hall, and their snide, witty paragraphs, putting no one the wiser, did Jenny no disservice; her final performances were SRO.

Dora and I attended the last, and gave a reception afterwards. Leaving Town Hall (with some relief), we took a cab home to 54th Street in the spring evening to make sure preparations were complete.

All was ready. Our handsome first-floor series of reception rooms was lighted and fragrant, Cook was sending up tray after tray of canapés, Franz and Mr. Conley, the hired headwaiter, making the punch and opening bottles (I laid in enough champagne before Prohibition to sustain us for the duration). The house was cool when we entered—I always lower the temperature before a party, for people heat up any space soon enough. Smiling at each other, Dora and I gave up our coats, and had just time to freshen up before our guests began to arrive.

It was marvelous to see these grumpy figures get out of their cars and cabs, put on their party faces as they climbed the steps and come smiling into our foyer.

Finally, the Cadillac pulled up and the Hons. emerged with an entourage of four or five young men—the exotic longhairs who handled the lecture's electrical aspects and who, Dora intimated, wished to take Tesla's place with Mama!

"Dora! Max! It went wonderfully! Brase, take my coat— Oh, will you, my good man? Thanks! Max, meet the 'fellers'— they do the magic onstage. And they all know Tesla! Imagine! Don't stand too close, you'll be *galvanized!* Oh, *ha-ha-ha—* "

And off she went to find the food and drink.

One of her coterie lingered behind, a handsome giant with flashing blue eyes, flowing golden locks and mustache, and an impenetrable accent. At sight of my beautiful wife his eyelids retracted, his eyes shone. Towering over her, Piotyr

Alexandreyevitch Primov grasped her long fingers. Her height for once nullified, she as it were quickened—as it were blossomed—as he clapped his heels together and kissed her hand.

A moment later he'd swept towards the punchbowl, leaving Dora standing as in the calm left by a passing windstorm, fluttering with laughter as though leaves were swirling in the air around her.

So I saw them meet, and sensed what was to come, even as they were doubtless innocent of any such intention.

11.

"MAX," SAID DORA one evening a few days later. We were still in town, in our mellow, muffled sitting room.

I closed my book.

"Dear?"

"Do you remember Dr. Primov? From Mother's lecture?"

"Piotyr Alexandreyevitch?"

"He's a scientist. He's invented an electric musical instrument."

"Oh really?"

"He calls it the *Primover*."

"Good for him," I said. "What does it sound like?"

"Apparently like nothing on earth. Mother raves about it. Max, let's invite him to play here."

I readily agreed. After all, we frequently gave musicales for 40 or 50 friends. Usually we engaged string ensembles, although I was known to contribute my piano to the odd trio or quintet, but something as novel as the *Primover* might be fun. Accordingly we made arrangements.

On the night in question, I arrived home as a crew of Russians was getting out of a truck at the curb. Only one spoke English, and he, to my astonishment, was Col. Dead Eyes—Sir

Joseph Duveen's shadow—dressed as a workman in gabardine coat and cap. Obviously, even if Primov didn't know it, he had a minder. Col. Dead Eyes directed the others in carrying the instrument and a trunk containing electrical gear into our music room, then left, having given no sign of having seen me before.

Primov soon arrived with the lady who was to accompany him on my Bösendorfer, and fitted everything together. I'd never seen anything like the instrument he assembled. The *Primover* resembled a fine cherry secretary sprouting copper rods. Lifting the lid revealed Bakelite dials—the one for volume, I was amused to see, went from *1* to *11*. Opening the back exposed an array like a radio's of vacuum tubes that made weird sounds as they warmed up. Placing diamond-shaped screens behind and to either side, Primov tested his apparatus by essaying an eerie, unearthly tune.

Pleased, he sat down with us to a leg of lamb.

After dinner, we welcomed our guests and seated ourselves on velvet folding chairs in the music room, a pretty space, if comparatively compact: Waterford chandeliers illumined Louis XVI wall panels painted with dancing peasants and framed by crystal pilasters etched with lyres and flutes.

Primov and his accompanist entered. He announced a piece by Martinů specially composed for his instrument, struck a pose and nodded. His accompanist played a chord and—a wounded animal cried out in agony.

No, not really; but the caterwauling commenced. How to describe that sound? Like nothing on earth—except rather like the hand saw employed in hillbilly music, but from the steppes of Russia instead of the hills of Tennessee, electrified and amplified!

I am prepared to admit the *Primover* to be an astonishing

technical advance, a brilliant invention; but listen to it with pleasure? That I could never do.

An hour later the wounded animal had succumbed to the final agonies. We applauded, smiled and thankfully got up for refreshments.

But Dora thought the weird quavering—to me, so supremely discomfiting—marvelous!

"You were dancing with your fingers!" she exclaimed to Primov.

He thought the image apt (she flushed with pleasure). To her questions as to how it worked, he explained that the two antennae set up a field of Shado-Rays, and that interfering, delicately and artistically, with that field resulted in sound—in "music."

As we went to bed, Dora suggested that we invite Primov to Ca'Dora to play another recital, this one for our country neighbors. I sighed, but how could I refuse her?

On a Friday in April, then, the station wagon as usual went out carrying Franz, Cook, kitchen maids and housemen, followed by William in the Cadillac driving Dora, the children and her maid. That day, a truck followed bearing a *Primover* and its attendant gear; I was careful to hire our usual piano movers, as I didn't wish to give Col. Dead Eyes entrée to Ca'Dora.

Also as usual, I took the train out later. Primov met me at Grand Central for the 3:51, and rode with me in the club car. The porter sold us set-ups of tonic and ginger ale and, eyes held high, passed from the car while everybody brought out their flasks.

"Civilized, this," noted Primov.

We talked while discouraging rear views of Scarsdale flashed past through windows foamed with cigarette smoke. It came as news to me that he planned to exploit further the

Shado-Rays that gave the *Primover* its eerie tone by developing what he called *Shadio*.

Although I didn't quite understand what *Shadio* might be, my sixth sense—dormant since the Crash—stirred.

"Perhaps I might come by your workshop one day, Dr. Primov?"

"Please, Mr. Berlin, any time at all."

The Cadillac met us at Katonah and carried us to Ca'Dora. Alas, we never built the gatehouse we once planned, but Mr. Albrezzi, our grounds supervisor, was waiting at the gates. Putting his back into it, he pulled them open and their steel wheels ground along the inlaid track. The car entered, and he closed them again; an innocent piece of theatre, for there were also two gateless back drives.

I particularly enjoy seeing Ca'Dora through the eyes of a guest. We swept half a mile through rhododendrons and leafless trees. At the circle where the old house had stood, marvelous horses' heads sculpted by Malvina Hoffman topped wrought-iron gates of the 18th-century. The car passing through, we had our first sight of the house, sprawling amongst trees beneath lofty red-tile roofs and twelve distinctive chimneys.

We took a turn around it; more theatre. The house always looks beautiful and enormous thus, the Music Room rising high as a castle over cellars, garages and lawns, rich light spilling through the rose windows. Dora's Afghan hounds chased us the length of their kennel opposite. We came around the caretaker's cottage to the West Wing, whose stucco wall drew itself haughtily up. Passing beneath the pergola leading to servants' cottages, we arrived at the long, sweet front, broken by a great archway to the courtyard.

Franz opening the gate, we entered, Primov exclaimed at sight of the courtyard, I pushed at the sitting-room door and indoors we went.

This brought us where I love most to be. The house smelled wonderfully of orchids and gardenias—cinnamon, sweet clover, vanilla—and felt warm and inviting. Blazes were going, and golden early-evening light filled the rooms. Persian carpets and polished wood gleamed. Lamps made from jade carvings of Kuan-Yin held glowing clamshell shades of figured silk.

Dora hurried in from her dressing room to greet us. Sinking into Adam club chairs, we chatted over cocktails, then showed our guest to his bedroom, the Loggia Room in the West Wing, which connects, past a bathroom and dressing room, to my library, a stunning 17th-century chamber from Burgundy painted with Old Testament scenes.

We had no other guests that night, so dined at the bay window of the breakfast nook a few steps up from the lacquer-topped table where 28 can (and frequently do) sit down to dinner. Afterwards we had brandy in the Music Room while a houseman in the musicians gallery tended to a phonograph, changing 78s of—in compliment to our guest—Tchaikovsky and Prokofiev.

In the morning we took a walk, accompanied by the children—who adored Primov. The grounds delighted him, as did the chilly weather, which reminded him of home. We followed the pathway through the "Juliet" gate and climbed our hill, where we had thrown up a turret, stone steps winding to the top. There we won a view that took in miles and miles of rolling hills just going hazy with a tender green.

That evening we had neighbors in for dinner before the recital. One of them, the industrialist Mr. Stanley, interrogated Primov over drinks in the sitting room. Primov guilelessly tried to explain Shado-Rays but, when he wasn't looking, Mr. Stanley winked at me and his wife rolled her eyes at Dora.

After dinner we went into the Music Room. It always elicits gasps from those who haven't seen it before, as the Stanleys had not. Dora and I took pleasure in showing them around, while on the stage Primov warmed up his instrument. This evening he had no accompanist.

When he declared himself ready, we took our seats—we were few enough to sit in the set of tapestry armchairs from Fontainebleau—and he announced his first piece as being by Khachaturian. Standing still as a statue, he went to work. Fingers danced, and his instrument thrummed responsively with weird high-frequency tones. Behind him presided a marvelous fresco (School of Fra Angelico) of angels bearing candelabra; contemplating it gave me such pleasure as I derived from that particular performance.

In town the guests at our musicales were music lovers, and even those not pleased by the *Primover* had been interested in its novelty. Mr. Stanley felt less obligated to be courteous. He sniggered that Primov had meant *Cats Fighting* instead of *Khachaturian,* and his wit brought guffaws. After several similar pieces, I led the applause, then tried to lighten the mood by playing a Mozart concerto on the Bösendorfer while Primov improvised an accompaniment. Our guests departed smiling.

In the Pope's bed I apologized to Dora for putting her through another ordeal-by-*Primover.*

"Max! You don't like it?"

"My dear! Do *you?*"

"Enchanting! So modern and musical! Dear, I want to learn to play. Dr. Primov has agreed to teach me, and I think he might sell us an instrument, too."

12.

OF COURSE I had misgivings; what man whose younger wife wants private lessons from a handsome young man would not? But I suppressed them, and visited Primov's studio the following Wednesday.

William let me off at its 25th Street address a hundred steps west of Fifth Avenue, in a canyon of ten-story buildings mainly devoted to the printing trades. In my youth this block had been a genteel residential offshoot of Madison Square, and the sooty gothic church across the street a Society stronghold; I believe Mrs. Wharton was married there.

My destination was on the fifth floor. Since the elevator didn't respond to my ring, I walked upstairs. Meanwhile shouts came tumbling down the staircase—foreign shouts. After passing lofts lighted by windows never washed where men in yarmulkes were tending presses, I arrived at Primov's landing to find the noise being directed at him from a gentleman flanked by porters. The shouter, I gathered from his noisy Yiddish, was Primov's landlord, speaking aggrievedly of past-due rent and threatening to evict him.

Primov stood at his open door, black velvet dramatically draped behind him, seemingly unperturbed.

Finally the landlord receded and Primov with a nod invited me to step inside, saying, "So good of you to come, Mr. Berlin. Welcome to the realm of *Shadio!*"

As I came through the door, he walked his curtain to the wall with a showman's flourish—revealing a scene that transported me to childhood!

I faced a room walled on three sides with glass divided and framed to resemble darkened shop windows. As Primov watched with a smile, I stepped curiously up to one and it came alive! Neon signs repeated his greeting: *"Welcome to the Realm of* Shadio!" That faded as I turned, replaced by, *"Like Terpsichore you dance!"* and *"Come closer and you shall see!"* Speedily I discovered that when I stood still, the mottos and slogans dimmed, but when I moved, they brightened and changed.

Primov put his arm through mine and led me around his magical walls. I was mesmerized! For as we proceeded, our passage was celebrated behind glass by objects suddenly made animate! There was a "toy store" where dolls danced, model cars and trucks rolled along, projections of children brightened the glass. As we passed on they rested, while in the next window mannequins spun, dresses and scarves danced a ballet. Next, place settings came to life, plates and saucers rolling off while others rolled in and cutlery marched. Toiletries paraded across a "drugstore" window, as prices streamed overhead. When we passed on, motion ceased and lights went down.

It was like a wonderful dream—like strolling through an enchanted forest. Magical!

Disengaging from Primov, I went back and experienced it again—but this time differently. Colors changed, intensities varied, dances went faster or slower as *Shadio* collaborated with my singular passing parade.

Finally I permitted Primov to seat me beside his desk in the middle of the floor and tell me how *Shadio* came to be. He explained that on coming to the U.S. he noticed that what we Americans appear to like best is selling things to one another (something altogether forbidden in his Russia!). In particular, he was struck by the industry, new to him, devoted to greasing the wheels of such exchanges: *Advertising.*

At first, he told me, he was dismayed to find how pervasive the sales pitch is in daily American life (except he loved billboards, especially the one for Camels in Times Square that ingeniously pipes steam through a giant cigarette). But, as he put it with a gesture of his wrist, *when in Rome.*

He explained that Shado-Rays act at short distance. Rather than going through people and objects (like radio waves), they are pushed and shaped by them like water, responsive to the merest flick of the fingers. Very well: With the insight of genius, it occurred to him that the same Shado-Rays that made the *Primover* shriek could enliven shop windows—could make money if used as an advertising medium. Hence *Shadio!*

Imagine, he said, a city street of store windows rigged with *Shadio.* Walk down it; passing a bar triggers in the window a "match" lighting a "cigarette" and the slogan: *"Smoke Old Gold!"* (Imagine it, Mr. Lorillard!) Go past a jewelry store, and necklaces and bracelets fly up. With another step, see displayed drugstore items emblazoned, *"On sale today!"* Drive down that same street, and larger signs—veritable billboards—spark to life.

Something stirred in me, something going back as far as the fairy tales I grew up with about marionettes coming alive, shoemakers animating whole villages.

Before leaving, I arranged to buy Dora her *Primover.*

Primov at first declared that she'd have to wait, for he built each one by hand—"like Stradivarius"—but when I took out my checkbook, he remembered that he had one almost finished.

13.

I LEFT PRIMOV'S studio with much to mull over. That *Shadio* in fact held vast commercial potential, I was instantaneously convinced. Thinking about how to develop and promote it gave me much pleasure, and I could see clearly some of the steps to be taken.

The afternoon when, a week later, its inventor personally delivered Dora's *Primover* to West 54th Street, I managed to be on hand. She was in seventh heaven as Primov positioned his instrument in the music room and plugged it in, eager to begin making music. But first I insisted on bringing Primov into my library for a tête-à-tête.

He accepted a seat and a snifter of brandy. I told him how much his studio had impressed me, and how dismayed I was to find him holding it under threat of eviction. Next door to my house, I told him, I owned another of some 6,000 square feet, at present vacant. I suggested that he lease those premises, as a combined work and living space, at a rent of $1 a year. He readily agreed.

Further, I suggested that he and I together, that very day, form a corporation for the purpose of exploiting *Shadio*. I would undertake to furnish, in stages, a capital of $500,000, if he provided the rights to *Shadio* plus his expertise. We would be equal partners. Again he agreed, and before he left my house that afternoon (stunned, thinking himself already a millionaire!), we had signed the written instruments that established the *Shadio Corporation of America,* and Dora had had her first, screechy lesson on the *Primover.*

My intention was to begin with a pilot project, to install *Shadio* in real stores on a real street. We would monitor its operation and its effect, if any, on store sales, and meanwhile take factory space, set up assembly lines, hire workers and train a corps of salesmen.

Then, I anticipated, we would announce *Shadio* to the world. Our salesmen would solicit merchants for monthly subscriptions, our technicians and artists would rig their store windows. If all went as hoped, if people responded to Primov's animated windows as I thought they might and began to take their trade to stores equipped with *Shadio,* money would begin to roll in — quite possibly roll in on a very large scale!

The start to our enterprise went as planned. Within weeks the Shadio Corporation was filing patent applications and Primov had transported his entire apparatus from 25th Street and set it up next door — the house's whole second floor was transformed into a *Shadio*-endowed "street." Also he set up in the basement an assembly line for *Primovers,* where soon one instrument a week was being completed and, I'm amazed to say, sold (frankly, I saw the *Primover* strictly as a novelty sideline).

Meanwhile, we rented space in the Paramount Building on Times Square, as being an appropriate neighborhood for such an endeavor, and there, on a high floor — as it happened opposite the smoking Camel billboard — set up corporate offices. I seconded one of my junior partners to exercise day-to-day executive authority, though I stopped by every week myself (very amusing). Primov himself set about training assistants in how to design *Shadio* installations.

While we did these things, Dora practiced at her *Primover*, and soon we ordered a second instrument for Ca'Dora. I loved watching her at her music, for there was an erotic component to seeing her wave her beautiful hands, long fingers pinching sound from the very air, her face emoting sensitively. But in fact it wasn't *music*, it was a screeching that skinned the nerves. *Excruciating*. I always had to retreat behind closed doors within minutes.

I encountered two complications in building up *Shadio*. One concerned Primov's existing business arrangements. It turned out that whenever eviction loomed, Primov had signed away rights to this or that idea to a slew of rather sinister "partners." These "partners" now showed up, papers in hand, and we had to deal with them. It was a tangled, costly mess, but we got him clear of every obligation, save for a deal with his compatriot Gen. Sarnoff to develop color television for RCA. (No matter; I see no future for such a toy.)

The second complication, of course, was Dora.

14.

WHEN SOMETHING happens — anything, really — it has finally so many causes that it's useless to try to single out any one of them. What happens would have happened, had to happen. In this case, I even expected it to happen — had an inkling, foresaw the danger.

Anyway, it happened. My wife took a lover.

Oh, I knew from the start. Primov was young and possessed a certain appeal, while I had inevitably thickened into a stocky little individual. My wife, after 19 years of marriage, with too little to do aside from daily routine, and ground down by four years of bottomless Depression, was susceptible. One day in July, I entered Primov's house on a business errand, using my passkey when no one answered my ring, and discovered Dora with him in circumstances that left no doubt as to their relations.

We all rather looked at one another. I excused myself before a word was said, and returned next door. No sooner had Franz taken my hat and walking stick than my gorge rose: I vomited over the terrazzo.

Helping me to a chair, Franz placed brandy in my hands, and soon my shaking eased and I felt a little better.

Of course, the dilemma was clear. I was in business with my wife's lover. But business had nothing to do with my marriage, which was ever a sphere separate and distinct! And if in some painfully uncharacteristic scene, I were to compel them to break off relations, I would be left with an aggrieved, unhappy wife, and a resentful and unhappy business partner. I could see no solution.

That night, and afterwards—pleading my stomach—I slept in my dressing room.

The next morning I threw up my breakfast. Dora called Dr. Kopplemann immediately, and he put me on the diet of Melba toast, white rice and carrots that seemed to him the obvious course if I was unwilling to give up the business responsibilities he blamed for my condition.

That afternoon, my strength bolstered with a few crumbs of toast, William drove me downtown. There Mrs. Pritchard brought me coffee and Graham crackers, which I was able to stomach. I sat for a few minutes, intending to get down to work. Instead I could only think about the situation.

But no thinking was required. I opened my desk drawer and took out my pistol. The heft of the semiautomatic Walther PPK .32 reassured me. I cleaned and oiled it, and slipped in a clip of seven bullets (best, I thought, to leave the chamber empty), while thinking how I was going to kill Primov.

Weapons are commonplace on Wall Street, and have been since the shootings of Frick and Morgan, Jr., not to mention the attempt on Russell Sage's life: One day a man walked into Sage's office, lighted a match, showed Sage the dynamite strapped to his body and demanded cash—$50,000, I believe—to blow out the match. Sage refusing, the man touched match to fuse. It was only Sage's presence of mind in grabbing a passing employee and shoving him between the bomber and himself an instant before the explosion that saved his life.

I wanted Primov dead. I wanted to shoot him, watch him bleed and die while I looked him in the eye and gloated. But to kill Primov would be to kill *Shadio* and its prospects, too, and probably to lose Dora forever — and quite possibly to strap myself into a certain crude direct-current device at Sing-Sing.

So I put my gun away, and telephoned Bob Argent, the detective, and asked him to come to my office right away. The only way I could think of to prevent myself from killing Primov was to set a troop of watchers on him. Only that could deter me — save me from myself.

Argent entered shortly thereafter, midafternoon of 1933's hottest day. Windows open to a sultry breeze, a tang of salt and fish and the rustling of papers on my desk accompanied our discussion. Much as I hated to open up my personal business to anyone, there was no alternative.

"Bob, I have a delicate subject to. . . propound." His face expressionless, I went on. "There is a man on whom I wish you to keep watch, a Russian national named Piotyr Alexandreyevitch Primov. He lives at 37 West 54th Street, in the house next door to mine."

I pushed a photograph of Primov across the desk. Argent studied it.

"Mrs. Berlin—" I continued, and in an instant could see him thinking, *So his wife's sleeping with the Russki!* "Mrs. Berlin takes lessons from him on the musical instrument he invented, the *Primover*. With my full knowledge and approval, they are much together, both at his house and mine. It is not their relations about which I wish to learn. Rather, I wish to know his movements and whom he meets. We are going into business together, and I don't want any surprises."

Argent nodded. I thought I detected the diminished respect the cuckold always gets. Though he warned me of the expense of keeping a 24-hour watch, the corps of agents required, in the event he accepted a sizable retainer, shook my hand and assured me that he personally would have Primov under surveillance beginning at 5:00 o'clock that afternoon.

There's a confessional aspect to putting one's problem before a detective. I felt better as I saw him out. That confession is not a sacrament of the Episcopal Church is possibly to be regretted. In any case, I had acted well: Primov was safe, and so was I.

Standing at my window after Argent left, I unconsciously tried to solve the harbor's familiar puzzle—boats of different sizes moving at different speeds, safely getting wherever they were bound—and remembered a railway bond renewal that required my attention. Turning away, I happened to glance at my watch, and realized (without meaning to) that if I wished to get this done I had to hurry, for already it was 4:00 o'clock! My golden hour of opportunity was ticking away!

Shoving my pistol in my pocket, I dashed downstairs to find a taxi.

As it rushed uptown, I marveled at the power that weight on my hip gave me. I trusted seven bullets would do for Primov. Dora of course I would spare, for—I loved her. Had I ever realized that before, really? It was so vividly apparent to me how much I loved her and that my love was the most important thing in my life!

I alighted first at my house to see if, perchance, she was home. Franz told me she was at her music lesson next door— had been since lunch. I knew the eerie sounds I thought I heard were only in my head.

After gulping some whiskey, I slipped out the front door. Pausing on the stoop for a deep breath—I needed oxygen—I walked down the steps and for 30 feet joined the sidewalk's homeward-bound throng towards Sixth Avenue, broke off from it and climbed Primov's steps. I had my passkey in my hand. I inserted it, turned it, entered the foyer.

So far, so good. Carefully closing the door behind me, I stood listening. I heard nothing.

Stairs or elevator? It didn't matter, I would find him and shoot him. There would be no colloquy beforehand. No words were necessary. A lover seeing the husband come in with a gun in his hand knows all he needs to know. If somehow Primov scrabbled past me, got out the front door, I would shoot him on the stoop or on the steps—in the back if necessary. I wondered just how much blood would spill out.

I stepped softly across the marble paving towards the staircase, and—*EEEEOOWWWOOO! EEEEOOWWWOOO! EEEEOOWWWOOO!* Weird, *Primover*-like tones sounded, but in ear-splitting volume, and a gate slid across in front of me and clanged shut! I stood there rattling it, flummoxed.

What I recognized as a small, circular television screen poised near the vestibule ceiling's sparked to life and resolved a greenish image of Primov's face. As though seeing me through an unseen camera, his eyes opened with surprise and through an invisible speaker he shouted, "Mr. Berlin? Is that *you?*"

"Piotyr Alexandreyevitch!" I shouted back. "What's happened? What's this *racket?*"

The noise ceased straightaway.

"Mr. Berlin, what are you are doing in my—in this house?"

"I'm looking for my wife."

"Um. My Detector Wave Reader says you are carrying—a gun? Is that possible, Mr. Berlin?"

"A *gun?* Why ever would I—?"

"It detects a metal mass on your person. Forgive me, there can be no mistake."

I delved in my pocket.

"This, perhaps?" I said, offering my cigarette lighter to the ceiling. "It's gold."

"But of course," Primov said rapidly.

"Piotyr Alexandreyevitch, I wish to speak with you. If you'll please open this gate—"

"Mr. Berlin, I'm sorry, but no."

I rattled it again. The gate was quite secure.

"I want my wife to come home."

"Your wife's not here," he told me.

What could I do? Taking out my pistol, I took aim at the screen, even as Dora's face, also green, shoved in beside Primov's.

"Max, what are you doing?" she asked, and screamed: *"Max, put that thing away!"*

"Move aside, Dora!" I shouted, and fired seven times: *bang! bang! bang! bang! bang! bang! bang!* Their faces vanished amidst explosions of glass and sparks and the echoing roars of gunshots. Acrid smoke wreathed up.

My frustration was enormous. Shooting the television dead gave me no satisfaction; not when the man still lived.

I shoved the gun back into my pocket, waited a minute to regain my self-possession, and went out to the stoop. A glance at my watch showed that my hour was up: 4:55. Looking around, I spied Bob Argent checking *his* watch as he walked briskly up in front of the Dorset Hotel. Seeing me, he rested a shoe on a brass standpipe and discreetly touched his hat and squared his jaw. I nodded, went back next door, put the gun safely away, had a drink, and then another.

Argent had Primov under surveillance. Everybody was safe again. All told, it was just as well. I had come close to ruining my life. It reminded me of when the blood stirs in adolescence, and like an animal one will do *anything*, take *any* chance, *any* risk to get at what the blood craves.

In other words, it made me feel young again, a condition I

usually was happy to have outgrown many years since.

By next morning I had calmed down, and even put in some, I hoped, useful thought regarding commercial possibilities for Primov's *Detector Wave Reader*. I was eager to talk to him about it, and to come up with a better name.

At the breakfast table Dora, greeting me quite as usual, rang for my plate of Melba toast.

15.

IN THE WEEKS that followed I exerted myself doing everything possible to develop *Shadio*. I wrote and telephoned business friends, soliciting—in some cases collecting—their investments in the Shadio Corp., while overseeing the hiring of a sales force; writing and pricing standard merchant contracts for *Shadio* subscriptions; helping set up the Brooklyn manufacturing facilities; preparing the common stock offering to come some time later, and of course consulting closely with Primov and monitoring his technical and artistic advances. Consulted in writing and by telephone, I mean; he refused to see me, which, after all, was understandable.

Also I monitored the installation of our pilot project. The display windows of the street-level shops in the brownstones I owned on West 55th Street would, I thought, be perfect for our purposes, and I knew I could persuade my tenants to cooperate.

One store was that of a jeweler who catered to the carriage trade. He was shocked at my proposal to animate his windows, but I invited him to read his lease, and Primov devised an amazing scheme whereby whenever anyone walked past, box lids coyly opened and necklaces flew up to collar a mannequin while bracelets traveled up her arms, rings slipped up and down her fingers, and lights shone through rubies and emeralds.

Similarly, the haberdashers next door were reluctant, until they saw how Primov could make their suits dance, make ties waltz with socks and belts, and project on the glass images of gentlemen dressed in the season's styles.

At the bookstore, volumes jumped off the shelves, pages opened, silhouettes of William Shakespeare and Rex Stout flared to life, while selected quotations streamed across the windows.

Next door, clock faces flew across the watch-repair shop's windows, time ticking visibly—and accurately—whenever anyone passed.

That stretch of the block became a wonderland! Everything operated just as we wished it to. Every day I found occasion to stroll around to it, my very sauntering causing magical effects in the windows. It was *enchanting*.

Others noticed, too. Daily, crowds began to converge, nor could onlookers just stand and gawk, for that brought the windows to a halt. No, they had to move, keep walking in order to keep *Shadio* dancing in its endless permutations. Many walked right into the stores and spent money; my tenants were *delighted*.

I felt more and more optimistic in regard to *Shadio's* money-making potential. But every day I had to emerge from this businessman's dream to remember that my partner was sleeping with my wife! And every day, put that fact aside again.

That autumn Dora made her public debut on the *Primover*, performing at three concerts. The first took place among friends (no press allowed) at St. George's church house auditorium. Of course I attended. Her friends at Fortuny devised a marvelous yellow silk pleated gown with, at the shoulders, fins straight out of Tom Swift. The applause was tepid, but Primov beamed (except that he scowled at me from afar when I went forward to kiss her).

Her next performance came a week later, at Aeolian Hall. The crowd was small, but the press notices encouraging. They praised Dora's musical phrasing, her sensitivity in fingering the Shado-Rays; anything harsh in the noises that emanated from the stage was laid at Primov's feet. Satisfactory.

Finally, she partnered with Primov at Carnegie Hall. A notable occasion: the first time electric instruments graced its stage. The program included Martinů, weird versions of Bach and Wagner, and what was claimed to be — Mozart. Carnegie Hall was filled to overflowing (I made sure of that), and the crowd deliriously receptive (I made sure of that, too). Reviews, however, this time reflected a certain reserve.

Meanwhile my nausea got worse. Nausea engorged me all day and night! I lost a great deal of weight, began to carry myself like a brittle old man. In addition to an inedible diet, Dr. Kopplemann prescribed bottles of stuff, and failed to hide from me his conviction that some unidentified cancer was eating away at me.

Bob Argent came by my office every week to deliver his reports on Primov. At our final such meeting, on a mid-November Friday, he came in, took a sheaf of papers out of his briefcase and slid them over the desk.

"It's all there, Mr. Berlin. Primov's sticking close to home — 54th Street, Paramount, the factory in Brooklyn."

I was glad to hear it, for the Shadio Corp. was preparing to announce itself to the world after Thanksgiving.

I looked over the week's reports:

𝔄𝔯𝔤𝔢𝔫𝔱 𝔇𝔢𝔱𝔢𝔠𝔱𝔦𝔟𝔢 𝔄𝔤𝔢𝔫𝔠𝔶
92 𝔍𝔲𝔩𝔱𝔬𝔫 𝔖𝔱𝔯𝔢𝔢𝔱 𝔑.𝔜. 𝔑.𝔜. 1
ℭ𝔞𝔟𝔩𝔢: 𝔇𝔢𝔱𝔞𝔯𝔤𝔢𝔫𝔱

```
Wednesday 11-15-33
Subject stays home on W 54 all day.
Visited 1 p.m. to 5 p.m. by
Mrs. Berlin.

Thursday 11-16-33
Subject works on W 55 shop window
installations until 2:30 p.m. Returns
home, is visited by Mrs. Berlin 3 p.m.
to 5 p.m.

Friday 11-17-33
Subject goes to Brooklyn, 9 a.m.,
stays to 2 p.m. Returns home, visited
by Mrs. Berlin 2:30 p.m. to 5 p.m.
Visits Horn and Hardart Automat, 501
Fifth Avenue 6 p.m. to 7 p.m., meets
two Russian nationals.
```

Et cetera, et cetera.

"Satisfactory, Bob," I said, locking the papers away. "Good work."

"Your orders, Mr. Berlin?"

"Oh, please keep it up, Bob."

The reports always included this Friday evening visit to the Automat with Russian nationals, one of whom, from Argent's description, sounded like Col. Dead Eyes. I wasn't bothered; *Shadio* being an advertising medium, it could, I thought, be of no interest to Stalin.

In any case, several weeks earlier I had asked Primov point-blank on the phone who his Automat friends were.

He was startled.

"Compatriots," he mumbled. "Friends from the old country."

I asked if they could possibly be Soviet agents, and this man who never made a joke said, "Oh, yes, you see Stalin covets the secret of the Automat. And one doesn't care to say no to Comrade Stalin!"

He barked an anxious, artificial laugh.

Non-New Yorkers may not be familiar with the secret of the Automat: It is that, after you put your nickel in a slot and crank the knob to open the little glass door and take out your sandwich or piece of pie from behind it, an Automat employee replaces it with a fresh item through the rear.

Even Stalin, I thought, could figure *that* out.

16.

SO: CALLED TO TOWN late at night and sitting in my Cadillac limousine across West Street from Pier 46 in a cold November wind, the highway overhead dripping on the roof, lights glowing from the inlays of the maple dashboard, the heater blowing. Occasionally a ship's horn blasted from the river.

A crane finally swung out from the ship's deck and lowered some cables. Col. Dead Eyes directed his crew in strapping them under the packing case. With a grinding mechanical protest, the crane lifted it into the air— precariously; leaning, it began to spin as it described a high arc up, up, up onto the deck.

And my heart soared along with it!

Unexpectedly, I felt a burden lifted. That box contained my hopes and plans for making millions of dollars, but when it vanished over the gunwales, I felt *joy*. A rush of relief and *joy!*

"Mr. Berlin, we can still get it done," said Argent, an edge to his voice. "One call to the Bureau. Otherwise the Coast Guard will have to board before she's on the high seas."

I sighed a long and profound sigh. Clearly the old vessel was preparing to cast off. At first light a few hours hence there would come some fuss of Customs, the gangway would be drawn up, whistles blown, a tugboat tow her to mid-river. The pilot, after guiding her out of the harbor, would board a tender near the *Ambrose* light ship, while the rusty and ungainly freighter went on to brave the North Atlantic. Finally it would sail into the Baltic and arrive at, most likely, Helsinki. From there Russia was but a railway jaunt away.

The promptness of Primov's abduction—on the day the U.S. recognized the USSR—made clear that it had less to do with any wish by Stalin to hear the *Primover's* uncanny throbbing than wanting the man and his electrical expertise, doubtless with a view towards war with Hitler; I'm sure Stalin knew as well as I that war was inevitable.

"Mr. Berlin?" Argent prompted.

"No, Bob, let him be," I said. I had decided; decided in favor of my marriage. In a low voice I explained, "I love my wife."

"You're sure, Mr. Berlin?" said Argent. "I think it's our duty—"

"I love my wife very much, Bob. Can I drop you anywhere?"

Assuring me he'd be all right, Argent got out and closed the door.

With a thwack of my walking stick on the back of his seat, I said, "William, back to 54th Street, please."

"Yes, sir."

William drove me home and we woke up Ernest the houseman and Elsa the maid—probably woke them up in each other's arms, but that's no business of mine. At my request, Elsa cooked me up a marvelous omelet, sausages on the side, and Ernest opened a bottle of champagne, for my symptoms had instantly and permanently vanished. I slept there, and returned to Ca'Dora late the next morning.

Dora greeted me with a look of concern, but I folded her in my arms and told her that I loved her.

17.

BOB ARGENT LATER reported that Primov did not disembark before the ship sailed.

Primov's absence was discovered belatedly. His assistants, unable to get into the house the following Monday morning, trooped over to the Paramount Building offices and telephoned me. I suggested they work at the Brooklyn facility until further notice.

Dora fretted. Later that day she asked me if I knew where Primov was.

Oh, has he not been around? I queried.

No; in fact, without explanation he'd missed a lesson. Perhaps she should call him up, even ask him to dinner? Even a genius has to eat, after all!

By all means.

So in front of me she telephoned next door, and was perplexed that there was no answer. I counseled patience, but she demanded that we enter the house.

I humored her, though I asked Argent to accompany us. When he arrived, we three stepped across and rang the bell. Passersby saw us neglected on the stoop. I inserted my passkey, but found that, though the door was securely shut,

Col. Dead Eyes in fact had broken the lock. But going down the areaway, we got in through the cellar door.

Walking upstairs to the ground floor gave us a bad scare: Not only was the gate askew, hanging loose from the wall, with several crowbars lying on the floor, but a man was speaking, speaking in Russian. Dora's face brightened. But it proved to be merely a radio, a short-wave unit in the front room. It was not immediately apparent how to turn the thing off, nor did unplugging it at first occur to us, so we left Dora in there, listening to Radio Moscow, I presume, while we combed through the house.

Many of the rooms were a litter of electrical gear and gadgets, others quite empty. In the kitchen were the remains of a meal. The top floor, where Primov slept, showed signs of habitation, but nothing was disarranged or out of order; nothing reflected anything but the dedication of a scientist at work on *Shadio*.

Finally, we reported to Dora that there was no sign of Primov. I told her, "My dear, I fear Piotyr Alexandreyevitch must have tired of us and gone back to Russia."

"Oh Max! But without a word!"

"Men returning to their wives can forget to say farewell." I was making it up, but she blanched. "Maybe he'll show up yet from some spree? I hope so, for from the business standpoint it would be a nuisance to lose him: Shadio Corp. owns his patents, but we can't get far without his genius.

"Dora? Dear, are you coming? We'll leave things as they are for now."

That winter, as 1934 replaced that eventful year, Dora grieved. She was quiet, sad and serious. I tried to be patient and considerate, but must admit to my own distraction: Business was finally showing a faint pulse, and helping it breathe required all my attention.

Not *Shadio*. That was over. Our pilot project began to break down. Tubes burned out, motors stopped, animations froze. We removed the installations, shut down in Brooklyn, vacated the Paramount Building. Although now without a teacher, Dora continued to practice on the *Primover*, by herself devising new screeches expressive of loss—laments that sounded like bagpipes breathing helium gas.

That spring she took action. Hiring a manager and promoter, she borrowed William and the Cadillac, and took her *Primover* on a three-week tour of New England. She performed in New Haven, Hartford, Pittsfield, Worcester, Portsmouth, Manchester, Boston and Providence, and returned to New York, not only with press notices, some of them favorable, but with a certain hard-won serenity. She had kept faith with the departed, and so was reconciled to the necessity of going on living.

She had her children, after all, and—it occurred to her—a husband, too. That husband, determined to prove his love, was so grateful for her small attentions! That husband she began to make happy again.

New in her was an ardency that reminded me of our honeymoon, when we were too absorbed in each other to notice the World War getting under way! She astonished me with new forms of sensation and exertion—introduced me to lovemaking *à la Russe*. Our union became *galvanic*.

One day, I astonished *her* by bringing home a picture I'd bought at Parke-Bernet. I imagine I was thinking of our meeting at the Armory Show when, on impulse, I bid for a large nude painted by M. Picasso, my costliest purchase in years (although, I believe, a bargain, too).

William carried it in from the car, unwrapped it and laid it on the couch in good lamplight. He looked first at it, then at me with an expression as though I'd made him upend a garbage can over the silk. Dora, too, was surprised. Picasso presents the nude—his mistress, I believe—as picture-puzzle, in colors of fire, desire, repulsion, conflict. *Beautifully* painted.

Before the evening was through, glancing at me as frequently as at the Picasso, Dora told me it was growing on her. The next day she said she liked it; soon, that she *loved* it. To me, too, sensuous, complex, rather violent, it seems beautiful, though I am hard-pressed to explain *why* or to trace its forms from the long traditions of art I cherish. It hangs today in Ca'Dora's Music Room, between the Canaletto and the Mateo di Giovanni, and maintains animated dialogues with both.

Ca'Dora may not be exactly what we set out to build, but no house, I verily believe, is so exquisite, and I am better and better satisfied that it expresses my love for my wife and hers for me.

In the early morning I like to move about it in my robe, coffee cup in hand, absorbing the rooms and their objects, the ideas and passions that lie behind them, their disparate histories, forms, lines, colors and textures. The maids and housemen going about their duties are apt to look at me somewhat fearfully (William tells me the maids think the house haunted!).

I watch the morning's new light steal indoors. In the Della Robbia, it first tugs at the Madonna's robes, at once floods her features. Sunlight lends fronds of shadow to the ivory of the nude courting youth, brings majolica villagescapes to life and wakes up Cranach's princess: Blinking, she peers past her velvet curtain. Meanwhile, in the crepuscular light Picasso's mistress tends to resemble a skull grinning sardonically. *Memento mori.*

But I'm afloat on art, on the stream of human feeling and passion and stories; soaring on a sea of joy that often ends in my sitting down to play at the Bösendorfer for half an hour.

A maddening thing about life is the sense that starts to come over one in one's 30s, that no sooner will one begin to get the hang of it—and to enjoy it—than it will end. I'm past 60 now, with every prospect of completing my three-score-and-ten, and those final ten are precious, precious to me. But another, different note sounds, too, as in a chord—a dawning sense that one day the world might best be left to those with more energy and heart for it than I can any longer muster.

Especially as another world war draws near. Our son, eager for it, afraid America will refuse to fight in it, has left Yale Law School to enlist, with the Hon.'s assistance, in the Royal Canadian Air Force (the Hon.'s cousin Winston Churchill, his power in sad eclipse, failed even to win him an appointment to the RAF). Our daughter, meanwhile, is married and ecstatic; I hope it lasts.

The world turns towards darkness from light, from dark to light in regular turn and turnabout. What one clings to is what doesn't change. I cling, in the house we built together, to my love for my wife.

Another's Fool

This one's for you, Al

Troilus: You cannot shun yourself.

Cressida: Let me go and try.
             I have a kind of self resides with you,
                 But an unkind self that itself will leave
             to be another's fool.

                              —Shakespeare
                              Troilus and Cressida

PROLOGUE

YOU MIGHT THINK, after reading what follows, that what I did was an awful thing to do and I must be a terrible person. But I invite you to look closer, to get to know and understand me, see why I could do nothing other than what I did. I'm not so bad!

David and I loved each other. That is the truth. But it was also more complicated than that. Isn't it the common experience that you can hate the one you love? I don't think I'm unique in that regard.

The root of our problem was an unequal endowment of talent. That the love of my life, my doppelgänger (as it were), had so much greater a musical gift than yours truly surely meant that it was natural I should feel just a little jealousy, a little resentment.

I accept the difference between us, I do, and always did the best I could to help David — always. But he was *living my life* — the life I wanted, the life *I should have had*. It's unbearable — you must agree! — how, through no fault of his own, he made me feel muted, silenced, unable to protest, so that for me to go ahead and do this supposedly terrible thing —

There, I suppose now I *am* protesting, even protesting too much. But what happened *was not my fault*. Read and you will agree.

And please ask yourself what would *you* have done?

Thank you.

1.

AS WE ROLLED through the tunnel, a dark man of mystery was blowing frost at me through glass iced with cigarette smoke. Harlem's daylight made him a ghost, but his hollow cheeks and uneasy expression haunted me over Westchester's snowy ground. *The hell he want?*

I would have preferred staying in the city that January morning. Nominally my day off, Monday tended to be a half-day victory lap at Nikolodimsky Concert Management, low-key and satisfying after the hectic week and weekend. Telephones rang with clients calling in grosses and audience counts, and Western Union messengers brought more, while my colleagues and I charted, kibitzed, gossipped, analyzed reviews, congratulated or consoled one another, generally caught up with how we were doing on our mission of bringing classical music to the masses.

David had called me at our apartment in Greenwich Village the night before, and the news as usual was good: an SRO house in Des Moines Saturday night, his Dvořák and Rachmaninoff applauded to the rafters, at Sunday's recital four encores demanded. No surprise: David Spegall was a genius and a star.

Acute, too. Asked if everything was OK, and it was all I could do to persuade him that yeah, sure, everything was fine—no trouble in Paradise or any place else.

In fact, though I could usually fool David—only when it was best for him, of course—I wasn't sure he bought it.

When the train slowed and the conductor came through calling "Katonah, *Katonah!*" I pulled myself to my feet and, rudely reminded of my shoulder, stepped off into the cold air and looked around for a taxicab. I'd not before been to this northern Westchester village, summer and weekend redoubt of horse-loving financiers. Opposite the station stood a block of old-fashioned storefronts.

"Mr. Harnes!" a voice called, the misplaced stress making of my surname an item of riding tack.

I focused on a big, wide-faced chauffeur my age in pearl-buttoned moleskin livery that hinted at brutality; in another context I might have looked twice.

He was holding open the rear door to a cream-and-black Cadillac limousine, one of those early 1950s behemoths gnashing twin chrome incisors in its grille, projections shaped like artillery shells. This one's custom padded roof, half a foot higher than normal, meant I didn't have to stoop getting in. As I was to find in a few minutes, Mrs. Berlin was herself tall and regal.

My boss had called me in as soon as I got to the office that morning, for all that I was, on purpose, early. Mr. Nikolodimsky was earlier still.

But then, that Russian-born force of nature who pulled the strings of American high culture, dedicating his whole intense being to music and ballet, did nothing *but* work. Since emigrating from Russia after the Bolshevik Revolution, Nickel-and-dime (his employees' mostly fond nickname, Aleksandre

Michaelovitch Nikolodimsky being a mouthful) had become a principality unto himself, dealing with governments as their equal to pull off such coups as bringing the Bolshoi Ballet to America.

Most days East-West relations seemed centered in his office as he worked to draw artists West from behind the Iron Curtain and send our best East. His taste was informed, catholic and more welcoming to the new than the American public's, which he privately scorned as having the hardened arteries of the Old Regime.

And did he make a good thing of it? Oh, yes: Lived like a count on Park Avenue and in Old Westbury.

"Mrs. Dora Berlin," he pronounced, lounging against his chairback as cars honked ten stories below on 57th Street. "Ring a bell?"

I hesitated. "Didn't her husband die?"

"Year before last," he confirmed.

Max Berlin, eminent Wall Streeter, art collector and amateur pianist; an Arnold Genthe portrait had garnished his *Times* obituary, index finger propping up a marble cheek burnished to wait out eternity. He'd often booked artists from our roster for private musicales at his town or country places.

"Well, Mrs. Berlin has an idea. Told her you'd go out to Katonah and talk to her. She'll give you lunch and drive you back. There's a train in" — he shot a look at the Richard Street longcase clock — "35 minutes."

"Yes, sir," I said.

"Call me from there," Nikolodimsky said, adding, "And don't mention your — weekend. Grandsons, young boys."

Hence rattling out of town in the smoking car and now swanning along in a limousine with an interior tufted like a casket's. What was the wily Russian up to, I wondered? Firing me?

I'd counted on his not finding out about my disastrous Saturday night, but clearly he knew all about it.

How? But—information being his lifeblood—why wouldn't Nikolodimsky have informants in the NYPD just as at the State Department and Soviet Embassy and every known security apparatus? Through Cadillac windows I surveyed the world quite possibly a ruined man.

Of course I attended my quartet's New York debut Saturday at the Carnegie Lyceum. Penguins swaying in unison, they played their Haydn and Schumann beautifully. I'd confirmed with the *Herald Tribune* and *Times* that critics, if of the third rank, would be in attendance, which meant short notices appearing on Tuesday. So much to the good, since the Enlightenment's performance meant the reviews would be positive, despite the tendency of critics (third-string ones especially) to pull at some extraneous loose thread and carp on it in a desperate *look at me.*

Afterwards I took them next door to the Russian Tea Room for a celebratory toast (not supper), before returning downtown by subway. Columns flashing past like sprockets on a film reel brought the evening's drama to a close.

On my way home to the Bleecker Street apartment I shared with David, I stepped into a bar on Sheridan Square. The Minstrel Man's a quiet place, more given to conversation than your average Village watering hole. It was still early—hardly 11:00 o'clock—when I took my seat at the end of the bar; midnight's the witching hour. Smoking, sipping Scotch, I ignored my surroundings, a man of mystery in black tie, handsome (if you say so), all cheekbones and hooded eyes.

Men in suits pressing inside, the bar gradually filled up with a clientele, if not exactly genteel, certainly a cut above.

I was halfway through a second drink and, spiderlike, sensing my prey about to strike—some predator brave enough to try to penetrate my mystery, shortly to discover himself ensnared in *my* web—when loud and fast there came *"Against the wall, you fucking cocksuckers!"* and *"Move it, ladies!"* and *"Raid!"*

My first raid, first arrest. The persuasive effect I tend to have on people—fed by my conviction that everything in life is negotiable, *everything*—held no sway at *"Raid!"* When the cops charged in flailing batons, nothing I could say differentiated me from anyone else. And set aside any repercussions with Nickel-and-dime, my relationship with David wasn't supposed to extend to meeting men in bars.

The cops corralled us into black marias, a gratuitous blow crushing my shoulder; fortunately I no longer play but for my own amusement. Downtown at The Tombs they jammed us into one big, stinking cell awash with vomit and crowded with a Saturday-night assortment of drunks and muggers who found sport in taunting us. The next morning, no one having slept a wink, we were released—photographed, fingerprinted and given desk appearance tickets for disorderly conduct; left to find our way home on the Sabbath in soiled Saturday night garb.

Such were the tactics of 1953: wholesale scoopings-up of homosexuals who forever after had police records, with whatever that might mean in job or relationship troubles. We were favorite scapegoats for a society filled with fear.

Why the fear? Having helped win a world war against Fascism, the U.S. was prospering as never before. So why hysteria about Communism, when it could make no inroads in a society getting rich on capitalism? Why the obsession with men who like men, police raids wherever we gathered? Don't ask me!

I went into work that morning hoping I bore no mark or taint, aside from my invisibly aching shoulder, but Nickel-and-dime's cultivated basso called me into his office and put me on my train.

The limousine swam down narrow curving roads. Out here the snow looked deep. The houses we passed ranged from large to larger to invisible, which meant enormous.

We turned into a lane, passed two antique barns, crossed an arched stone bridge — and entered a magical realm. For all that it was January, I could tell we were in a manicured garden precinct, its outskirts a village of stucco cottages, farther on a sprawling stucco mansion whose red-tile roofs sprouted a dozen fanciful chimneys. This was the back way onto Ca'Dora, Mrs. Berlin's place.

Going through a pergola entwined with leafless wisteria, we pulled up at a marble balustrade near the long vine-covered front. Beyond were snowy lawns and hedges.

"Thank you," I said when the chauffeur opened my door. Ignoring his possibly meaning smile, I walked to the cast-stone archway that broke the façade, was just reaching for a bell-pull beside the wrought-iron gates when a silver-haired butler stepped out of the house.

"Welcome, Mr. Harnes," he said, his emphasis correct.

Clanging shut the gate behind me, with a bow he opened a door. I had just time to cast a glance over the arcades of a large flagged courtyard before entering a most pleasant sitting room.

"Hat and coat, sir?"

He carried them away, leaving me to inspect over the fire a glittering view in oils of, as I later learned, the ballroom of London's bombed-out Halliwith House, one of Mrs. Berlin's girlhood homes. Precious objects in bronze, jade, cloisonné enamel, Italian majolica and Ch'ien-lung porcelain surrounded me, and layers of fabric: needlepoint upholstery, silk brocade on the walls, on the floor a superb Bokhara.

There was a step, and into the room wearing tailored tweeds and carrying a riding crop came a handsome, imposing woman who appeared younger than the mid-50s I knew she was.

"Mr. Harnes? Dora Berlin. So good of you to come all this way."

2.

THAT AFTERNOON MRS. BERLIN dropped me at Carnegie Hall, opposite Nickel-and-dime's offices.

Her limousine growled off, a whale among minnows. The overcast was so pronounced that, at not 4:00 o'clock, lights were coming on. But there's glamour to New York's early winter dusk, the city's nerves and energies throbbing as people stride onto the pavements eager to get on with it.

Pulling my fedora low so as not to meet some man's gaze or brush his knuckles and reflexively end up in his bed – there was no time! – I crossed the street and, nodding at the doorman, entered the building.

The grimy brown brick edifice, a mixture of studios and offices, was dedicated to the music trade. At any hour one could hear expert touches on piano or violin; our office game was to guess who was working where: Firkušný, Rubinstein, Horowitz? Heifetz, Zimbalist, Menuhin? A baritone was vocalizing as I waited for the elevator. Robert Merrill?

When I'd telephoned from the country, Sophie, Nikolodimsky's secretary, had me hold the line while our boss railed away in Russian from his supposedly sound-proofed office, whether at his wife about dinner or at the Soviet

Ambassador — quite possibly in person — about exit permits for artists he wished to present.

Finally the savagery ceased and Sophie connected us.

"*Well?*" It came out *Vell?* "How do you find our lady friend?"

"Very nice. Fed me well, and now she's showing me around."

"*And?*"

"Ambitious plans, with no time to spare. But I told her I'd do it."

"*Goot!*"

"Look, Mr. Nikolodimsky, I'm going to Chicago tonight to break the news to David. Back Thursday — working lunch with Mrs. Berlin."

"David? *Goot!*"

House policy required that client-management changes be made face-to-face, for, as Nickel-and-dime put it, "Music is *people*, and people you treat with *respect*." My other clients happening to be in town, I could deal with them on my return.

Another house policy — the generous expense accounts that allowed me to travel first-class, the better to bolster the prestige of the arts — would make the round-trip bearable.

"Train's at 5:00? Come in before," Nikolodimsky told me.

David. We'd been together five years, and I was in love with him still. David Spegall was handsome and supremely talented; I *had* to love him, even if, loving him, I was tied down, domestic, not myself, living a persona that, however pleasing, wasn't *me* — and with jealousy decreeing I forever had to hear *You're not good enough!* (Not that *David* would dream of saying such a thing.)

But now Mrs. Berlin proposed hiring me to start a summer music festival at Ca'Dora, and I could no longer manage David's career. Someone else had to take over; I had to set my lover free.

That I felt some relief in doing so reminded me of what a shit I was. Mind you, young people often have to be, having their way to make in a world not very welcoming to them. And I was never as bad as some might claim.

Worst was the jealousy of my own lover that constantly gnawed at me. What it could drive me to! Especially given David's obliviousness, off in the artist's comfy cloud-cuckoo-land of vagueness, while I had to subsist in the most real of worlds.

A music festival outdoors on a great estate! So much to do! Dates; programs; artists; publicity. Parking! My God, *chairs*! My God, what if it *rained*? And so little time!

But I was thrilled, gone from fearing I'd lost my job (though apparently I had) to having a niche of my own in the music world.

The usual progress of a career at Nickel-and-dime's was glacially slow. I personally managed two pianists — David one of them — plus the Enlightenment Quartet, a cellist, a flautist, a fiddler, a chorus and two conductors: Booked their appearances and negotiated their fees, collected commissions, wrote program notes, arranged interviews, under their by-lines ghost-wrote articles for the music press (*On First Hearing Delius; The Best Advice Toscanini Ever Gave Me*), advised on repertoire, attended recording sessions, even posed them at keyboard or music stand to photograph them, and all for a pittance.

And this I'd been doing since being hired out of the Juilliard School of Music three years earlier with bachelor's and master's degrees in music criticism — hired at David's behest, with every prospect of continuing for another 30 or 40 years. Counting on promotion, much less succession, was pie-in-the-sky; though he'd been around forever, Nickel-and-dime was by no means over the hill.

So I couldn't pass up Mrs. Berlin's offer. Founding a festival? I could do that!

Nickel-and-dime's corner office was a former studio paneled in walnut. Behind his desk, clocks displayed the time across North America and in London, Paris and Moscow, and antique weathervanes from his collection studded the wall opposite. The grandfather clock, lacquered in *chinoiserie,* shaded the passing seconds into majestic *tocks* and *ticks.*

As I went in, my boss was sitting as still as the Buddha across from two visitors in gray suits, white shirts, dark ties whose heads snapped towards me in tandem. They stood up menacingly. Crew-cuts made their faces those of boys. One had the physique of my football-player father, the other was slender and willowy; the first somewhat older than myself, the second younger.

"Ah, here's Mr. Harnes," said Nickel-and-dime, remaining seated. "Bruce, these gentlemen are from the Federal Bureau of Investigation."

The elder—Special Agent Nolan—grabbed my fingers, his jaw telegraphing his intention of crushing them, but pianists have strong hands; I was gratified to make him wince.

The blond offered his hand gravely, and I pressed it with equal gravity. Palm and fingers were warm, his eyes enormous; I rather fell in. His name was Goddard. It surprised me to find a fairy among the G-men.

"I told them you're going to help Mrs. Berlin stage her festival. Am I correct?"

"Yes, and about that, Mr. Nikolodimsky—forgive me, gentlemen, but I have a train to catch—I want David Spegall as Music Director."

"*David Spegall!* Get out of here!"

"No, sir: I need him. Can offer a very good fee."

"Listen to yourself!" he exclaimed, closing the topic for the time being.

I was confident he'd come around. David's reputation was as a pianist, but he was also a gifted conductor. Directing my Festival would be a big boost for his career, even place him in the running to lead the New York Philharmonic should Mitropoulos ever pass the baton, while permitting me to keep hold of—not to say, the leash—but the *reins* in whatever remained of our relationship.

"Special Agent Nolan wishes to speak with you."

Standing at angles to each other, Nolan and Goddard boxed me in, the younger's pelvis thrust out, body arched like a bow pulled to highest tension.

"What can I do for you?" I asked affably.

"It's not for *us*—" began Nolan.

"—but for your *country*," Goddard finished.

"And what does that mean?"

Disgust clenching his features, Nolan declared, "Two nights ago you were arrested at a place for perverts in Greenwich Village."

Nickel-and-dime turned to look out the window.

"Apparently you know all about it."

"Disposition of the case?"

"Desk ticket for disorderly conduct," I said shortly. "I'll pay a fine at my arraignment."

The younger man relaxed, the bow going slack as the arrow hit its mark, and both sat down, as did I.

"Mr. Harnes, we're not here about *that*," said Goddard, leaning forward, "but in connection with your relations with Mrs. Dora Berlin."

This was surprising. "Why would Mrs. Berlin interest the FBI?"

Nolan answered, "Given her ties to the Soviet Union—"

"*What!*" I was astonished.

"Oh, yes, 20 years ago she had an affair with a *Russian*, until Uncle Joe personally intervened."

"Plus, she was married to a *Jew*—" put in Goddard.

"Now, listen here—"

"—and her daughter to a *Hungarian*."

"Look here, Mrs. Berlin's as distinguished a lady as we have," I said, "not excepting Eleanor Roosevelt." Better not to have mentioned Eleanor Roosevelt. "One grandfather was Lincoln's Minister to Paris, the other a Union Army general. For goodness' sake, her stepfather's Churchill's *cousin!*"

Better not to have mentioned Churchill.

"*Churchill*," sneered Goddard.

Nolan summed up, "Mrs. Berlin travels in circles that include Russkis, Jews, Commies, Brits and queers. Given the present climate, we need your help."

The present climate of hysteria, he meant, Americans convinced that liberals—abetted by queers (etc.)—were bent on handing the country over to Stalin. Truman, President until the week before, boasted of purging hundreds of homosexuals from the State Department.

"Gentlemen—" I began deprecatingly.

Goddard interrupted. "With your police record, Mr. Harnes, you'd be well advised to cooperate."

"Ah." There we were: Already I was being blackmailed— and by a little faggot. Kafkaesque! Orwellian!

"Call it cultural counter-espionage," Nolan suggested. "It's a matter of national security that we monitor Mrs. Berlin."

"Bruce, you must agree," Nickel-and-dime said flatly, revolving towards his weathervanes.

"Inform on my new boss?" My old one shrugged.

"Special Agent Goddard will be your contact," said Nolan as his colleague handed me a card bearing a telephone number. "You are Confidential Informant DB-2. Call every week, and he'll set a meeting. If you don't call, he'll find *you*."

I studied the card.

"And Confidential Informant DB-*1*? Who might *that* be?"

The agents looked askance at each other, but said nothing.

I didn't see what choice I had. Not to mention that my train wouldn't wait.

So did they give me anything in the way of tradecraft to go with my code name? Any training, any hints that might have helped prevent the catastrophe to come?

Nope, nothing at all.

On my way out I stopped at my desk – already cleared – to grab the suitcase I kept under it, and used the phone to call the Palmer House; David was playing the next evening with the Chicago Symphony Orchestra.

He was at rehearsal, but I dictated the message of my arrival in the morning, and ran to Grand Central.

3.

I BOARDED *The 20th Century Limited* with a minute to spare.

The gleaming, streamlined machine was shuddering in the terminal's depths, alive with anticipatory vibrations, its glamour, as I trotted to my car, a little spoiled by someone's flushing a toilet in defiance of the ban on doing so when stopped at a station. Waste spilled onto the tracks.

Handing my bag to a porter who took it with seeming delight, I was shown to my roomette as the train began slipping through the tunnel. A man of mystery already regarded me as I sat down. Soon we emerged into the waning light of the Hudson's bank, metallic river waters vanishing into darkness. The man of mystery reaching out in mute appeal, I lowered the shade.

My day had passed with the weight of one of rare destiny.

"Please, Mrs. Berlin, call me Bruce."

"Bruce, do you ride?" she asked warmly.

"Western, yes."

"Next time, then."

Indicating a Louis XV chair of tortoiseshell lacquer, she excused herself. Reappearing in a silk print dress, she poked the fire before alighting in my chair's mate.

"Where to begin? Well, why don't I show you?"

Springing to her feet, Mrs. Berlin led me down a terrazzo corridor past oaken linenfold doors, around a corner and along a passage with snowy lawns to one side, to the other a covered summer porch overlooking the courtyard, and through a magnificent dining room of gilded *boiserie*.

I was lost by the time she pushed open a 16th-century Spanish wrought-iron gate and brought me into the largest room I've ever seen in a private house. Ten rose windows — their stained glass taken, I later learned, from medieval cathedrals — pierced the thick upper walls.

"Wait," she said.

At the wall she punched buttons, and flame-shaped bulbs sprang to life on chandeliers 25 feet above the floor.

The room thus revealed reminded me of the Palazzo Vecchio's lofty, crowded *Salone dei Cinquecento*. There were Louis XIII armchairs, marquetry tables, Gothic wooden statues, Renaissance busts in ceramic and marble, painted *cassoni*, carved *credenze*, a ceiling of walnut rosettes, friezes painted by Paolo Veronese and, ranged round the walls, Old Master paintings. On high at one end presided a musicians gallery; at the other, steps ascended to a stage where a grand piano stood next to some sort of contraption.

"Magnificent," I murmured.

"Our music room," said Mrs. Berlin. "My husband was devoted to music. After our son died in the War — "

"Oh, I'm sorry." *That* I didn't know; I was startled.

"Your age. Would have been, I mean: Max Junior. Bomber pilot, shot down over Germany. Were you in the War?"

"Army," I answered.

Did she really wish to hear about my Special Services stint as Entertainment Specialist, playing piano at USOs on two fronts, never having a better time in my life until, caught near

Mannheim with a desperately pretty corporal, they sent me to Yale to learn Japanese? Probably not.

"My daughter doesn't want this house — these big places are old-fashioned — so after our son's death my husband and I decided to leave it for the public's benefit. All very complicated, I'm afraid. When I'm gone Ca'Dora will go, with an endowment, to the Max and Dora Berlin Foundation for Music and the Arts. *Anyway.*"

She was leading me in a slow circuit of the room, past Cellini bronzes, Han Dynasty figurines, *Quattrocento* temperas, paintings by Canaletto, Cranach the Elder and, unexpectedly, a raw Picasso nude. Everything was beautiful, as well as priceless. The jumble was of the sort that can only be redeemed by taste — but taste abounded.

"They tell me we could seat two or three hundred. The acoustics, I assure you, are *marvelous.*"

I followed her up onto the stage, like the rest of the room handsomely floored in teak. The piano was a Bösendorfer, and the contraption beside it, of inlaid maple and protruding copper rods —

"Why, surely that's not a *Primover?*"

"Yes, it is." She beamed. "I've another in town."

"My goodness!"

I'd never seen the world's original electronic musical instrument, weaver of spooky soundtracks for horror films and science fiction flicks. And wasn't there a story about the mad Russian who invented it, Piotyr Alexandreyevitch Primov? Kidnapped in Manhattan by Russian secret agents, repatriated and shot? Something like that?

"My husband was Dr. Primov's great patron, and I play, didn't you know? '*Its foremost advocate and artiste.*' *Herald Tribune.* Well, not so much anymore. Now we don't seem able to find the right kinds of tubes. We're going mute."

Watching her caress the instrument, I realized the FBI wasn't just whistling *Dixie* about her having an affair with a Russian.

In the encouraging beams of her smile, I sat down at the piano and, murmuring, "My shoulder's a little sore," embarked on—yes, *Ravel*. Somehow I knew that polishing the prisms of *Pavane for a Dead Princess* would ravish her.

Disconcertingly, I was hardly a dozen bars into the piece when, her smile fading, she spoke up: "Yes, well, I wanted to show you the Florentine Cloister?"

Through French doors she took me into the courtyard, remarking that its columns came from a Tuscan monastery. It was overlooked by the house's upper story, chimneys looming.

"Charming," I noted.

"We've had music here, too. Better acoustics than you might expect. They say it could seat 350 or more?"

Her butler leaned into the courtyard and harrumphed, "Madam, lunch is served."

"Thank you, Freddie!"

We stepped indoors and, after I'd washed up in a powder room extracted from Fontainebleau, took seats, not at the dining room's main table, but a few steps up at a glass-topped one in a bay looking out at a marble terrace. But first Mrs. Berlin went outdoors and scattered birdseed, bringing doves, cardinals and sparrows descending in waves around her. It reminded me of medieval tapestry.

Then, spooning lentil soup and slicing a veal cutlet, she explained her summons in a delightful old-fashioned high-class drawl: She wished to start a music festival that coming summer—in the classical music world, tantamount to *overnight*—using as venues her music room and Florentine Cloister, as well as the Colonnade Lawn (which she promised to show me after lunch), and on Nickel-and-dime's recommendation wanted *me* to take charge.

Her husband's and son's deaths had torn her asunder, she said; inaugurating the Festival they'd dreamed of would help her cope. She mentioned also the generous salary she proposed paying me.

All this in accents rather English, featuring the dropped *g's* of Oscar Wilde's day and reflecting her upbringing in Britain after her mother divorced her copper-magnate husband and married a younger son of the richest commoner in England.

As the butler cleared she said, "Freddie, both cars in an hour, please? Tell Joe we'll stop at the Lawn."

"Very good, Mrs. Berlin."

"Bruce, let's go upstairs. Where I hope you'll wish to live."

Retracing our route up the corridor, this time we pierced a velvet curtain and climbed a spiral staircase as into a boys' clubhouse. We emerged into a delightful room with a peaked, beamed ceiling, a fireplace my height and latticed windows overlooking courtyard and lawns.

"This should do for the Festival office," she said. "My son's study?"

Past a spacious bath tiled in a challenging purple, we found her son's bedroom, a comfortable chamber with a hooded mantelpiece and furnished in Henri II pieces that, despite being 400 years old, resembled modern Danish design. Casements commanded the lawns, and it had a spacious dressing room. I felt at home immediately.

"Wonderful," I said.

"Oh, *good*," said Mrs. Berlin. "I *think* you'll like your rooms in my house in town, too."

After gawking my way behind her through the West Wing's palatial reception rooms, and remembering to call Mr. Nikolodimsky, I tramped in hat and coat with her through a swinging door into the butler's pantry and down to a garage where her chauffeur helped us into the Cadillac, while maids and housemen crammed into a wood-sided station wagon.

We set off down an unplowed track the car didn't much like—the main drive. After sliding a few hundred yards Mrs. Berlin said, "This will do, Joe," and the limousine skidded to rest beside towering spear-tipped gates flanked by plunging horse heads sculpted by Malvina Hoffman.

"Just a quick look," she said.

Getting out, she opened a door within the gates and passed through to an icy stone staircase, which we didn't venture down. It descended to a long flat lawn bordered by laurels and cedars at whose far end arose two dozen Roman pillars of marble and porphyry joined by arches and defining the edges of a stage. A Doge of Venice had assembled the colonnade for his gardens, Mrs. Berlin told me, where it stood for half a millennium.

"There's room onstage for a symphony orchestra," she said, "and on the lawn for a thousand spectators. Acoustically challenging, though. Really we need a bandshell or something. But you do see what I have in mind? Something like Glyndebourne or Aldeburgh?" she asked, naming two famous English festivals.

I did see. We returned to the car. It turned around and motored out the plowed and sanded back way, the station wagon falling in behind. Refusing the eye of the ghost in the glass beyond her, I thought about what to say. Though I wished to be encouraging, someone had to throw the cold water of reality on her scheme—had to screw up the courage to broach what was, after all, *sink or swim* and *make or break*.

"Well, Mrs. Berlin, your Festival's a wonderful idea," I said. "And at the risk of sounding immodest, I'm the perfect choice to run it. But—with apologies for being crass—I must warn you: The thing above all needful is *money."*

"*Oh!* Don't worry about *that."*

I was getting hungry. Raising the shade, I double-checked that there was nothing out there.

Leaving David would hurt him, I knew, but do no permanent damage. No, *art* would save him, work its transformative magic. He would rise up over his pain, *use it* to make music even more probing, more beautiful. My leaving would make him a better artist!

That's the thing about art, and the difference between us, I considered resentfully. Arrested and jailed, I suffered until I was free, glad to be out but left with nothing from the experience but heightened wariness.

Whereas art was David's sole element; to art he assimilated *everything.* Consequently, his art deepened as his knowledge of the human condition expanded with anything and everything that happened to him. At the keyboard or on the podium David could redeem any experience—delve into any humiliation, suffer any hurt over again—to make his music more personal and more honest. Not without anger himself, to be sure, but that anger fueled his creativity. Thanks to his *art,* nothing entirely *bad* could happen to him!

Was it *fair?* Fair that David had his art when I had none? Fair that I was left high and dry, in this life necessarily out for myself alone? Fair that David was living the life that should have been *mine?*

No, not one little bit fair!

AT THE SECOND SEATING I found my way to the dining car and was put at a four-top where only one other sat, a rather spectacular kid. Brooding mysteriously, I penciled my choices of entrée and vegetables—rainbow trout, with new potatoes and green beans—before reluctantly letting my tablemate, a grad student headed back to school, draw me into conversation. Discovering that he liked behind-the-scenes music stories, I invited him to my roomette for after-dinner brandy. There was a flask in my bag.

The porter had pulled out the bed and turned down the sheets. We sat down, I poured, and the rest was delightful: the breathless reaching over, not knowing what would ensue, the kisses, toyings, unveilings of flesh and bone, and building to the moans (suppressed).

I couldn't sleep with anyone but David — perhaps because we so seldom had sex — so packed my trick back to his seat and turned out the light.

4.

I KNEW MY showing up in Chicago the day of an important engagement wouldn't throw David off his stride: He was a professional. Of course I intended waiting until after the concert—next morning, actually—to break up with him; he deserved that consideration.

Arriving at the Palmer House at 9:00 a.m., I went upstairs and knocked on the door to his suite. David answered, coffee cup in hand, smile on his face.

"Brucie! Glad you made it!"

Glad he may have been, but really he was off wherever he goes in the hours before taking the stage—wherever you dwell, not touching planet Earth, when you're to play Rachmaninoff. After doing some scales at the piano, he abruptly pulled on his mittens and announced he was taking a walk, did I care to join him?

We plunged into the one downtown that rivals Manhattan, braving icy blasts up to the Art Institute. What engaged us that freezing morning of course was the huge Seurat, that notation of summertime sunlight on the banks of the Seine. Under a guard's gimlet eye we leaned into it until the scene dissolved into dry meaningless dots.

"*Ha!*" said David.

Soon we were hauling ourselves against the wind back to the hotel by means of ropes considerately strung along Michigan Avenue, I marveling that Chicago was ever settled.

Upstairs, I suggested, "Shall we have lunch in?"

"Whatever you're having," David said. "You sounded funny on the phone the other night, like something's up."

"Well, I have news. A widow named Dora Berlin wants my help starting an outdoor music festival in Westchester this summer."

"Aleksandre Michaelovitch is OK with that?"

"His suggestion."

For a moment David looked serious, then he shrugged and reverted to concentrating on the evening to come. He would revolve the matter before recurring to how my new job might affect *him*.

I ordered up sandwiches and salads while David played oompah band music (odd preparation for Rachmaninoff, I thought, but who am I to question genius?), and we ate.

The afternoon passed with David's nervous hovering between keyboard and windows, radio and newspapers. Not a word about *us*; unconsciously, he was postponing facing facts.

After a light supper, from the lobby of golden piers I saw him off resplendent in white tie and tails and mittens. People could see, so it was with merely a handshake, and round to Orchestra Hall he went.

Needing a pick-me-up, something to help me get away from myself, I went into the bar. A few minutes later, a shoulder pressed mine and I looked up to find an engaging young face. That man of mystery had a useful allure when he wasn't spying on me.

We just had time. Upstairs, we peeled back the wool, got at that hard red flesh, brought each other expertly over the brink.

"My goodness," I said when my voice came back.

DEPLETED AFTER MY little adventure—but it had done me good—I hurried around the corner ready for the high altar of art. Fritz Reiner was to lead the CSO in Berlioz and Strauss before bringing on David for Rachmaninoff's *Third Piano Concerto*.

Really, I thought, listening to the opening pieces, no one compared to Reiner. And watching David cross the stage, I was free to feast on him as I couldn't when alone with him, when he grew embarrassed and suspicious. People always told us we looked like brothers, but I thought David much better looking, with his noble high brow, warm cushioned eyes, mouth of passionate joys, the determined set to his jaw and hair that hinted at the fires within. Older, too, of course— pushing 40.

Express like an angel, he went to the piano, bowed, sat down, reached to the keyboard as to a lifeline, awaited Reiner's downbeat and bounced!

A battle royal! Everyone knows how driving and powerful the *Rach Third* is, but David made it intimate, too. The sheer beauty of the sound he produced stunned us in carrying us to higher dimensions of limpid, all-encompassing logic and beauty. We wept, David's touch sounding each note's lament as he suffered exquisite torture that we might hear the music to its depths without being distracted by pain.

Of course, gnashing my teeth like one condemned to Hell, I found it as unbearable as I did beautiful.

It was at Juilliard that we met. David, a recent defector from the USSR, was in his first year of teaching, and I was studying piano on the G.I. Bill.

David's people were *petit bourgeoisie* for whom the Revolution meant a hard fall and who suffered greatly until

their boy's astounding talent improved things for them. But
came the War, and with everybody else David was swept up
into the Red Army, fighting for his city's and country's
survival.

He seldom spoke of Leningrad's siege; all I knew was that
he drove trucks over frozen Lake Ladoga, and that his parents
and bride — oh yes, he'd married very young — starved to
death. (I never understood why, a million frozen corpses
piling up, Leningrad's meatpackers didn't can a "siege
chicken" product that might have saved thousands.)

After the War came European tours, then a fateful trip to
Britain and David's escape to the West. Nickel-and-dime was
instrumental in bringing him to America.

At Juilliard — in those days on Claremont Avenue, near
Barnard and Columbia and the seminaries — we lived within a
reverberating hive, music resounding from every surface.
Thus, I heard David before I saw him: Walked enraptured
down a cork-walled corridor as somebody wove from Bach's
Well-Tempered Clavier a momentous narrative undergirt by
unsuspected soul — *Russian* soul!

After loitering in the hallway, I breached every rule of
decorum and went in. Had to see who was making me fall in
love. Raising his head from the keyboard, hair flying, face
shiny with sweat, David's eyes burned through me and — after
harrowing me to the bone for five seconds — he nodded as
though to say, *Oh*, there *you are. Hold on a sec, be right with you.*

Now, in Chicago, after the ovations and encores, I rescued
him from well-wishers and brought him and his bouquets to a
reception in a Lake Shore Drive penthouse Mies van der Rohe
designed in clean lines of glass and marble. The lake sparkled
with lights as we drank champagne.

When we finally returned to the hotel and — with a
vengeance — David came down to earth, I was receptive,

knowing it was our last time together, and also that for him it had been a while. He was faithful to me, but I'm afraid I tended to keep him in a sex-starved condition. We fought the passionate mock battle, taking and mauling without let or mercy, simultaneously scaling the peaks. Sobbing in my arms with ecstasy or agony — all one — he fell asleep.

At breakfast the next morning he asked, "Brucie, occurs to me, for this Festival will you be staying in Westchester?"

"Yes, and until then at Mrs. Berlin's house in the city." His eyes widened with hurt surprise. I added, "I've proposed engaging you as Music Director."

He brightened. "Have I dates open this summer?"

"We'll work it out."

"Mozart's so effective in the open air. Tchaikovsky, too. Has she family, Mrs. Berlin?"

"Her son died in the War."

"Oh, does she want a new one?"

The Russian sense of humor can be elephantine.

"But there's a daughter I haven't met, a divorcée. Interested?"

David peered to see if I was joking, whether he should laugh. Decided not to. Already his mind was on getting himself to Louisville for his next performance. He would be fine, I knew. The moment was come.

"But David, I can no longer manage you. To run this Festival I must leave Nickel-and-dime."

"Are you leaving *me*, Brucie?"

"Yes, but it's not *you*, feels like *fate*. I *am* sorry. We'll always be friends."

David was looking out at the Loop when I said this, but he heard me; weighed my words and turned on me the saddest look in the world.

"Your Festival will be a big success," he told me. "You're

the kind of person destined for success, Brucie—like a mirror all over. Sorry, it's something we say in Russia. *Slick,* is that the English?"

"Oh, thanks so much," I said.

Later I dropped him off at the Central Station to catch his train, on my way to the LaSalle Street Station to catch mine.

5.

SOMEWHERE IN OHIO I sat down to dinner with a married couple who didn't linger and a long-lashed looker of 20. Alas, while shoveling in his second piece of apple pie à la mode, this beauty spurned my suggestion of after-dinner brandy with that youthful cynicism you see more and more often.

Having no better luck in the club car, I rumbled solitary through the night — a free man at last, and horny, but alone.

Which invited me to brood again about my dashed musical ambitions, in turn bringing up the disapproving image of my father's face, forever subjecting me to his *I told you so*.

It began so hopefully. I loved sitting beside my mother at her piano, from the age of two tried to help out. My father would tear me away, of course, just as he did from my sisters' dollhouses, where the relations of dolls and stuffed animals entranced me, and drag me outdoors to toss a pigskin that made me flinch and flee crying. More than once my father told me I was no son of his.

He was a Michigan gridiron star — *All-American!* — who, as a lawyer rising to eminence, came practically to govern a vast district of Idaho: A judge, forsooth! I never knew him as anything else.

Unendurable. With every word, every gesture he laid down the law. Sometimes I'd see him biting his tongue, eyes amused even as he tried to suppress a witticism. And he wonders why I don't speak to him?

Given lessons from the age of four, I made piano my focus, my chosen field, my obsession. After Mother's death (I was 14) and that USO apprenticeship, my gift took me to Juilliard. But when Juilliard began pushing me away from piano into criticism and management, Father said, "I told you so."

Yes, Juilliard shunted this boy—hailing from a town home to three spinsters teaching at two spinets—away from performing. No matter that I had no interest in writing about music or musicians, steadily, with kindly intent and ruthless realism, everyone—David, too—pushed me clear off the piano bench. How David praised my literary turn of phrase! My insight into performers! While silent as to my playing.

Good as I was, however talented, I wasn't good enough for a professional performing career.

Gall and wormwood.

Thus did David help *squelch* me, deprive me of the instruction that would have ripened *my* talent, too, transformed my glib touch at the keyboard to lift *me* to the lofty, austere realms where artists like him dwell.

So why couldn't *I* live and die in a phrase of Mozart's, like David? Why couldn't *I* push Beethoven to the very edge of what music *is*, as David could? Because *no one taught me how!*

Finally I accepted that if I wished to remain in the music world, reviewing or administration was the best I could do. Hence Nikolodimsky Concert Management.

It was a bitter reckoning, and to be steered to it by my own lover was hurtful and humiliating. But David had too much integrity to encourage me to enter realms where I had no business being.

Thus, of necessity I found myself his servant. After all, you couldn't expect *David* to know how to drop off dry-cleaning, fill out a tax form, renew his visa, bank his cheques or pay an electric bill—he was made of finer stuff. That his fingers might convey what Chopin, Mendelssohn or Mussorgsky, communing with the gods, compressed into notes, he had to be free of the quotidian, of the ordinary stuff of life that mires the rest of us; free to breathe of Parnassus.

This was why, shit that I am, I was jealous of him and his *art*.

I didn't necessarily dispute that my highest possible contribution to mankind was to keep David Spegall warm, fed and happy, for I loved him. Didn't dispute it, but I did rebel: Live *my* life on such terms? I was *jealous!* And what can you do with jealousy when you can't accept, accommodate or ignore it? It eats at you, crushes you, makes life hell. To escape it—to stay alive—I used such diversions as came my way. *Had* to, knowing that ultimately I would have to leave him; though better *that* than, as my fantasies sometimes had it, *kill* him.

Now, thanks to Mrs. Berlin, I had the excuse I needed.

Wondering who would keep David warm at night, I yanked the shade down on the smirker in the window. The wheels, chanting *hypocritehypocritehypocrite* (no idea *why*), finally lulled me to sleep.

What happened to David in the meantime seemed prophetic of something or other. A nervous traveler, not yet of such eminence that a Nikolodimsky factotum accompanied him, that evening he stepped off in St. Louis with no notion he wasn't in Louisville until enlightened by a taxi driver.

In a panic he called New York, and the junior associate he reached through the after-hours answering service calmed him down, looked up a flight that would get him to Louisville in time for rehearsal the next day, and instructed him how to get to the airport and buy a ticket. Judged to have proved his mettle in doing so, the youngster was named David's new manager.

And the performance with the Louisville Symphony? Apparently quite up to snuff.

6.

IN THE MORNING New York's *sis-boom-bah* — the roar like a rollercoaster's — greeted me as I stepped from Grand Central onto 42nd Street, Park Avenue coursing overhead. The racket made me smile. Thinking *Now for it!*, I carried my suitcase round to Mrs. Berlin's on 54th Street between Fifth and Sixth Avenues.

It's a charming block, running from Stanford White's opulent University Club past grand townhouses and Art Deco apartment buildings to the Dorset and Warwick Hotels, though surely it was even more charming before the Rockefellers tore down their mansions to make way for the Museum of Modern Art.

Mrs. Berlin's limestone Beaux-Arts house was flanked by brownstones that also belonged to her. In fact, it was from the one just to the west that Stalin's agents abducted Primov. Opposite was the gray brick wall to MoMA's sculpture garden.

I climbed the steps, rang, and soon Mrs. B. was greeting me warmly. She introduced me, too, to her "companion" (like a character in a Victorian three-decker), telling me that Miss d'Orsay was eager to help with the Festival in any way she might. I nodded genially at this anxious-seeming person where she hung at the wall scrubbing her black-clad hips.

Delighted with my news that David Spegall was coming to lunch Wednesday next to discuss her Festival (I rather preened myself), Mrs. B. took me up in the elevator to her late son's fifth-floor domain.

Just as six or eight rooms taken from European villas and palaces had been installed at Ca'Dora, her city house boasted some half dozen period rooms. Max Junior's study, which would serve as the Festival's Manhattan office, was a lofty Piedmontese painted library of the 17th century overlooking the street and sculpture garden—I could see Rodin's thumping big *Balzac* and, behind it, the RCA Building sawing away at the sky.

The bedroom next door was a fine chamber with beams and paneled walls taken from the Stratford-on-Avon house of Shakespeare's baker friend whose oven fire incinerated the manuscripts; the beams were charred with *Hamlet*'s smoke. It had a spacious bath, fortunately of the 20th century, where I would occasionally hear footfalls from the servants' floor above.

Mrs. B. left me to settle in. Nowhere had I felt more readily at home. Everything was just as I could wish it; I reveled in my rooms. My only difficulty was deciding which I preferred, those in the city or country.

At lunchtime I descended into chaos.

"*Tibor!*" a woman commanded as I pushed open the elevator door. I couldn't see her, but her voice was like—like her mother's, I realized. "Put that down *instantly!*"

And instantly a seven-year-old boy in a sailor suit smashed a Dresden figurine to the parquet.

"*Really*, Tibor!"

"Bring him in here, dear," Mrs. B. called calmly from the

dining room, telling a maid, "Please sweep up the pieces for the menders."

Another young sailor already sat next to her, observant and quiet, his head against the chair.

"Bruce, may I introduce my daughter, Elyse Ferenci? Elyse, this is Bruce Harnes."

"*Music* festival!" said Elyse, advancing with flashing eyes.

Oh dear, thought I.

Their resemblance was striking, Elyse being as tall as her mother, save that she had her father's frizzy hair and was 25 years younger. In fact, aside from a perennial expression of discontent, she was beautiful.

"Oh yes, Mrs. Ferenci, and the way it's shaping up—"

"*Really*, Mother, haven't you better things to spend your money on? *Tibor!* If I have to tell you one more time!"

Crash!

But lunch got under way, Miss d'Orsay and I sipping our soup, Tibor erupting intermittently. Eventually even he settled down to eat, freeing his mother to grill me on my qualifications and intentions.

It was clear that Elyse Ferenci and Bruce Harnes were not destined to be friends, but we took each other's measure and so avoided outright war. This was, after all, the dismal dawn of Mutually Assured Destruction. The Soviets had just developed their own atomic bomb (our countrymen convinced they had American connivance, probably from us pesky homos), and MAD kept the peace.

So with Elyse and me. Respecting each other's spheres of influence, we avoided the Armageddon that might have been expected from two people who loathed each other on sight.

Meanwhile, like a mother too wise to interfere in her children's battles, Mrs. B. conversed with her grandsons.

I found watching her with them instructive. After lunch,

that transparent Tibor went up to her with a gleam in his eye, affectionate, charming, wheedling. He wanted a bonbon from her Steuben dish, but even if he got his wish, he didn't put one over on her. She assessed his charm even as she enjoyed it, and was manipulated to none but the foreordained grandmotherly result when, grasping his foil-wrapped prize, he scooted off triumphant to gorge in solitude.

Miss d'Orsay filled me in later on Elyse's divorce the year before. She'd married a gifted but impoverished cellist from Hungary and, after ten years of his wandering ways, two boys and a solid start to his famous collection of Renaissance drawings, divorced him. The crisis came after Max Berlin's will made his daughter a rich woman with an unshakable grasp on her own money, and she discovered the pockets cut out of her husband's favorite weekend pair of denim shorts, making her wonder why he required ready access to his genitals.

Settling into my digs, I soon formed new routines and found new pleasures. Mrs. B. cosseting me as though I were the son of the house, artichokes and Alaska King Crab began to appear on her table, and *Variety* — bible even to the classical music trade — on my desk. Also she pleased me by permitting me to escort her to see *Der Rosenkavalier* from her Golden Horseshoe box at the Met.

Though someone who often found women rather irritating, I hit it off with Mrs. Berlin. And as I sounded the voids left by the deaths of her son and husband, it seemed there was much we could do for each other, though I knew I could never replace them completely.

Living in his rooms permitted me to get to know Junior, too. Leather-framed photographs showed him to have been a good-looking youth with a mop of hair and easy smile — rather a heart-breaker. I perused his photo albums from Middlesex and Harvard (where he roomed with David Rockefeller!); never a shadow as he wielded tennis racket or baseball glove in open-faced poses with schoolmates.

His most persuasive portraits had him snuggling into his mother as a boy, or as a youth entwining her shoulders or claiming her waist as he steadily regards the lens. From me they elicited a clench of emotion that he should have met fate so early.

My new salary enabled me to improve my wardrobe, too. With some thought I adopted a modified resort-wear style, based in fact on Junior's, as best accommodating professional and personal demands.

I particularly liked the way Junior carried off his ascots, which I hadn't previously associated with young men. Consequently, I thereafter often appeared with a flourish of silk at my throat. In giving me that slight self-consciousness that sets one off to advantage, they helped me project an air of leisure that, I hoped, the activity of my days belied.

Alas, Junior's own wardrobe had been donated to a Bowery mission, the recipients no doubt ever since sauntering along with ineffable *insouciance*.

7.

WEDNESDAY ARRIVED, a bright February morning bringing a foretaste of spring, windows open to the warmth (and soot, in that era). Mrs. B. sent the Cadillac to Grand Central to collect David Spegall, who was just touching base before starting the New England leg of his tour.

From my office, I heard a cacophony of honking horns — *An American in Paris* played in outraged New Yorkese. Putting my head out the window, I saw a procession: A redhead strolling towards me beneath the University Club, a tall Cadillac keeping stately pace, behind it cars and taxicabs honking in apoplectic fury — wanting to pass but finding themselves enlisted in David's parade.

For it was he. Looking curiously to left and right, David marched at the head of his own orchestra (brass section, at any rate). Turned out that, wanting exercise, he declined the lift.

I dashed downstairs to alert Mrs. B. and, cars honking self-righteously past the limousine at the curb, we met David as he tripped up the steps, a dashingly handsome and well-made man, blue Viking eyes blazing intelligence. Taking a step backwards to forestall his embrace, I murmured introductions and looked on benevolently as they clasped hands.

But possibly my smile faded as, her eyes widening, Mrs. B. looked flirtatiously aside, bosom thrust out as if carelessly while David bent to kiss her fingers. *She liked him!*

Did he like her back? More than once he'd put me off by chortling "*Vive la difference!*" in regards to the sex. Sometimes when with me the sight or scent of a passing female had yanked his head aside. But this one was already *mine!*

We had drinks and ate lunch, David paying court to his flustered, stammering hostess. Regardless, I plowed ahead, laying out my Festival plans and setting forth the responsibilities and emoluments of its Music Director. In this first season I meant to produce just two weekends of music, in late June: orchestral concerts Friday and Saturday nights at the Colonnade Lawn, Sunday afternoon recitals alternating in the Florentine Cloister and music room. If all went well, I would expand the schedule the following year.

Like any great musician, David had his businessman side, so though what I said had to compete for his attention with Mrs. B.'s charms, he recognized it for the opportunity it was. Allowing as how he might be interested, he cautioned that before undertaking to alter his schedule he needed to inspect the ground — see the three venues with his own eyes.

Fine; Mrs. B. ordered up Joe and the car and, scooping me up, too, however *de trop* I imagined myself, we embarked on an excursion to Katonah.

They chatted easily through The Bronx, around the Hawthorne Circle and up the sweeping curves of the Sawmill River Parkway, while from my jumpseat's window a man of mystery glared at me balefully.

I was kicking myself. It had seemed so simple: David was the best — sufficient reason to make him Music Director. And it would be convenient to work with someone I'd worked with before, especially in the rush required to stage this Festival.

And the *jealousy* that shadowed my *love* for David decreed that he be kept close, if only for purposes of torment: I wished to flaunt my millionairess and my new role as, in effect, her adoptive son—show him I needed him no longer. The *art* he might have, the *talent*, but *I* had the *power* and the *comfort*.

Not the highest of motives, but surely harmless?

But I hadn't imagined that she'd *like* him—or that he might play along! So I kicked myself, my jealousy flaring.

Soon we were turning into Ca'Dora's main gates—the drive clear of snow—and David was exclaiming at the beauty of grounds and woods.

At the Horse Heads we got out and, hands clasped behind his back, David approvingly surveyed the Colonnade Lawn, before turning to ask, "Toilets?"

Of course! And we'd forgotten. Mrs. B. gave me a look of reproof.

Returning to the car, David helped her skirt a puddle of melting snow, and she giggled. I hadn't before heard her giggle.

The car circled the house before fetching up in front. If not the gigantic pile the Berlins for years planned to build—as fate would have it, they waited to begin until the eve of the 1929 Crash, and the Crash necessitated building a smaller house— still it was one of Westchester's showplaces, especially imposing seen thus, going round the back, past the cellars bearing the immensity of the music room, the dogs barking in their kennel opposite. David whistled.

We entered through the front gate and inspected the Florentine Cloister, and David, his approval instant, nodded impatiently. Into the music room we went. The sun full on one wall's rose windows, the vast space glowed with color.

"How remarkable," he said. "This will serve *beautifully*."

And when he joyfully recognized the Primover, Mrs. B.

glowed, too. She flipped switches, and with squeaks and squeals the tubes began to warm up, while David sat down at the piano.

This was too much for me. Excusing myself before they could musically consummate their relationship in front of my face, I went upstairs and fussed around the office.

In fact I threw papers about with cathartic fury: David was poaching on *my* territory! Not that I took his interest in Mrs. B seriously—but *she* wasn't fooling around. Either they'd embark on a disastrous affair—*she was too old for him!*—or she'd suffer all the pangs on offer in unrequited love. Though I didn't want him for myself any longer, neither did I wish David to steal or hurt *Mrs. B.!* But I'd invited him in!

Just as in the days of siege and counter-siege (but is there a more apt description of modern life?), I was hoist with my own petard: *Hoist!*

Finally Mrs. B. sent the caretaker to fetch me. I entered the music room just as she and David were finishing a keening duet of the Martinů *Fantasia* she happened to have commissioned, he sight-reading at the keyboard, she gesticulating at the Primover, playing together in—of such weird sounds I could never say *harmony*—but in perfect time, and *smiling smiling smiling* at each other.

After her last note died of its quavering grief, she turned to tell me she and David were staying the night so that the car could take him on to his Hartford engagement the next day; Joe would drive me back to town and fetch David's suitcases. It would be like camping out, she exclaimed, only the caretaker and his wife to tend to them!

I went quietly.

My main point was achieved, after all: The Ca'Dora Music Festival's first press release announced that David Spegall had been named Music Director.

A coup indeed, except that David was shoving me off the bench—again.

I seethed all the way back to town, burning with resentment, even as I reminded myself that it was *I* who dropped *him*.

8.

THOUGH POWERLESS TO transform into *art* the pain of losing Mrs. B. to David — whether platonically or worse — I found certain compensations nonetheless. That evening I entered upon the congenial role of lord of a stately Manhattan residence.

In their mistress's absence Freddie and Ernest, Swiss servants long in her employ, took splendid, respectful care of Miss d'Orsay and myself; a testament to how smoothly Mrs. B. ran her homes. Freddie served us drinks in the sitting room overlooking 54th Street, Miss d'Orsay enjoying a nonalcoholic cranberry-juice decoction and myself excellent Scotch as we chatted pleasantly. In the dining room, coming around the table in tag-team fashion, Freddie brought the chops, Ernest the mint sauce.

After dinner, Miss d'Orsay and I returned to our Adam club chairs in the sitting room, where presided a great Philco television set, twin to Ca'Dora's, its bulging round screen serving up our reflections. The man of mystery looked replete and thoroughly at home.

The TV stayed off, however, for after living in the house a week I thought it time to get to know Miss d'Orsay better.

She was a small, angular, nervous person in her 40s or so, with dyed black hair. My impression was that, despite her name, she was neither French nor a maiden lady; later I heard tell of an unhappy early marriage, though for the truth of that, as for much else regarding her, I could never vouch.

Certainly she was the least *obtrusive* person I ever met — seemed to make it her study to fade into the background. In both houses she slept near Mrs. B's bedroom in rooms that were formerly maids' rooms. Wearing black as if in perpetual mourning, one day she modeled a string of small pearls, the next a chain of little gold links. And there she was — if hardly distinguishable from walls or furniture, she was always there.

Miss d'Orsay described herself as *Dora's great friend, Dora's lifelong friend, Dora's devoted friend.* No salary attached to her position, but she lived expense-free. She sang for her supper, however, serving informally as Mrs. B.'s social secretary, telephoning as requested and writing notes in an extravagant hand. Seconded to the Festival, she proved an efficient assistant — effective on the phone and an expert typist, saving me a ton of labor and Mrs. B. a salary.

That evening she expressed excitement, remarking, "This Festival is so close to dear Dora's heart."

"Clearly," I said.

"I quite liked *Maestro* Spegall. Dear Dora did, too, I think."

"So it seemed."

"Vigorous sort of man," she declared. "Musicians so often are, don't you find? He is — a Russian national?"

"Yes."

"A political refugee?"

"As it happens, yes, he is."

"Communist?"

"Surely not!"

"His visa's in order, I hope?"

This finally startled me. "Oh, yes: Nikolodimsky Concert Management represents him, and they see to such things efficiently."

"That's good," she said with strange enthusiasm.

I let it pass, but light was beginning to dawn. Full daylight came a little later when she was reminiscing about her father.

"His parents brought him from Poland—the part Russia held?—when he was a boy," she said, recounting her family history in the manner, I imagined, of an émigrée *comtesse* after the French Revolution. "A comedown, The Bronx, but he adjusted. Never heard English until he was twelve, but at 20 graduated from the City College as a structural engineer, and of course did *very* well. Built the Presbyterian Hospital."

"Really!"

"In the Depression he did what he could to help others." Her voice dropped. "That's when he joined the Party."

"The *Communist* Party?"

"*Hmm-mmm,*" she affirmed, sipping cranberry juice, eyes upturned to mine. Her matter-of-factness stunned me. "From the highest ideals, of course. But then came August 23, 1939? The Hitler-Stalin Nonaggression Pact? *Well,* the disillusionment killed him. He hanged himself."

"I'm so sorry!" I said, thinking *Wow!*

"His death shattered me."

"I should imagine."

"Though his politics weren't mine—not at *all* mine. Forgive me if this is too personal."

"No, no."

I couldn't make out why Miss d'Orsay was telling me these things, unless, however clumsily, as an overture of friendship; though I didn't much care for her, clearly it was best to take it so.

At any rate it enabled me to put two-and-two together and

answer, thus swiftly, the question looming since I stepped across Mrs. B.'s threshold: *Who was Confidential Informant DB-1?* Obviously it was she. Miss d'Orsay's father's history gave the Bureau the same hold over her that my arrest gave them over me. At least I knew to tell her nothing I didn't want whispered into J. Edgar Hoover's ear.

But I did think to ask about Primov, Miss d'Orsay striking me as the sort that knows where the bodies are buried. And indeed, though the episode occurred before her time, she knew every gaudy detail and told the tale plain.

Gaudy, because what happened resulted in part—to my surprise—from Max Berlin's *jealousy.* That (I thought) cold-as-marble figure discovered Primov was having an affair with his wife, so one day took a pistol next door where the Russian lived and, unable to penetrate further, shot up the foyer!

Later the private detective he sicced on Primov reported that Russian goons were spiriting a crate from the house. Suspecting it contained his wife's lover, Mr. Berlin rushed after them to the docks, where, declining to interfere, he watched as the box was winched aboard a freighter. From that day to this nothing more was known of Piotyr Alexandreyevitch.

It was a dramatic story, and moving, too, for I couldn't doubt Mrs. B.'s love for her husband, whatever her feelings for Primov. I found it curiously considerate of Max Berlin that, once past his murderous impulse, he let the situation be resolved on, as it were, a minor chord, thus permitting a wash of poignancy to linger in his wife's memory. Miss d'Orsay assured me husband and wife lived happily together until his death.

Needing another drink after this recitation, instead of ringing for Freddie, which seemed silly, I got up and walked into his pantry, thus stumbling on the evening's comic relief.

Seeing me, Freddie reared back in surprise from the sink,

Scotch bottle in hand and the tap running.

I took the bottle and refreshed my drink while Freddie forced a smile and said, "Mr. Harnes, sir."

There was a mark on the bottle's side well above the level of the liquid within and, seeing me notice it, Freddie blinked.

Thus was I introduced to a custom of the house, or rather to two of them: Max Berlin's of marking his bottles with a grease pencil at the level of the liquor, a practice loyally kept up by his widow, and the servants' of helping themselves, then at the tap refilling the bottles to those same marks.

I inscribed myself in Freddie's good books by returning the bottle with a wink. No skin off my nose. Seemed a practical arrangement, in fact, especially as I take my Scotch with water anyway. Everybody was happy, and if Mrs. B. ultimately bought more spirits than she or her guests consumed — why, she could afford it.

When Miss d'Orsay showed signs of preparing to retire, I announced that I was going out.

She looked startled, but simply advised, "Don't forget your passkey. Freddie's grumpy about answering the door after 10:00 o'clock."

It had decided to snow that evening; the thaw had been a hoax and a fraud. Sound was muffled, a correlative to the white erasing everything. Fresh snow is so beautiful in Manhattan, so lovely the sensation of being the first to crunch across it. I wandered the neighborhood until, just blocks away, I found myself in front of a nightclub called Tony's 52nd Street, and sensed it would do.

Couples enthralled by a combo playing bebop half-filled the red-striped showroom; the whole world was going bebop. Every head in the room shook to melodies fractured into ecstasies, and some of those heads followed my progress to the bar. Because Tony's was patronized by jazz fans of both sexes, the chances of a police raid were *nil*. In fact, the city's crackdown had the effect of opening up every bar in Manhattan to cruising, albeit of a nuanced, subtle sort.

So, smoking on the end stool, I brooded.

Good hunting grounds indeed. I did have to rebuff an out-of-town smile, but soon a sexy Eastsider was asking me why I looked so sad, and we went to his place. I had decided against bringing anyone back to Mrs. B.'s. Besides, in sleeping around, one's safer away from home — giving *them* the problem of disposing of the body helps deter the worst.

Just the relaxation I craved — to fuse my face to another's and work out my anger against David.

9.

AS IT HAPPENED, Miss d'Orsay and I had the house to ourselves for some time. Besides rearranging his schedule to suit the Festival, David canceled several engagements "due to illness" so as to remain sequestered at Ca'Dora with Mrs. B.

The music world was concerned — *What could have felled so vital a man?* — until word spread that it was *love;* love and interest combined. Those things it understood.

What *I* didn't understand was what they were actually *doing. Were* they lovers? I doubted it, though I recognized that of course I'd *want* to doubt it, which meant I had to doubt my doubts.

Meanwhile this period, however *comfortable,* wasn't my easiest. I felt distinctly left out as the station wagon made round trips between city and country, bringing firewood and hothouse flowers to town, taking staff and supplies to Ca'Dora.

The Cadillac also made the trip once or twice, Mrs. B. suddenly appearing in the city for a few hours. At her first such visit, after seeing David off at Idlewild Airport for a Los Angeles concert too important to miss, she was relaxed and animated. And casting an eye over my Festival preparations, she pronounced herself pleased.

I beamed as if Mother had stuck a gold star in my music book, until she came out with two jewel boxes and asked which pair of diamond cufflinks David would prefer. Rather coldly, I said I had no idea.

Meanwhile, distasteful though I found it, as instructed I'd gotten in touch with my FBI handler and was meeting him when and where directed.

I first telephoned the day after David came to lunch. Stammering an excuse to Miss d'Orsay, I ventured out to Sixth Avenue to find a phone booth — but of course she expressed no curiosity in my errand, no more than I did in hers next day when she ducked out to shop, as she said, for a lampshade. I imagined her handler to be Nolan.

In any case, Goddard had set a meeting for that afternoon at the Horn & Hardart Automat on Fifth Avenue.

I showed up at my most nervous. But the meet only involved drinking coffee, eating lemon pie and my passing on the innocuous news of Mrs. B.'s new friendship with David Spegall. Under no circumstances would I tell the FBI anything that could threaten her; my first loyalty was to her. But the whole world knew about her liaison, platonic or otherwise.

Unfortunately, Goddard appeared to think Mrs. B.'s being friendly with a Russian news of grim import indeed, if in line with Bureau expectations.

FEBRUARY GAVE WAY to March.

Already by 1953 it was rare to learn of earthshaking events from the morning papers. Radio had kept the airwaves atwitter with bulletins for a generation, now TV was doing it. But on Friday, March 6, I went downstairs for breakfast to find it a new world. The New York *Times* headline hit like a hammer:

STALIN DIES AFTER 29-YEAR RULE

Miss d'Orsay sat stunned. Living next door to where the man had personally sent his thugs, I felt chills, too.

Appreciating her emotion, I said nothing as we ate. Finished, Miss d'Orsay in her nervous fashion pushed in her chair, flecked a crumb off the cloth and, not looking at me, said, *"Well!"*

"Indeed."

Muttering, "We shall see, we shall see," she toddled out of the room.

That morning Goddard called *me*.

The phone rang and Miss d'Orsay answered.

"Hello? *Hello?"* she said into a void. Perplexed, she hung up.

It rang again a minute later, I happened to answer, and it was Goddard commanding a noontime meet, not at the nearest Automat but at one over near Third Avenue. Stalin's death made it a busy day for the FBI, I gathered.

I wasn't surprised to learn that Miss d'Orsay was lunching out, too. Joe appeared in the city that morning and she asked him to drive her to a Long Island City upholsterers; he demurred on account of the Cadillac's needing an oil change on Eleventh Avenue, and she showily engaged a car service instead.

At 12:00 o'clock sharp I walked into Horn & Hardart more apprehensive than hungry. It was busy. I stepped up to the desserts, put in my two nickels, turned the knob and took out a wedge of lemon pie. Grabbing coffee at the geyser, I crossed the black-and-white tiles and claimed a table for two.

Moments later Goddard joined me, setting down a tray of turkey, stuffing, mashed potatoes, gravy and cranberries: Thanksgiving for a dictator's death?

He was a different man from the one I'd met at Nickel-and-dime's. There his face had been pinched and remote, registering distaste. Every week since, his features were softer, more mobile. Frankly, I was beginning to find him an attractive package.

"Hello, Mr. Harnes," Goddard said.

"Bruce, please."

"Heard the news?"

Putting fork to meringue, I nodded.

"Well, and how did Mrs. Berlin take it?"

"Mrs. Berlin's still in the country, so I don't know," I told him. "Do you suspect late-night Kremlin phone calls? Microfilm bonfires? I must say, Miss d'Orsay didn't seem at all sorry." Said this to needle him, but he didn't take the bait. "Does Stalin's death change anything?"

"Everything." He couldn't help but look important as he chewed.

"How old are you?"

He blushed. "Twenty-seven."

"You look younger."

He winced. "Thanks—I *think.*"

"Married?" I took a bite of pie.

He fumed, his forehead solid and resentful, but admitted, "No."

"Girlfriend?"

"No. I'm the one asking questions here."

"Ask away."

No *wife?* How could he expect to have a government career without a *wife?* Most homosexuals were married—just the way it was. Accidentally—I was *not* putting the make on him—my loafer slipped on the tile and touched his wingtip. He pulled his foot back, but sighed, managing to seem both put upon and interested.

What have we here, I wondered? Could I get him to bed? Might be amusing, not only for the notch—one more body, one more cock—but also for the *frisson* of putting myself in the hands of a G-man (though not, I imagined, into his reports).

But he stood up and plucked his hat from the table.

"Well then, Bruce. Till next week."

"My pleasure, *Phil.*"

After hearing radio bulletins all day to the effect that no one knew who was running the show in Moscow, Molotov or Beria—names to make the blood run cold—after dinner I found my way once more to Tony's 52nd Street.

10.

AN IN-DEMAND MUSICIAN lives the life frenetic. So with David Spegall: Returning to the concert circuit — accompanied by Mrs. B. — every day meant another city, auditorium, hotel, another trip by train, plane or limousine. Waterbury, Springfield, Worcester; a brief respite at Ca'Dora; Providence, Boston, Portland.

Which made things hard on us back at HQ. David was to conduct the four Colonnade Lawn concerts, but before we could contract with soloists, much less launch a publicity campaign or start selling tickets, our Music Director needed to choose his programs, and decide about the Sunday ones, too. But for days on end no one heard from him, with the result that Miss d'Orsay and myself came rather to a standstill.

At Mrs. B.'s next flying visit, I mentioned my need to consult with David, even as I appraised her appearance. Hair and lipstick brightened, clothing more youthful, she *gleamed*, but I sensed something somewhere was beginning to fray. Her pageboy, despite my compliments, was distinctly wrong. Her trying to be a girl again hinted that David wasn't making use of the woman she was.

I mentioned also another matter proving a nuisance.

Though Mrs. B. had earmarked for the festival a princely sum in a dedicated account, its leather-bound chequebook, three cheques to the page, was entrusted to Miss d'Orsay, who since Mr. Berlin's death had taken on the burden of paying bills. Now I asked to be made a signatory.

Seeing the sense of this, Mrs. B. picked up the phone and spoke to her husband's successor as managing partner at Dillinger Muenster, which in part was a private bank. That afternoon, while she returned to David, I made the trip downtown to provide my signature.

Dillinger Muenster had six floors at the top of an old skyscraper on Broad Street. Its upstairs lobby, wood-paneled and dark, was furnished with Jacobean chairs and highboys — redolent of the Twenties. Behind the scenes, things were updated but decidedly utilitarian.

The serious young man assigned to take me in hand brought me to a conference room where I signed a card and was assured I could now write cheques on the Festival account.

At my request, he then showed me the corner office formerly Max Berlin's, familiar from photographs that showed him radiating an attractive aura of power in front of a view of New York harbor. Alas, his successor ruling from a different floor, Mr. Berlin's old room now was shared by three junior partners who at sight of me smiled and spread their hands over their papers. The walls, denuded of Mr. Berlin's Renaissance prizes, were garnished instead with bond-sale "tombstones." It gave me a sense of time's remorseless passage. Only the view remained Mr. Berlin's old, incomparable one.

Inadvertently, but usefully, becoming a signatory on the account helped me gain at last an upper hand over Miss d'Orsay. In poring over the chequebook she relinquished to me, I was perplexed by several items. Festival outlays as yet were modest, but cheques already cut for tuning pianos and buying music stands — costs I knew well — made me almost fall out of my chair.

I then made so bold as to look over the household chequebook, too. Working for Nickel-and-dime had taught me about budgets and balance sheets, so although I couldn't know what Mrs. B.'s grocery bills or heating oil expenses ought to be, from what I saw I suspected that they, too, were inflated by kickbacks to Miss d'Orsay.

Mrs. B., I knew, in addition to being a financier's widow was heiress to a copper fortune — but that shouldn't make her a mark! My first impulse was to go to her. But after considering the matter, I spoke to Miss d'Orsay instead.

It was like stepping on a hornet's nest.

"That's *spillage!*" she screeched. "In any great household there's *spillage*. *Always!* Anyone can tell you!"

"*Spillage?* Not theft? Or embezzlement?"

"*No!*" she screamed. Calming herself, she spoke quietly, if bitterly. "I see what it is: You want yours."

"No, I don't want 'mine.' Mrs. B. pays me a salary, a good one."

"But she pays me none, you see — prefers I make out by mopping up the occasional *spillage*."

"She's said as much?"

"Nothing need be *said*, it's *understood*. Really, Bruce, you're too young to realize that dear Dora's a woman of her class: Howevermuch money she may have, every *penny's* precious, because money represents *more* than money — it means *everything*. It would *kill* her to pay me a salary. But so long as I provide for myself without bothering her, all is well. She knows only that I never ask for anything."

Murmuring that I saw no need to bother Mrs. B., I left it at that, confident Miss d'Orsay henceforth would be in my pocket.

And finally, through several long-distance brainstorming sessions, David and I managed to complete the Festival programs.

Our first Friday would feature him conducting Mozart, Rimsky-Korsakov, Brahms and, from the keyboard, Tchaikovsky's *First Piano Concerto*. Saturday would bring an all-Beethoven program, and Sunday afternoon Marian Anderson would sing in the music room. Splashy debut weekend!

The following week would feature Rachmaninoff, Stravinsky and Copeland, plus the Enlightenment Quartet performing in the Florentine Cloister.

Over pie and coffee I mentioned these arrangements — soon to be public knowledge, after all — to Goddard, and for whatever reason the G-man asked about David's visa status.

I objected that, as a Fed, he must already have access to such information. Irritated, he put me through a short course in intragovernmental relations that boiled down to *Does Macy's tell Gimbel's?* Apparently not. So I repeated what I'd told Miss d'Orsay: Nikolodimsky Concert Management was efficient about that sort of thing.

That David's visa situation in fact was complicated I didn't care to volunteer. Mustered out of the Red Army in '45, he toured Eastern Europe that year and the next, giving state-sponsored concerts and docilely returning home.

Greedy for foreign currency, the USSR in '47 sent him on a Scandinavian tour, from which he brought back for his masters suitcases stuffed with Kronor.

Having earned unusual trust, David next conquered Paris at the *Salle Pleyel,* and flew to London for his Wigmore Hall debut. There he defected to the West — eluded his escort and made a bobby famous by approaching him in Piccadilly Circus and asking for refuge.

Britain granted him political asylum. Like all defections, David's caused an uproar, being what passed for a Western victory in the Cold War. What he really wanted was to come to the U.S., farther from the long arm of the NKVD (soon succeeded by the equally long-reached KGB). Nickel-and-dime bestirring himself, the U.S. issued David a visa, and here he came, to a teaching post at Juilliard and a concert career.

This visa he duly renewed every year, performing in Montreal or Mexico City so as to meet the State Department's requirement that applicants leave the country for 48 hours and apply from abroad. As a refugee admitted to Britain, now annually renewing an American visa, David's status remained too tangled for comfort. At some point he had better apply for permanent residency.

But until a minute ago he'd lived with *me,* and the moral turpitude my new police record proclaimed might well taint *him,* too—even make him *persona non grata* to the U.S.: *Hello, Moscow!*

After Goddard's query, I telephoned my old boss and asked him please to send over David's visa paperwork—said I'd take it from there.

A manila envelope arriving by messenger, I opened it to find David looking out in sepia quadruplicate, with a note from Nickel-and-dime pointing out his current visa expired at midnight on June 20—which happened to be about the moment our inaugural concert would end. There was no choice, therefore, but to whisk David out of the country and renew it, however busy the run-up to the Festival. Failing to do so would win him a knock on the door and a free trip home.

Not that I looked forward to any contact with government.

Homosexuals were being lumped in with Commies in every witch hunt that came along. In April, President Eisenhower issued Executive Order #10450 banning us from Federal jobs. People like me walked on eggshells, trying to keep out of sight of the lynch mob milling around the next corner.

I had to wonder how Goddard coped, for leading the charge was his own Bureau, under the sway of the unfortunate-looking J. Edgar Hoover. Ironically, rumor insisted that Hoover was a homo himself, even that he frequented a house on Maryland's Eastern Shore where steamer trunks were stuffed with plus-size women's clothing (Hoover supposedly being that kind of queer). Certainly he shared a house in Washington with his deputy, Clyde Tolson, and they often wore identical suits and ties to the office.

The public had nothing to go on but a single charming, damning photograph, Hoover and Tolson sitting in beach chairs, legs crossed mincingly, wearing shirts (with plunging necklines) that looked suspiciously like silk.

Perhaps Goddard was more secure than might be apparent? Protected at high levels?

I put David's visa file on the corner of my desk so as not to forget about it and, leaning back, found *Balzac* trying to catch my eye from MoMA's sculpture garden.

11.

HIS TOUR OVER at last, David—Mrs. B. in tow—returned to the city with a homecoming embrace that crushed the breath out of me. I noticed no one had shooed this lion of a man to the barbershop lately. His locks were almost worthy of Stokowski.

I noticed also Mrs. B.'s still overdoing the powder and the perfume, and how unflattering her new wardrobe was to a figure no longer a girl's. Previously, she'd been accustomed to boast with great good humor about being the masterpiece of her husband's collection. Now, newly acquired by David, and these touches inadvertently emphasizing their age difference, she took on a contingent quality, as if fearful she might have gone out of fashion.

My heart bled for her—*I* would never have visited such indignities upon her.

I tried to buck her up by proposing that she promote her Festival by giving a party for the music press. She not only accepted but threw herself into it, asking the leading critics to dine and 60 friends for music afterwards, when her guests of honor—Miss Marian Anderson and Mr. David Spegall—would perform.

But I had a piece of mischief up my sleeve, too. Asking

myself what I could possibly do to rescue Mrs. B. from the clutches of unrequited love, I made sure her daughter would attend. Miss d'Orsay scrawled invitations to everybody else; I called up Elyse Ferenci myself.

"Mother's court jester!" she exclaimed, after first pretending not to recognize my name. "What do *you* want?"

Inviting her for the musical portion of the evening, I urged her presence as honoring the father and brother to whose memory the Festival was dedicated, and she accepted. She *adored* her father and brother; her mother, possibly less.

The evening arrived.

May has to be New York's loveliest month, when the sunset sky's an electric-blue cyclorama that conspires with the fragrant air—cherry, apple and pear trees bursting into bloom up and down the sidewalks—to soften the city's stone and brick. The house looked splendid, its first-floor rooms opening *en enfilade* in stunning succession. In the music room upstairs, gilt banquettes were pushed to the walls and red-velvet folding chairs set out.

Dinner went well, although Mrs. B., ensheathed in Fortuny pleats, put on the brittle, giggly manner of a younger woman. It didn't suit her. Moreover, the way she interleaved her fingers with David's verged on the unseemly.

Her guests adjourning upstairs after the meal, she went to the foyer and, flanked by Miss Anderson and David—myself posted just behind—welcomed those asked for the music. The double front doors were propped open (but quite adequately manned) as cabs and cars let off guests at the curb.

The last to arrive was her daughter. Elyse Ferenci emerged from her glossy black Cadillac limousine, its grille jutting silver bullets, and climbed the steps with her mouth screwed up, clearly come from duty and not for pleasure. But what a splendid animal she was, her mother's features, bone structure, complexion and bearing in an alluringly youthful edition!

As Mrs. B. presented her daughter to him, I watched David closely. And saw his eyes light up! Saw every vein and sinew stiffen! It was comical; I could almost hear him burbling, *"Vive la difference!"* Elyse seemed taken by him, too.

You can't always predict sexual attraction, but sometimes you can, and then it's *Katie bar the door!*

Mrs. B. swept upstairs, and I followed, leaving Elyse and David to gape at each other.

The 54th Street music room was lovely, but of course much smaller than Ca'Dora's. Eighteenth-century French crystal pilasters engraved upon musical themes marched down the walls in counterpoint to panels painted by a contemporary of Watteau's. Chandeliers of Waterford crystal shone like aerial fountains.

Her face lighted up by the prisms overhead and the Renaissance jewels at her throat, Mrs. B. discussed her Festival, as well as the son and husband who inspired it. She introduced me, and I spoke a few—I hope gracious—words, as did David when he finally appeared (Elyse taking a seat just inside the door).

Then David took his place at the Bechstein. At dinner he'd asked Mrs. B. what she wished to hear and, *à la* Diaghilev, she replied, "Astonish me!"

Now he gave us Satie's *First Gymnopédie,* and made it a revelation—played it as if it were some Russian Constructivist collage he had a blood affinity to. Mesmerizing to watch his fingers hover, to strike whenever an unseen wheel, as it were, came spinning around, giving the piece an immediately addictive off-kilter rhythm, each audible note alluding to notes *not* played. An eccentric exercise, one might think; so why did tears well up in every eye?

As David sat back, looking surprised at what issued from his fingers, I heard the old, *He's a fucking genius, dammit! And you're just not good enough!*

Next came a piano arrangement of the *Lt. Kije Suite* — a treat, as Prokofiev was seldom heard in those days. Then David accompanied Miss Anderson as she stirred us with spirituals — *My Lord What a Morning* and *Nobody Knows the Trouble I've Seen* — and sang Donizetti exquisitely.

Afterwards, while they circulated in clouds of congratulation, I slipped into David's place on the bench to noodle at Gershwin and Rossini while bantering with guests; worst come to worst, I could always be a cocktail pianist.

Mrs. B. proved an excellent hostess, working at it without being seen to do so in making her guests feel welcome as they nibbled canapés, drank champagne, chatted about the Festival and finally prepared to take their leave. But I perceived a worried element to her manner. Looking around, I realized neither David nor Elyse was to be seen.

Abandoning the keyboard, I quietly took the staircase up, pausing to listen at every landing, but hearing nothing until the fifth floor, when something registered as coming from my office. I stood at the door, the silence perfect, and opened it.

The room was dark, the only light what flared indoors from the RCA Building, but I could have sworn I smelled ozone, as though the lights had fused. Flipping on a light switch, I found my Chippendale porter's chair occupied, Elyse sitting on David's lap and their mouths pressed together. Beyond them the man of mystery leaned into the room leering at the carnage.

"*Oh!*" I exclaimed. "Excuse *me.*"

Pulling the door to, I returned downstairs and helped bid guests farewell. When the only ones remaining were those irreducible few so encouraged by liquor that they intended never moving on, Elyse and David appeared, shamelessly hand in hand and their faces artificially bright.

I hovered close as Freddie brought her wrap. She adjusted it while David smiled dazzlingly at her mother and announced, "Marvelous party, my dear. I think I'll sleep out tonight. Tomorrow, then?"

Without waiting for a reply, he gave his arm to Elyse and she, eyes shining in victory, walked him out the door and down the steps. Her car arriving at precisely that instant, they got in, and off it rumbled, exhaust pluming up featherlike beneath each scarlet taillight. Miss d'Orsay—who had kept to the walls all evening, when not passing trays of caviar toast rounds—looked on in horror, a hand clapped to her mouth at the stunning betrayal.

Saying nothing, Mrs. B wobbled into the sitting room. She looked overheated, her dress tight; was in a moment *old*, like Jane Wyatt in *Lost Horizon* going in a trice from youth to dust. *Thus healing begins*, I thought to myself. Longing to comfort her, I joined her but, pleading a headache, she excused herself and went to bed.

Just as well, actually, for a meeting with my handler loomed. Goddard had rung up before dinner with an urgent summons, though leaving it to me to choose our rendezvous. Asking, *How much lemon pie can a man eat?* I named Tony's 52nd Street.

Now, triumphant—close to reclaiming Mrs. B. as *mine!*—I went out to meet him.

12.

NEXT THING I KNEW, I was waking up with a ferocious thirst, my head pounding. But before getting water or aspirin I wanted to work out who this naked man lying against me was.

Naked *man?* On *54th Street?* Anyone I knew? Despite the pain — like a shovel thwacking me — I opened my eyes.

"Morning, sleepy head," murmured Special Agent Goddard.

"*Christ!*" I said, jerking away as from a snake. I was horrified.

"Sleep well, Bruce?" he asked, stretching skinny and alluring.

Had we done it, I wondered? Of course we had; despite my hangover, I was already hard, my body eager.

It was coming back to me.

Tony's had been subdued, the music bluesy and slow. Perfect for the man of mystery at the end of the bar communing with glowing bottles. Still good hunting grounds, though as time went on I was having hollow-eyed encounters with men I'd already been to bed with, each of us looking through the other without recognition.

Foolishly switching from champagne, I drank Scotch in

celebration of my little plot's success. Just goes to show, I thought, how an artist's loyalty goes to his art alone, and also how simple at bottom *sex* is. Poor Mrs. B.!

Goddard entered, took the next stool and bought me a drink. Toasting him, I remarked that being a Confidential Informant wasn't so bad, after all.

The G-man seemed thoughtful, listening to the music with his head cocked. I wondered what he wanted. Dirt on Mrs. B.'s nest of traitors and fellow travelers? Her guests had discussed Schubert's modulations, cross-over hand positions for Debussy, the themes of Tchaikovsky's *Sixth Symphony* ("The Self-Pity," I always call it). Treacherously, I was willing to divulge it all and name names.

I should have been more on my guard as Goddard kept buying me drinks. Whether I reported the conversation about Schubert, or that David Spegall had gone off with Mrs. B.'s daughter, I couldn't remember. The G-man's urgency? Less to do with the Red threat than a young man's *ex-officio* horniness. More my *métier*.

Now, throwing on a robe and handing Goddard his clothes, I said, "OK, you've got to get out. *Christ*, but without anyone *seeing*. Anyone sees you, I'm *sunk*."

He yawned, from behind his hand mumbled, "Get Joe."

"Joe?"

"The chauffeur? He's one of the family, he'll know what to do."

One of the *family*? Joe a *faggot*? OK, but I didn't even know where he lived, upstairs or nearer the car, which was garaged across Sixth Avenue.

"Ring," Goddard suggested.

Gingerly, I rang.

Freddie's emollient voice soon came at the door.

"Sir?"

"Can you find Joe for me, please?"

"Yes, sir."

When I heard the back-stairs door, I opened mine and—I don't know why—feigned surprise at the sight of Joe in undershirt and knowing smile. Funny how taking off a uniform makes for a kind of nakedness. He was solid, fleshy, very confident. The dowsing rod that informs my instincts tingled.

"Oh, it's you," I said.

Goddard darted forward, kissed Joe. "Hey, honey."

"Need him *out,*" I told Joe. "With no one the wiser."

"Righty-ho."

Taking Goddard by the arm and moving with exaggerated care, Joe vanished down the hallway. I was on tenterhooks, but when I came across him later in the course of that long and difficult day—Mrs. B.'s first without David—Joe gave me the high sign.

Crisis averted.

13.

WE SOON MOVED to Ca'Dora for the summer. Leaving the city house to a caretaker's charge, Mrs. B., Miss d'Orsay, the servants and myself piled into limousine and station wagon, a hired one-ton truck bringing up the rear with wardrobe and kitchen necessities.

During the drive, Mrs. B. looked silently out her side of the car, probably meditating the painful reunion the Festival would force with her faithless David.

I pitied her, really I did. Even if I'd engineered David's leaving her myself, I hadn't expected the loss to hit her quite so hard — not when she had *me* at hand. But Mrs. B., bereft, for the moment was beyond my consolation. Which definitely put a dent in my triumph.

In one particular she'd already deftly altered arrangements, assigning her daughter Ca'Dora's best tenant cottage, a Colonial presiding from a hillock over the back way; so both at any rate were out of the house.

As I looked out from my jumpseat, the man of mystery trapped in the window's laminations unmistakably began to croak *revenge* — croak that Mrs. B. must be *revenged*. The appeal of revenge is that it makes things right — restores justice, order and peace to the world. Any child can tell you that.

In my luggage was David's visa folder. Not very smartly, I'd been putting off his trip out of the country to renew it. If I got a move on, there was just time for him to dash up to Canada and get a new one before the old one lapsed.

But what if I forgot? My own plate was piled so very high, after all, mightn't I just *forget?*

Revenge.

As we flew along the Parkway, I found myself studying Joe's haircut through the partition. There was something brutal to the planes of the back of his neck. Once at a party I heard a leading lady lament that her co-star didn't return her interest. "Then look to the wings!" an elderly supernumerary commanded with the authority of The Duse. "Look to the wings!"

At that, it might save some furtive traipsing across the countryside. What do they do out there, anyway, I wondered—loiter on train platforms? Stalk the aisles of hardware stores?

With a flourish, Joe turned the Cadillac through Ca'Dora's gates and up the drive. Mrs. B. and Miss d'Orsay heaved sighs as the grounds opened up around us in a riot of color. I marveled at the beauty—the gardens were in full bloom, flowers flourished everywhere. What first I'd seen covered with snow was become a vernal paradise.

As Joe held open the door, I thanked him looking straight into his eyes. They lidded and fluttered, and his mouth went into a sidelong grin.

OUR AFFAIR BEGAN a few days later. It took just a little doing, given the discretion required.

First I found out where Joe slept. Turned out he had a cottage to himself, one of a group like a Tuscan farmyard with walled courtyard, garages and clothes-drying areas. The house was actually quite fine—the Berlins had stayed there while building the big one. Though Festival electricians already were lodged upstairs, they had their own bath and exterior staircase, so didn't infringe on Joe.

As part of my stratagem, I offered to walk Mrs. B.'s Afghan hounds on the famous Bedford bridle paths that, skirting the meadow past Joe's, wound for miles through hundreds of acres of woods, Ca'Dora's and neighboring landowners'.

The first time I brought Towser and Bruno by, Joe was smoking on his porch; he hadn't much to do during the Festival but ferry people to and from the station. He waved, invited me inside and helped park the dogs in a garage.

So enormous was the Berlins' collection that I shouldn't have been surprised to find even their chauffeur's cottage furnished like a museum. I admired the living room, and he offered to show me the rest.

Not that I'd describe him as a *keeper*, but Joe turned out to be great sport in bed. And afterwards, glowing with that temporary membership in the human race that good sex grants, I found it *nice* to have someone to talk to.

For one thing, having been with them since his discharge from the Navy, Joe knew the scoop about the Berlins that I couldn't get anywhere else. For instance, how the Old Man was always on the lookout for disparaging information about his employees—another tradition Joe said the Old Lady kept up: Had dirt on everyone, but was always avid for more.

"*Everyone,*" he specified. "Freddie and Ernest, Cook, the maids, housemen, gardeners. For that matter, you and me."

"*M—*" I started to say. "*You?*"

"I'm a lavender lad, didn't you know?" That was a phrase of the period.

"And *me?*"

"Another one, but one with a record."

I stiffened. Hadn't known that she knew.

"How?" I asked. "And how do *you* know?"

"'Cuz I know everything," Joe snorted, "except how you'd ever find another job. Think you'd pass a lie detector? Strap you up for the electric chair, they so much as ask your name you shiver and shake like someone threw the switch."

He was probably right. Take Nickel-and-dime's promptness after my arrest: No sooner had I stepped into the office than I found myself headed someplace else altogether, lucky — *lucky, lucky!* — to have the referral to Mrs. B. Without that, where would I be?

Or *was* it luck? Or had the FBI engineered raid and all so as to install me as a spy in Mrs. B.'s household? I tried to shake off my paranoia, but for once had to wonder who ol' Nickel-and-dime answered to — Uncle Sam? Uncle Joe? Or was it more complicated than that?

"What's she got on Miss d'Orsay?" I asked.

Surprisingly, *not* her father's Party membership; apparently that wasn't known (nor did I mention it; useful to hold some things in reserve).

No, it was that habit of mopping up *spillage*. Turned out Miss d'Orsay was right that Mrs. B. knew all about it.

"But she's getting value for money, promise you that," scoffed Joe. "She's way ahead of Miss *d'Orsay*."

"How do *you* know about it?"

"Told you, I know everything. Including why the Old Lady's going around like her best friend died."

"Oh? Why's that?"

"Because *you* introduced Mr. Spegall to her daughter," Joe said, "and *he* dropped the Old Lady like a hot potato."

I was startled.

"Everything," Joe repeated. "Told you. What I don't

understand is why you dropped him in the first place—a looker like that?"

"Well, you don't understand," I said, and tried to explain how David always left the mundane to *me*, while *he* enjoyed the glory.

"Aw, that's no good," he said, clicking his tongue.

Joe's sympathy led me to declare how I'd made a mistake bringing David on board the Festival in the first place, but had to live with it now, except—except—(and it just slipped out) *except*, having forgotten to renew his visa, one little phone call to the FBI and he was history! Not, of course, that I'd *do* such a thing.

Joe roared with delight. How we cackled at my fantasies of revenge! Giddy with letting loose!

Recovering at last, I remarked, "Guess I always felt torn about David."

"How about *this?*" Joe asked, doing something with his hand. "Feel torn about *this?*"

Which brought us back to sex. A meaty, beefy man, not really my type, Joe happened to be just what I needed.

Refreshed, I gave the dogs a little walk and returned to the grind.

14.

FROM DAY TO DAY my Festival machinery chugged along. Buses brought for rehearsal New York Phil and Met Opera musicians furloughed for the summer whom David whipped into an orchestra. With house and cottages filled, meals were served *al fresco* on the summer porch off the courtyard or on the terrace outside the dining room. Voices chirruped over the estate all day and all evening.

Within doors, too, we slaved away. Advertisements appearing in the broadsheets and on WQXR, ticket orders poured in. Every concert was selling out! Miss d'Orsay efficiently counted out tickets and dispatched cheques to Dillinger Muenster that in a small way repaired the festival's deficit.

And Mrs. B. immersed herself in every aspect of preparations, made herself available to solve any difficulty. Save that she moved somewhat gingerly, even dowager-like, no one could have guessed she was mourning a lost love. But it seemed to me that the Festival she planned to honor her son and husband now would memorialize her, too.

Her melancholy pained me, but she wouldn't be comforted. My intentions in fixing up David with Elyse had been the best: David was too young for Mrs. B.; in the long run she'd have suffered worse heartache and humiliation (fortunately that pageboy was already a thing of the past). Now, pulling in her head, she grieved privately, wouldn't let me in, even seemed cool towards me. A shame, when losing David, after all, was something we had in common.

Speak of the devil. On the day before our first concert, I was heading out to leash up the dogs when I ran into David getting a drink of water in the pantry. Had hardly seen him since the party; we were successfully avoiding each other. He was glowing with sweat, having made the house resound with chords from the music-room stage, and concentrating so deeply he didn't notice me until I greeted him; barely acknowledged me then.

After the usual stop at Joe's, I walked the dogs onwards. They were sloppily friendly beasts apt to yank me after squirrels or rabbits. From atop Mount Aspetong we took in a view that ranged from Long Island Sound to the Hudson Valley, from which thunderheads were skidding our way.

The wind picking up and thunder rumbling, the hounds pulled me home on a mission. Just after I put them back in their kennel—they fled into the shed—lightning crackled and the heavens opened up, raindrops falling in machine-gun fusillades. (Fortunately, no one caught at the Colonnade Lawn need get wet, not with great striped canopies ranged along the sides.)

Upstairs, I found Miss d'Orsay stuffing envelopes as the storm raged. It seemed an opportune moment to get my little revenge play going. After all, she was cast in an important part.

Silently, I took out the chequebooks and conducted a review. Paged forward to lightning, backwards to thunder; frowned, muttered, tapped my chin, opened my mouth as though to question particular items; then slapped them shut and stowed them away again.

Though she pretended not to notice, I was sure Miss d'Orsay missed nothing.

There was a crash overhead and the lights went out— lamplight vanished from beneath the parchment shades, leaving us in darkness punctuated by lightning flashes. *Couldn't have planned it better.*

At the next flash, with theatrical *shock* I noticed David's visa folder where I'd placed it so I wouldn't forget it after bringing it to the country. *My jaw dropped with very horror!*

"Oh *Lord*," I said sepulchrally, pulling it towards me. "Good *golly!* Miss d'Orsay, you asked about David Spegall's visa? Meant to renew it, but I just realized that I—forgot."

She gasped. "You *forgot?*"

"Unfortunately. No idea how it happened, but here 'tis. His visa expires—when?" Cue the lightning! "My goodness, *tomorrow*. David turns into a pumpkin midnight *tomorrow!* Well, too late now."

I handed her the folder, and she studied its contents with the crazed eyes of a terrier chasing a ball: *Here* was a morsel for C.I. DB-1 to serve up to J. Edgar!

"Our secret," I cautioned. "If the Feds were to find out, they'd haul him away."

"But dear Dora would be *delighted!* That snake in the grass?"

"Awkward for the Festival, though. I'll run him up to Montreal Monday. Should be OK. What difference can a few days make?"

Storm over, I excused myself, putatively to go check on the Colonnade Lawn, really to let Miss d'Orsay get on the horn to her handler and set the wheels in motion for David's arrest.

The power came back before anyone had to crank up the

generator, but this eve of our day of days brought one crisis after another. A bus bearing musicians had a flat tire, another got lost and called for directions from Ridgefield, Connecticut. But everything got fixed, sorted, found and guided and, though going to a late hour, the rehearsal was triumphant — David's Tchaikovsky stirred the very creatures of the forest.

I watched from the rear, with Joe rubbing the small of my back.

15.

FRIDAY — OUR BIG, historic day — dawned clear and bright.

The grounds were already abuzz with activity when I emerged — lawns being mowed, raked and rolled, hedges trimmed, flowerbeds weeded, chairs set out in precise rows. Everyone was so busy that I realized I should get out of the way. It's the hallmark of efficient music administration that *on the day of* there's nothing left to do at the top.

Except: Though I was confident Miss d'Orsay would see to David's deportation without my doing another thing, there was no harm in making *sure. Belt and braces,* as the English say. After breakfast, then, I decided to make a call from the Katonah train station's phone booth.

To get there I needed a car, so took from the pantry rack the key to the yellow Oldsmobile convertible. Mrs. B. in offering its use had told me how, after the War, her husband took to the joys of driving with the top down and purchased this 1948 model. Five years later the odometer recorded 3600 miles. I backed out and drove off, the dogs whining behind me.

Five minutes later I pulled up at the station, but had to wait while someone's portly unmet arrival noisily announced himself before slamming down the receiver and coming out of the booth fuming.

Going in, I folded the door shut and quietly told the Operator I wished to make a person-to-person call to Phil Goddard at the number he gave me at the FBI's New York office. Goddard told me the FBI had space in a commercial building downtown, over a drycleaners that served as its street entrance. I identified myself as C.I. DB-2.

"DB-2?" the Operator repeated, making sure.

She made a nasal announcement of how many nickels to deposit, we waited through the *dings* as the phone swallowed them and a man's voice said, "Federal Bureau of Investigation."

Goddard wasn't available, but I told the Operator the man who answered would do.

Turning, I saw the indignant arrival pacing some distance off, so said at my normal volume, "David Spegall, the Russian musician? His visa expires at midnight tonight. He's at the Ca'Dora Music Festival in Katonah this evening. Please don't disrupt the performance."

And hung up.

Treachery? Letting the government know a *Russian's* on the loose in *Westchester?*

As I stepped out of the booth, Elyse's limousine heaved itself beside the platform and her chauffeur called, "Judge Carlo?"

Moments later the impatient visitor was being driven away.

Catching up as the Cadillac turned into the driveway of Elyse's Colonial, I could hear David relaxing at the piano, boogie-woogie Mendelssohn melding into ragtime Wagner in a wedding-march mishmash that made me laugh out loud; all seemed well with my Music Director.

The day wore away sunny and beautiful, if just cooler than what would have been optimal; better to have scheduled the Festival one week later. But the grounds dried out from the storm, and the flowers, refreshed, were glorious. When supper was laid out, Mrs. B. appeared in silver Fortuny, wearing her grandmother's pearls and her mother's tiara, and looking as though she anticipated a wonderful evening.

I was touched when she took me aside, into her husband's barrel-vaulted dressing room, to present me with a gold Cartier watch engraved with gratitude for helping start her Festival. I kissed her cheek, happy to have things back on track.

My gift to her — David's exile — was due within hours.

Curtain was at 8:30, sunset past 9:00. Around 7:00 o'clock, fine cars began streaming up the half-mile drive between banks of rhododendrons. Gardeners and their sons parked them, as their occupants, faces pinked by the setting sun, dragged their shadows to the Horse Heads. There they showed their tickets to Miss d'Orsay, who, in a bluer shade of mourning than usual, was manning a booth, and Mrs. B. greeted them as cherished friends.

Stepping into Mrs. Dora Jessup Berlin's exclusive company caused everybody to radiate that joy in being together you see in Renaissance assemblies of saints, angels and donors. Exuding satisfaction, they promenaded along the white-graveled circle and the turf pathways wending through the cedars, or wandered the walled gardens, or patronized the new restrooms that showed off the latest in plumbing.

It was like a dream, that foregathering of the privileged so pleased to find themselves chatting with one another in the flattering light — unmolested by mosquitoes, too (I'd had clouds of DDT wafted over the lawns). People loved coming to Ca'Dora; being there flattered them. Flattery enhanced and animated the scene, the estate transformed to a stage set and them to players. Curious how art serves the self-congratulation of the rich, but when was it ever different?

Among the couples, I was relieved to see, were Mr. Hoover's emissaries Nolan and Goddard. We exchanged crisp nods, and when Nolan looked aside I winked at Goddard.

And among the cars was Nickel-and-dime's weighty black pre-War Rolls-Royce Wraith. Aside from showy auto (and showy driver), and jewels at tie and cuffs, he was inconspicuous, satisfied with the note after David's name in the program, *"By arrangement with Nikolodimsky Concert Management."*

More conspicuous was his henna-haired wife, as bedecked with diamonds as a battleship with guns, diamonds blazing at hair, ears, throat, bodice, wrists and fingers. She was a sweet, earthy woman who spoke, or pretended to speak, no English.

When the stage lights atop the columns finally came up, making the scene glamorous and otherworldly, and the orchestra began tuning up in competition with the calls of mourning doves and nightingales, everybody trooped to the thousand chairs on the lawn to be seated by scrubbed young persons from John Jay High School.

Meanwhile, letting go inch by fractional inch behind the trees, the sun ceased to cast light, though the sky remained full of it through the concert's first half.

I was taking a seat in the back row when, just as in a New York apartment a mouse will sometimes scamper across one's field of vision, Miss d'Orsay appeared at my side.

"Isn't it *marvelous?*" she whispered.

Indiscreetly, I whispered back, "I see your friends wangled tickets. Who knew they were music lovers?"

She looked perplexed. "Yes? Whom do you mean?"

178

I merely thought, *Fine, be that way.*

It was time for Mrs. B.'s speech of welcome. Those of us in the rear couldn't catch a word, though I could tell when she was eulogizing her dead. Her arm sweeping towards me as people turned, clapping, I rose and smiled in acknowledgment.

Mrs. B. exited the stage on one side to applause and on the other David mounted like the Angel Gabriel, masterful and sexy in a white dinner jacket. Turning to his players, he tapped his baton, raised it high and with his downbeat struck from them *Eine Kleine Nachtmusik.* Mrs. B. came back and took her place on my other side and — however stormy her feelings — sat listening calmly.

Everybody was rapt as Mozart swam us past the stars and the gods to one of his crazy calm climaxes at the heart of the universe. We surged to our feet, applauding David, the orchestra, ourselves. David bowed, raised up his soloists, we clapped ourselves silly, then heard *Scheherazade.* At the interval we drank champagne and told each other how marvelous we were. Then came Brahms' *First Symphony* — meticulous and emotional, the slow movement enlivened by screams when bats flitted overhead.

During the second interval, a Steinway was rolled to the front of the stage. We reassembled to watch David come on, shake his mane, take the bench and with the mighty opening chords of Tchaikovsky's *First Piano Concerto* hammer himself into the air.

For two-thirds of an hour he surfed the crests of passion, carried us through its crashes, burials and rebirths. Whenever he snapped his head, sweat flew, giving him a momentary halo in the lights.

I watched David's final performance in the West in utter serenity; for once, not a particle of jealousy did I feel.

That's the beauty of revenge.

He finished, bowed to a storm of applause, walked ceremoniously off the stage, but—just like Tinker Bell!—was clapped back to life, and encore after encore brought us to the dot of midnight.

At last the clapping failed to draw him from behind his pillar and the Ca'Dora Music Festival's premiere passed into history.

Instantly, the G-men were on the move, rushing down the aisle, I at their heels. My new watch told me that David had already been in the USA illegally for two—going on *three!*—minutes.

"David Spegall?" said Nolan, leaping onstage and displaying his badge. Smiling, David eyed it as though it were a decoration offered by a grateful nation. "FBI. You're under arrest for violation of Section 242, Immigration and Nationalization Act of 1952."

David beamed, would probably have thanked him, save that Goddard clapped a silvery bouquet of handcuffs to his wrists, saying, "Holding you for the immigration authorities."

He began to get the drift, did David. Not wishing to witness his humiliation, I was turning away from the flashbulbs of the press photographers there to record our first night, when Elyse ran up screaming, "What's this *nonsense?* Take these off my husband at *once!*"

Husband?

I goggled, but the agents ignored her, dragging David offstage and bulling him up the aisle, his knees apparently forgetting how to hinge.

Elyse turned to Judge Carlo and appealed to him to *"tell them."*

And tell them he did!

Launching a barrage in that stentorian voice so familiar to

the U.S. Court of Appeals, Judge Carlo filled us in as to how his client's marrying David Spegall—in a ceremony that afternoon at which he himself had officiated!—made the fact that his visa might have expired five minutes ago *irrelevant* and altogether *moot*, his marriage putting him in line for *permanent residency* and *American citizenship*.

The spray flew as he repeated: *moot!*

Although—he added—the agents were certainly free to haul Mr. Spegall away if they were prepared to face the career-ending consequences of an action so *reckless, feckless, ill-advised, illegal, unnecessary, unjustified* and *unconstitutional!*

Balked, having lost face, Nolan fell back and glared at Goddard. Goddard uncuffed David—while giving *me* the evil eye—and they left amidst more flashbulbs, the crowd parting as though they carried the plague.

Frowning, David rubbed his wrists and embraced his bride, then, flanked by her and Judge Carlo, stalked on to the courtyard reception he'd been headed for before being so rudely interrupted.

As for me, I was stunned—simply *stunned*—at this turn of events. After doing everything necessary to deliver up David on a silver platter, to be foiled by *Elyse?*

In the Florentine Cloister *la crème de la crème* drank champagne into the wee hours. Corks flew, water spilled from the mouths of marble dolphins and compliments from the people's, and the Judge held forth. Tides of congratulation flowing over her, Mrs. B. ordered up more bottles from the cellars.

I don't know how she did it. Sick as *I* felt, I could only imagine what *she* was going through!

Making my excuses finally, I went indoors and pulled myself up the stairs, hounded by the merriment ringing out behind me as corks popped and fountains plashed.

16.

NO HONEYMOON FOR the artist! Saturday night's triumph followed Friday's: David slashed open Beethoven's *Fifth Symphony* with lightning bolts. Afterwards the calls of *bravo!* were thunderous.

Of course, I'd expected my back-up to conduct. I'd signed Artie Bowers, young sub-conductor of the New York Philharmonic — made sure he was comfortably ensconced upstairs in the West Wing, and enjoyed hinting he might get a chance like that which made Leonard Bernstein famous.

Instead, David was at his post, *Mrs.* David beaming.

The Sunday papers competed in praising the charm of our opening night — its setting, the power of the program, above all David Spegall's artistry, reserving for sidebars the amusing story of his secret wedding and subsequent arrest-and-release.

And Marian Anderson never sounded better than singing Bizet and Verdi in the music room Sunday afternoon.

Nothing could lighten Mrs. B.'s mood, however; her daughter's marrying *her* beloved was a blow. Nor could anything shift my gloom.

Monday morning birds voicing tiresome joy at the coming sunrise woke me up and I couldn't get back to sleep.

As sun began to catch at the chimneys across the cloister, I slipped down the grand staircase beneath Mrs. B.'s most extravagant portrait. The place felt deserted as I stole outdoors and followed the pergola to Joe's cottage.

Not my style to keep going back to one man. So why? What was I getting from Joe?

A *soupçon* of degradation, I suspect, the piquant humiliation of having a *chauffeur* master my every response. For Joe, animal reality sufficed: So far as he was concerned, there was no man of mystery! But for the moment I couldn't get enough.

When we rested, he remarked, "The other night with Mr. Spegall? Must have been tough on you."

"Shot my bolt," I said, "and it was a *blank*. Oh, that clever Elyse! I'm just sorry for Mrs. B.'s sake."

"Know what you should do?"

"What's that?"

"You want the dirty Commie back home where he belongs, right?"

"For sure. Well, I mean, Mrs. B. would be loads happier."

"So send him back!"

"Great idea," I laughed. "But I tried, remember?"

"No: What they did to Primov? Russkis boxing him up and carrying him away?"

"Yes?"

"So put the dirty Red in a box, call the KGB, and you're done. No big deal. I'll even help."

"*Genius!*" I exclaimed at the ridiculous notion. "After all, what have I got to lose but my job and my freedom?"

I soon took my leave; plenty to do, after all.

But I couldn't shake Joe's idea—couldn't stop thinking about it nor, no matter how hard I tried, poke holes in it, either.

Joe might not have been too quick on the uptake (no big *deal?*), but his scheme happened to be *brilliant*. Had all the power of *simplicity*, and would accomplish everything I'd hoped to do with my expired-visa gambit (in retrospect so pathetic): Mrs. B. would be happy again, and my revenge complete.

So for a day or two I mulled things over without actually intending to do anything. But when I challenged him as to practicalities, Joe was ready for me.

Leading me into the cellars, he showed me a varnished crate custom-made for the Primover upstairs. He even lifted me into it, thereby letting us realize what it lacked, and we fitted a plank on its cross-bracing to serve as a seat, and also, with a hand-drill, bored air holes.

Then, while the estate drowsed in siesta, we drove it up to the Colonnade Lawn and stood it beside a pathway in the cedars behind the stage. There, not so very far from boxes and trunks having to do with the lighting, it didn't even look out of place.

Joe also showed me, nestled in his palm, a little amber bottle of chloroform; I didn't inquire into ways or means.

Nothing in these actions committed me: a plank in a box, a box on a path, a bottle in a pocket?

But by Thursday I found myself actually considering doing this unthinkable thing. And Friday morning, a good night's sleep having sealed my intention, I woke up determined to carry it through. I sought out Joe, who agreed to proceed after that evening's concert.

I repeated my drive to the station, from its phone booth calling—not that bumbling Bureau—but the Soviet consulate on East 91st Street.

Asking for the KGB—what else could I do?—I was connected to someone who, while stoutly denying having anything to do with such an outfit, courteously heard me out, even had me repeat where the crate in question would be found — clearly he knew who David Spegall was — before again disclaiming any affiliation and demanding (in vain) my name.

I hung up confident they would come a-calling while David dreamed his chloroform dreams. And on Saturday, after David so mysteriously failed to turn up, Artie Bowers would get his innings after all.

At the close of the day, then, I knotted the black tie I willingly put my ascot aside for — *We may not be Glyndebourne*, I told myself, *but Lord knows we try, we try* — while peering into the eyes of a dark man of mystery.

Downstairs, supper was laid on at the summer porch. After eating, everybody progressed to the Colonnade Lawn, where the scene replicated that of the week before.

Trees and shrubberies retreated benevolently into shadow from sunny emerald lawns as cars purred up to land bejeweled and silver-headed people who regarded one another with marvelous complacency.

Running into Elyse and her groom, I neutrally remarked on the evening's beauty.

"Queen's weather," replied Elyse.

"*Queen's weather?*" David repeated. "What's that?"

"A saying from Mother's girlhood?" she said. "It was always sunny at Queen Victoria's functions, never rainy or blowy: *Queen's weather.*"

"*Hah!*" barked David. "Same in Russia: *Tsar's weather.* Only it's 20 below zero! And snowing!"

They laughed maniacally, even as Nickel-and-dime arrived in state, his wife stepping out of the Wraith rather too Christmassy in rubies and emeralds.

Mrs. B. herself, in yellow Fortuny pleats, presented a somewhat novel appearance: For the first time, silver peeked from her hair, giving her features something newly *distinguée*. She had a suitable escort for the evening, too, a handsome, stiff-backed uniform aglitter with medals, General So-and-so. They sat on the aisle in the third row; Miss d'Orsay and myself again took the rear.

People milled about, sipping pre-concert champagne — that week's innovation — until birdsong (or the orchestra's tuning up) called them to their seats and, brilliant in the lights, David strode out and swept us away with Rachmaninoff's *Second Symphony*, in the second movement somehow levitating the entire orchestra and flying it across the heavens!

Then Copeland, Stravinsky and — the music over — it was time to *get it done*.

17.

IT TOOK ALL of five minutes. *Easy-peasy*.

The concert ended with David leading a third encore, Grieg's *In the Hall of the Mountain King*. Across the lawn a thousand people came roaring to their feet!

As the ovation died, *hoi polloi* moved to the parking field — eventually to follow their headlights down the drive — and an invited ultra-select portion of the audience began gravitating towards the courtyard reception.

Meanwhile David congratulated his players, his face and dinner jacket transcendent in the lights until one by one they began to snap off. Elyse Ferenci — *Mrs.* Spegall — waited offstage, impatient to claim the lion of the hour.

I swallowed. *Time*. Went up to him.

"*Maestro*, just terrific," I murmured.

"*Brucie!*" said David, grabbing me in a vise. My breath escaped in a regretful-sounding sigh. "Really think so?"

"Have a minute?"

"Sure, sure."

Concern flitting over his features, and making a sign to Elyse, David followed me. In response she stamped her foot with a moue of rage (always rage with that woman; how can anyone live like that?) and in a marked manner trailed after her mother, already strolling towards the house on the arm of her modern major-general.

I took David down the steps at the rear of the stage, through electricians calling to one another as they coiled cables and packed equipment away, past musicians snapping instruments into cases, and for some 20 yards through the cedars, deserted and dark but for fireflies' tracery, and halted beside the Primover crate, where Joe was standing guard.

"*Joe?*" David asked with a note of doubt as my confederate flicked his cigarette into the ferns.

"David," I said.

As David turned towards me, Joe stepped forward, crooked an arm around his neck and wrapped his face in a chloroform-soaked handkerchief.

The chemical gave the moonlight an off scent as David flinched and fought. I'd expected the result to be instantaneous, as in detective stories, but it wasn't. He struggled for a good minute before finally sagging and Joe, grunting, breathing hard, lifted him into the crate and sat him on the plank. It was fortunate no one came along.

David's head lolling, we tightened straps intended to secure a Primover to make him snug and, as was regrettably necessary, Joe taped his mouth. Bending down to assure myself that he could breathe, I was terrified when his eyes snapped open, the whites of them *right there*, and he began to thrash and moan. I hastily stood up, Joe brought down the lid and, even as the box started rocking, slipped a padlock through the hasps: *Done!*

And just like that, that crick in my side? That nail in my shoe? That gob of meat in my gullet? *Gone!*

Along with the refrains of *You're not good enough!* and *I told you so!*

Yes, I damn well *was* good enough: Look what *I* did! If only Dad could see me now!

I couldn't wait to see Mrs. B's joy, or her daughter's rage! How buoyant I felt, and so *happy!*

Revenge?

Revenge!

We headed towards the house. We'd done our bit, Joe and I, *got it done*. Out of our hands now, but the Russians would know what to do. No need to superintend; probably best not to witness it, in fact. I hoped they were following my advice to take the back way in and not trying to fight the Lincolns and Buicks slipping down the drive.

David Spegall would be on his way home before Freddie handed me a flute of bubbly in the Florentine Cloister — before dawn probably be aboard a ship bound for the USSR.

I'd make sure Joe got champagne, too — as much as he wanted. Bottle of his own, even.

But going down the path, I realized he wasn't with me.

Annoyed, I turned and with some asperity called, *"Joe?* They're waiting!"

Special Agent Goddard — *Phil* — stepped out of the trees, colleagues massed behind him.

"Hold it right there, Mr. Harnes," he said, forgetting we were on first-name terms.

And with the evening's concluding tonic chord he clasped handcuffs on my wrists, placing me under arrest for a litany of crimes.

The only one that registered was *kidnapping*.

18.

HANDCUFFS?

Worst for me was to see *Joe* toggling a cigarette up and down and pulling at the crotch of his livery as he joshed with FBI agents. Why wasn't *he* under arrest, too?

There came the growl of a truck approaching from the direction of the house. A special agent dashed off waving, it stopped and he returned ahead of a crew in gabardine jackets and caps, one man pushing a handcart.

What ensued was a brief, silent, historic spectacle — a top-secret Cold War interlude of cooperation, apparently overseen by a little man with a cane, his eyes two blots of darkness. I dubbed him *Col. Dead Eyes*. Nothing was said, but nothing needed to be. Federal flashlights picked out the crate, someone jammed a Soviet handcart beneath it and, steadied by hands of both powers, it was borne away, its wheels gouging twin tracks in the turf.

Goddard guided my elbow as far as the drive. There we watched them push the crate up a ramp into a truck whose side advertised a Russian deli on Second Avenue. Several climbed in after it, while Col. Dead Eyes and two others slammed the doors shut and, tugging at their caps with murmurs of *"Spasibo,"* got into the cab. The truck backfired out of sight.

They walked me to the house and put me in the sitting room. G-men—Joe, too—crowded in, filling chairs, settees, even the reading nook's cozy window seat. Vines and leaded glass filtered moonlight, silken shades the lamps. I could see and hear the reception in full swing, until someone drew the curtains.

I looked around, remembering my first visit, when snow covered the ground. Glimpsing a figure poised on the convex tip of the TV screen, I bent to take a closer look. A distorted little man of mystery wriggled like a worm on a hook.

Sitting back, I broke the silence.

"I'm a fool," I declared, "and being Mrs. Berlin's I think I could just stand—but *Miss d'Orsay's?"*

"Miss d'Orsay?" scoffed Goddard.

"How she got onto me, I haven't the foggiest," I announced, "but I know she's your *Confidential Informant DB-1."*

And everybody laughed! Funniest thing ever heard!

"No, she's not," Joe said, grinning. "That's *my* moniker."

The man of mystery reeled! The bait danced!

"You?"

"Really thought it was Miss *d'Orsay?"* He nodded at the G-men. "Nope, whole thing was *their* idea, soup to nuts, crate to chloroform—and you swallowed it hook, line and sinker. That egg you smeared on their faces last week? Wanted some on *yours.* A twofer, you *and* the Commie. Miss *d'Orsay!"*

A fool, and I didn't even know whose!

Dread filled me. What was I in for, anyway, prison? Wait: *Kidnapping.* Didn't the Lindbergh Law make kidnapping a capital crime? Yes, of course it did—a thought to conjure with the day after Sing-Sing's electric chair fried Mr. and

Mrs. Rosenberg!

We were there a long time. I could hear the Florentine Cloister slowly emptying out. This was taking too long, I thought; what was the hold-up?

But finally cars pulled up in front and, Freddie opening the gate (but avoiding my eyes), they walked me out to a line of black Fords and shoved me into the middle one's backseat, Goddard climbing in after. The dome light was illuminated; it felt like a fishbowl. To every side I saw reflected a face that didn't resemble mine in the least.

Nickel-and-dime's Wraith was sitting near by, puffs of exhaust the only hint of life. After a while, his driver opened a door to what looked like a crowded drawing room and, to my surprise, Mrs. B., her daughter, Miss d'Orsay and Nolan got out, along with Nickel-and-dime and his wife.

Giving Nolan one of his stogies, Nickel-and-dime lighted up, and everyone lingered in conversation beside the car, Elyse hugging herself as if for warmth. Her mother seemed solicitous of her as my former boss repeatedly indicated the car where I sat.

I knew what it was: He was filling them in on my amorous past with David.

Oh, and how that history altered *theirs! Gutted* theirs! Made a liar and impostor out of *me*, and a *monster* out of David Spegall! Proved his disappearance to be a blessing and a boon! There would be no diplomatic protest, no private detectives, no hard feelings, even; just a quiet annulment.

Trying to catch my old boss's eye, I waggled my head grinning like a maniac. No response.

Lunging, I managed despite the cuffs to roll a window partway down and shout, "Mr. *Nikolodimsky!* Mr. *Nikolodimsky!*"

Reaching across, Goddard smartly rolled the window back

up, but Nickel-and-dime never even looked over. A deliberate snub. I was down the *oubliette* for good.

Kissing fingers and shaking hands, he and his wife eventually ducked into the car and were silently driven away. The ladies, leaning on one another for support, dragged into the courtyard past my Ford with never a glance at it, save for a wayward flicker from Miss d'Orsay accompanying the ghost of a smile. Freddie closed the gate after them with a definitive *clink!*

On the other side of the bars stood Joe, hands in his pockets, sneering out at me.

Then Nolan piled in next to the driver and we drove to New York, one Ford in front, another behind. No one said a word and, unaccountably, the dome light was left on. I felt rattled and tossed around. A bumpier ride than the dampened springs of Mrs. B.'s Cadillac!

It was an uneasy sensation to be driven down dark roads in a lighted compartment. Nor did I know where to look, so intent on catching my eye was the man of mystery left, right and center. Goddard, his expression wiped clear as a mannequin's, kept his thigh well away from mine.

At first I meditated David's fate instead of my own: Not so bad, not really. They wouldn't shoot him, not when his homecoming meant good publicity for the Motherland, such a ringing victory over the USA!

No, they probably wouldn't shoot him. Might even make him a Hero of the Soviet Union, and permit him to give interviews proclaiming his joy at being home and decrying the American way of life! Most likely give him one of their great orchestras for his very own!

Yes, I could see it: David would enjoy a stellar career. He might never again cross a border, but recordings and broadcasts would secure his international reputation. Isn't it

Milton's Satan who proclaims the joys of being a big frog in a little pond?

Art would give him that.

Well, art and *myself!*

Alas, of art I still had none. At best I would rot in prison. At *best;* at worst, be made a holocaust to the upriver gods.

But as in silence we rounded the Hawthorne Circle and headed through The Bronx and down the West Side Highway, I could swear that inescapable man of mystery was winking at me!

For it occurred to me the Bureau had a situation on its hands: Helping the KGB abduct somebody on American soil? As I would happily testify? Somebody married to an American millionairess, yet? The powers that be might not be so pleased—and the public most certainly not, not when a Soviet Cold War victory meant an American defeat!

Questions would arise—awkward ones—and aspersions be cast.

In getting back at me for his own failed wedding-day arrest of David, surely Nolan had overplayed his hand?

Surely the government would prefer to leave J. Edgar's boys out of it, and say it knew nothing about how David Spegall might have left the country? Let his disappearance slide, even if that meant letting me go instead of strapping me into Old Sparky?

Which is how things fell out, and sooner than I could have hoped.

The cars pulled to the curb in pre-dawn Manhattan, far downtown in a neighborhood I didn't know, in front of a drycleaners I was surprised was open, until I remembered. *We keep you clean or your $$$ back,* the window said. Everybody went indoors except my car's driver and myself.

We waited. Like a heater starting to glow, the sky went a

more intense orange every moment. I needed a cigarette, also needed to pee, and said as much, but got no response.

At last Goddard returned. Opening the door, he perched on the edge of the seat and worked at my cuffs — took them off!

"One word to *anybody*," snarled my G-boy. "OK, *scatter*."

Shoulders slumped, he went back inside.

So there I was — summarily *un*-arrested. Startled, but pretty happy about it, I sat rubbing my wrists while the driver brought his face around. I sprang up then, bounded down the sidewalk unconsciously going "*Mommy!*" just as on that night across the Rhine when German mortars found the USO's range.

Scrambling around the corner of Chambers Street, I found myself on a deserted block near the water, orange already going gray, and relieved myself in an areaway while watching a freighter slip down the North River.

Thought I saw Cyrillic lettering on the bow, then that *David* was standing at the gunwales, looking reproachfully at the passing skyline even as his hair caught fire in the rising sun.

I doubted my own eyes. Surely David's captors would confine him, if not all the way to Murmansk, at least until after the ship dropped its pilot at the Ambrose Light? So, why, watching, did I feel the worst pain of my life? Flayed alive, *skinned*, my hide ripped off and sent flying bunched and shapeless after the ship?

Agony, when really I was so glad to see him go?

I zipped up, adjusted cummerbund and tie and consulted my Cartier watch.

Where to? Bleecker Street? The old apartment and old life, *sans* David, *sans* job, *sans* everything?

Or 54th Street? Use my passkey, settle in, wait for tempers to cool, attitudes to adjust and everybody to come back to town?

Or Grand Central? Take the train to Katonah, a taxi to Ca'Dora, tell Mrs. B. I was *home,* and we could live *happily ever after?* Though first we had a concert to put on this afternoon!

Knowing I'd figure something out, I began walking uptown.

EPILOGUE

THERE YOU HAVE IT: *It was the FBI's idea.*

The FBI made me do it.

At the height of the Cold War, the depth of McCarthyism, *the FBI made me do it!*

I didn't say so earlier, because I wanted you to make up your own mind about me without, as it were, being coerced. Told you I'm really a nice guy, and now you see it's so.

Sure, it sounds terrible, packing up the love of your life and shipping him behind the Iron Curtain — but now you see why I had to do it.

And notice how I only have good things to say about David Spegall? He deserves them, too!

However, this is a man completely incapable of maintaining a relationship. I mean, we'd be sitting there in the same room and he'd blank me out completely while he concentrated on his damn music when I just wanted to hold a civil conversation.

If I were to remind him that it was time to go out to a party or to eat or go for a walk, he'd look at me blankly. Unbelievable. So I say only nice things about him — praise his talent and sweetness, even his appearance — but there was this whole other side I was expected somehow to cope with every day.

Well, anyway, what would *you* have done?

And don't worry about me: All I ever wanted was to live my own life.

I Remember Caramoor

A Memoir

For Chris Benda, George Clark and Max Stanbach,
dead friends of my youth

Thank heaven for the ambivalence of truth.

—Frederick Kiesler
Inside the Endless House

I FIRST STEPPED inside Caramoor's "big house" in April 1970 for my job interview. Mother drove me over. She parked in the lot beneath the West Wing and I walked around to the front and yanked at the bell. Hilton Bailey, assistant to Executive Director Michael Sweeley, stepped out of the house with a severe expression. "Mr. Meyers?" he asked, before opening the courtyard gate and bringing me indoors to the sitting room.

Mr. Sweeley was waiting. He shook my hand and gave me a seat in a Venetian Louis XV chair of tortoiseshell lacquer and green silk.

The room was charming, with its bookshelves, reading nook, blue silk brocade on the walls and, over the fireplace, Sir John Lavery's sparkling view of the ballroom of Wimborne House, London. Through the windows — some panes bubbled and faintly purple — I caught glimpses of the Spanish Courtyard. Beside us, Kuan-Yin carved from palest jade stood in intricate balance beneath a boat-shaped, embroidered and fringed silk lampshade on an 18th-century *chinoiserie* table.

Mr. Sweeley was a bulky man my father's age — 45 — with a trim beard, a gaze generally aiming aside from one's eyes and a low, cultivated voice; I immediately knew, homosexual.

What we talked about I forget, but the facts could not have been in my favor. I was articulate, self-possessed and tall, but only 17 years old—a bespectacled, bepimpled high-school dropout with no work history aside from mowing neighbors' lawns and stuffing envelopes for Mother's boss. Mr. Sweeley did perk up at hearing that Daddy was a member of *Fortune*'s Board of Editors.

The job I was applying for had just been vacated by one William, whom I'd not met but who went to high school with my friend Chris Benda, two years older than myself. William, a favorite of Mrs. Rosen's—so the Clarks later told me—had worked several years at Caramoor, but grown restless since her death in November 1968 and now was moving on. Chris told me about the vacancy, and I looked up Caramoor in the phone book, dialed and offered myself for the job. My advantage was that no hiring process had started yet.

In the middle of my interview, Mr. Sweeley was called to the Music Room. He had me tag along. It was of course my first sight of that marvelous chamber—vast, lofty, crammed with wonderful things. A tall ladder was set up and Robert Clark—Caramoor's butler and caretaker—was watching his son Ronnie Clark, the grounds superintendent, replace light bulbs in a chandelier, while Ray Mulligan, one of the gardeners, held the ladder. They wished Mr. Sweeley's judgment on some point or other.

Mr. Sweeley introduced me to them as they stood some ways off. I said, "I've already met Mr. Clark."

This startled Mr. Clark. A big man in black pants and short-sleeved white shirt, 60 years old, groaning at every movement—"*Ouch! Ouch!*"—and with broken veins in his face, he creased his forehead and asked, "Did you go to John Jay?"

"No," I replied, "but I know George."

George was his younger son.

And apparently that clinched it. Remarking, "I'm glad you know George," Mr. Sweeley walked me out to my mother, waiting in her Citroën DS 21 Pallas, and liked her right away, as people always did. He sent me away feeling optimistic.

Mother was curious as to where we might be—I hadn't said anything—and impressed. Only the weekend before Daddy had sat me down and told me to get a job, go back to school, or move out, and I'd been glad to tell him I had an interview scheduled.

Mr. Bailey called a few days later and asked me to begin work the following Monday.

MONDAY, APRIL 20, 1970 was thus the most important day of my life, marking my liberation from my family; a beautiful, showery spring morning with forsythia blooming brightly along the back way into Caramoor.

I dropped off my cardboard boxes on the screen porch of the "chauffeur's cottage" where I was to live, thanked Mother, walked round into the big house's garage and pounded on the door. Mr. Clark opened it warily and gave me two keys, one for that heavy, balky door and another for the cottage.

He also introduced me to Martha Clark, his wife, George's and Ronnie's mother and Caramoor's housekeeper and cook. She was a short, plump woman of about 50 with curly hair dyed black and a peaches-and-cream complexion she was rightly proud of. From the start she seemed to find me beguiling; around me she usually bore a secret smile.

Right off she handed me a big old ostrich feather duster and marched me down a dark, winding way through the cellars beneath the Music Room over to the West Wing. I despaired of finding my way back. We passed storerooms, a laundry room, a bathroom (where I was shortly to see Mr. Clark sitting on the toilet with the door open, laughing at my shock), the boiler room, musicians' dressing and shower rooms that stored hundreds of red-velvet folding chairs, and up first a utilitarian flight of steps and then a grand marble staircase beneath the straight-backed, aureole-haired gaze of Mrs. Rosen's most stately portrait, to the second floor.

My task was to dust and dry-mop that upstairs—the hallway, the four bedrooms off it, the family room at the far end, and the bedroom at the top of the stairs.

That bedroom—which was where William had lived—looked out over the Clarks' attached caretaker's cottage. It had an antique bed of japanned iron, an armoire and one of the house's 17 or so excellent bathrooms. During the Festival a few months later Christopher Parkening stayed there, and later such artists as Maralin Niska.

The upstairs was substantial and beautifully detailed rather than grand like the downstairs. The other bedrooms were spacious and filled with light, each pair linked by a foyer and sharing a bathroom, one tiled in cobalt blue, the other in purple. Floors were teak, and casement windows overlooked the Spanish Courtyard. Several had antique Austrian floor-to-ceiling ceramic stoves and were furnished in suites of 18th-century Tyrolean peasant furniture—cheerful, cartoonish renditions of Louis XV—and bedside trays bearing ewers and water glasses, plus a miscellaneous scattering, like a seaside cottage's, of books and objects.

But in the first bedroom stood a magnificent bed lately brought out from Mrs. Rosen's New York house.

"Hope it doesn't bother you," Mrs. Clark said, "but the Old Lady died in this bed."

Bothered her. Its huge gilded headboard resembled an

altarpiece, and the bedspread, also 16th-century, was of stiff red brocade shot with gold thread. Mrs. Rosen had died in her house at 35 West 54th Street — discovered dead by Freddie, her butler, when he brought in her breakfast tray. Mrs. Clark was sure she'd felt ill in the night and rung for help, but that Freddie declined getting up to respond, and consequently found her body lying half out of bed. Sir John Lavery's 1926 *Mrs. Rosen's Bedroom* makes this bed look as big as an aircraft carrier; Mr. Bailey told me it had belonged to the famously flamboyant Marchesa Luisa Casati, who received visitors to her Venetian palazzo lolling in it next to her pet cheetah.

Mrs. Clark said Mrs. Rosen, 78 at her death, should have lived years longer, but that an accident ten or twelve years previous shortened her life: One night her cream-and-black Cadillac limousine with custom raised roof rolled over on a backwoods Connecticut road, and thereafter she was confined to a wheelchair. The Clarks suspected that, despite his denials, Joe the Chauffeur fell asleep at the wheel. He'd lived in my cottage; hence its name. (Mr. Sweeley told me the Rosens had occupied it while building the big house, coming out weekends with picnic hampers.)

One afternoon a few weeks later I found Mrs. Clark feeding a shifty-eyed chap in a cloth cap sitting on a stool in the kitchen: Joe the Chauffeur, back for a final visit.

While I dusted upstairs, Mr. Bailey, then about 30, a slender, attractive and invariably pleasant graduate of the University of Virginia, was driving Mr. Sweeley and their colleague Miss Renée D'Arcy out from Manhattan in the white Chevy station wagon.

Arriving at lunch time, they welcomed me to Caramoor.

I HAD MET my friend Chris Benda at Saturday morning group therapy presided over by a rather likable man of the world. I remember Dr. Warren's account of attending, while on leave during the War, a concert conducted by Leopold Stokowski; at one point the young woman sitting in front of him turned, presenting a profile so perfect it took his breath away—Gloria Vanderbilt, then married to Stokowski. He'd also seen Jacqueline Du Pré perform at Caramoor (as had Chris), and remarked on her sexy manipulation of the cello between her legs.

The group consisted of four or five boys. One had witnessed his best friend burning to death after they built a bonfire and the friend swung a gas can's contents onto the flames. Another lived for the day he'd be old enough to enlist and become a sniper in Viet Nam.

Chris had briefly attended Fordham University, dropping out for reasons I don't know, and had a car, a new green Buick Skylark with a vinyl roof. As tall as I but even skinnier, he wore glasses, too, chain-smoked, was smart, funny, frail and effeminate, and I always liked him.

I took the decisive step in our becoming friends, one day in April 1969 asking if he'd like to go see the David Smith exhibition at the Guggenheim Museum. We thereafter spent much time together, in his car and at his parents' house in Katonah—never at mine. We toured Lyndhurst together and went to the movies in Stamford, Connecticut. Also we saw foreign films—*Black Narcissus* and *La Strada* among them—in the beautiful auditorium of IBM's Saarinen-designed Watson Research Center in Yorktown Heights, where his mother worked.

Chris liked going at night to Beaver Dam, a towering stone

rampart with a rush of white water at its base, but another joy was to park on the deserted, dirt Hook Road and follow a trail through the woods to Caramoor's grounds. It felt deliciously illicit to run past looming shapes and structures gray in the moonlight, including what Chris said was called "the Pope's bathtub," a Roman sarcophagus near the Venetian Theater. We also drove in via the back way, though never venturing to circle the big house.

I never introduced Chris to my parents, and it strikes me now how trusting (and fatalistic) they were in giving me entire freedom. I had dropped out of high school in September 1967, but in the fall of 1968 went back, this time to a Mount Kisco school that specialized in rich kids expelled from prep school for using drugs, but which had memorably good teachers, class sizes ranging from one to four, and (need I say it?) interesting students. I dropped out again in January 1970.

Chris was friends from John Jay High School with George Clark. Once we visited George, home from the University of California at Berkeley, where he was a psychology major — Mrs. Rosen having left money for his education and those of gardeners' children — in the caretaker's cottage. This was the occasion when I met his father, who ignored us as he sat in front of the TV (probably watching *Benny Hill),* not moving save to lift his glass or fill his pipe. The house had the worst ammoniated air I ever encountered, from Mrs. Clark's eight or ten cats. It hurt to breathe.

George had a car, too — a four-door Corvair. The summer of 1969 his dad got him a job with Pinkerton's, and every day George went off in uniform, shoulder-length hair tucked beneath his visored cap, to an abandoned quarry near Peekskill, where he lay in the grass with his shoes off reading *The Diary of Anaïs Nin* instead of shooing off the boys swimming in the quarry. Chris and I visited once or twice.

One day George drove us all the way to Newport, Rhode Island, where we gawked at Ocean Drive's mansions and explored abandoned stables. Also, we sometimes drove around Greenwich and Cos Cob, and several times went to New York, seeing *The Movie Orgy* at NYU and a Miles Davis – Thelonious Monk concert at the Wollman Rink. Another time as we were heading for the city the Corvair broke down on the Taconic State Parkway and we limped home. George soon acquired a new, powder-blue VW Bug.

In July 1969 when I went to Chicago to visit an elder brother and his wife, George kindly drove me to the airport. A dedicated marijuana smoker – aficionado, as well, of LSD, peyote, mescaline and hashish – he shared a joint with me on the way to LaGuardia. I'd tried pot with him and Chris, but failed to feel much effect, and now he wanted me to take off while high. Perhaps I did feel something extra.

From Chicago I flew to Tulsa to join another brother and his wife in a drive through the West. Their friend who joined us at a commune near Taos, New Mexico recounted meeting Jack Kerouac a year earlier: "like a drunken truck driver."

My plan was to fly home from Denver on the eve of the Woodstock Music & Art Fair, to which, very excited, I'd bought a three-day ticket with the proceeds of piecework – folding informational materials into packets – for Mother's boss at a Mount Kisco engineering firm. George had offered me a seat in his car for the drive upstate.

Accordingly, when I got home – exactly when I'd said I would – I called to ask what time he was picking me up next day, and he said that, not having heard from me, he'd given my place away. And that was that. I was not consoled by hearing later his and Chris's accounts of their rainy, muddy, sleepless, miserable experience; my heartsickness at missing Woodstock never ebbed, nor did I ever quite forgive George.

Unfortunately, though it was he who told me about the Caramoor job, Chris dropped me as soon as I was hired. The night before I started he told me over the phone that he was tired of me: "tired of your—" (ignorance? intensity? cluelessness? I forget). It was a painful shock; it had been a life-saving friendship, however limited.

Painful, and a nuisance, too, as until I got a driver's license and car I was pretty much stranded at the chauffeur's cottage. Oddly, I don't remember whether Chris kept up with George during my time at Caramoor.

In 1971 George Clark had some kind of breakdown, left college and took up a very quiet life at home. He stopped driving, saw psychiatrists, was given medication and—briefly committed to a psychiatric hospital—shock treatments, too, after which he seemed but a whisper of himself. He occasionally came over to watch my snowy black-and-white Panasonic portable TV or listen to music and solicit my help in killing himself.

I TOOK TO my duties immediately.

My day generally began with Mr. Clark's good-natured wake-up call at 9:00 a.m., when I was supposed to be bringing Mr. Sweeley his breakfast. I'd throw on my clothes and rush over, coming through the garage. Mrs. Clark, waiting in the pantry, would pour hot coffee into a silver carafe and place it on an 18th-century Venetian tray of japanned *papier-mâché*, next to a pink half-grapefruit topped with brown sugar and a maraschino cherry, its segments carved out that no untoward squirting might occur, while from the warming oven Mr. Clark retrieved a plate of scrambled eggs, bacon, toast and jelly, and covered it with a silver dome.

Off I would whisk the tray, greeting in passing Miss D'Arcy and Mr. Bailey at breakfast at the glass-topped table two steps up from the dining room proper, beside French doors to the terrace never used in my time.

Taking the short way, up steep spiral stairs, I would knock at Mr. Sweeley's door, await his answering grunt, go in saying, "Good morning, Mr. Sweeley," and set the tray on the bureau beside his big oaken 16th-century bed, opposite the mantelpiece bearing bronze John Harvard bookends and an inscribed photograph of the pianist Gina Bachauer.

Shutting his door on him, I would find feather duster, dust mop and dust rag in a hallway wash closet and begin cleaning the office. Mr. Sweeley occupied the bedroom of the Rosens' son, Walter Bigelow Tower Rosen, a graduate of Harvard and Yale Law School who joined the Royal Canadian Air Force before America entered the War. In 1944 he was piloting his flak-damaged Halifax heavy bomber back from a bombing raid over Germany to its Yorkshire base when it crashed several miles short of the runway, killing him and his crew. Mr. Clark said he was engaged at his death to the Miss Coit who later married Lloyd George's grandson (Mr. Rosen actually left her an income).

The son's beamed sitting room served as the office. Its window seat and row of latticed casements — with stained-glass and bottle-glass inserts — overlooked the Spanish Courtyard. The overhead light fixture by E.F. Caldwell & Co. was a painted globe girdled with bronze signs of the zodiac, a reminder the room was built for a teenager who appeared to have an interest in the stars.

After emptying ashtrays and wastebaskets, I dusted everything, working from top to bottom, ceiling to floor; ostrich feathers are magically effective at knocking dust aside without disturbing objects. I ran a dust mop sprayed with

Endust over the floorboards, and as needed vacuumed the rug.

Meanwhile I would scan any papers exposed to view on the refectory table used as a desk; never saw much of interest, save for statements from Ladenburg Thalmann showing the assets of the Walter Tower and Lucie Bigelow Rosen Foundation for the Arts to be ever dwindling. (Mother was shocked to hear that Mr. Sweeley's salary was $25,000, a large sum for the day.)

Eventually Mr. Sweeley would progress in the silken dressing gown Mrs. Rosen gave him from bedroom to bathroom to office, but by that time I was cleaning the sitting room downstairs, where my first task was to clean out the previous night's ashes and lay a new fire; Mr. Sweeley enjoyed a fire the year round. Mrs. Clark showed me how to set layers of kindling, line the grate with crumpled newspaper—a twist sticking out for the match—and position a big back log and smaller front one.

Emptying ashtrays and wastebaskets, I dusted and swept the sitting room, adjoining stair hall and the staircase, with its Cecil Beaton watercolor of an elongated Mrs. Rosen in yellow.

Ashes and trash I carried to the boiler room beneath the Music Room, where ash cans lined the floor sloping up to double doors, above the pit where lay enormous boilers like recumbent missiles.

As I came through the pantry Miss D'Arcy would be in conference with Mrs. Clark in the kitchen, ordering the day's meals—a lengthy process, involving much gossip, and clearly the highlight of her day. Mrs. Clark's deference washing over her, Miss D'Arcy would dance about beside the butcher-block table in front of the kitchen range, something puppet-like and deeply uneasy to her movements: "Oh, that's *marvelous*. And I think perhaps lentil soup, Michael *so* loves your lentil soup."

Menu planning focused on the weather and, consequently, on what might not be too "heavy" to eat, and of course on Mr. Sweeley's preferences.

Meanwhile, Ronnie Clark would drop off the *Times* and mail (fetched from the post office) on the pantry counter, and I'd carry them up to the office.

Early in the week Vito, the Italian longtime head gardener (I never knew his surname), would lay his flowers across the pantry's stainless-steel center table, whose scratches always looked circular in the overhead light. There were snapdragons, asters, marigolds, chrysanthemums, gladioli and often orchids.

Mr. Clark would line up his dozen vases and, concentrating deeply, arrange each and tell me where to take it. Vases went always to sitting room, office, bedrooms, Music Room, and several to the dining room; after the house-museum opened, West Wing rooms also. It amused me that this Tennessee native who never lost (or cared to lose) his Southern accent pronounced *vase* with a posh broad *A*. Often the old flowers were still beautiful and I'd take them home.

A quiet murmur emanating from Mr. Sweeley *et al.* at work in the office, I would make their beds and clean their rooms, bathrooms and hallway, even unto the candle sconces. Mr. Bailey had the room with double bed over the sitting room, with windows overlooking both the courtyard and the front of the house, and Miss D'Arcy the small maid's room (as Mrs. Clark said it had been) next door, with a window over the courtyard, a narrow bed and lovely little prizes arrayed on shelves.

My mornings were thus occupied until 11:30, when I knocked off and returned to my cottage. Generally I took a nap and showered, returning refreshed to the big house promptly at 1:00 o'clock.

Lunch at the glass-topped table just starting, Mrs. Clark

would lure me into her kitchen to show the meal she was leaving for me, and suggest I eat while it was hot. I'd protest I was too busy to eat just then, but she'd prevent me from getting back to work by launching into *talk talk talk* while serving up plates and cleaning up.

Mrs. Clark was a talker with a keen sense of the drama and mystery of her life. Taking up a defiant stance, she would declare with flashing eyes, "You don't know me very well, Steven," and tell stories of the hard early years when the Rosens' European staff snubbed her and her husband, stories also about the Old Man and the Old Lady.

"She would have liked you," she said frequently (Mr. Clark chimed in with agreement).

The Old Lady was beautiful, she told me, aside, of course, from that sharp nose, thin hair, problem with body odor and the pallor that prevented her from wearing her favorite color, yellow. Impatient with rivals, the Old Lady tended to avoid high society ("had to be queen bee"). Her best friend had been Lady Ravensdale, Lord Curzon's daughter. One former cook (Elsa?) ate jelly all day long and on her frequent trips to the toilet left trails of shit across the kitchen floor. Oh, the criticism heaped on her when Mrs. Clark put the extra-active child Ronnie out in the yard in a harness on a rope!

One of her refrains was, "I hope you don't think of yourself as a *servant*." ("No, no," I assured her.)

Getting away was difficult; I developed a slow backwards walk that would eventually take me into the pantry and freedom. This at least prevented Miss D'Arcy's finding me eating an unauthorized free lunch when she brought Mr. Sweeley's extensive compliments to the chef, though I suspect everybody knew Mrs. Clark fed me.

After lunch, Mr. Clark would plop on his hat and take out the station wagon to do Caramoor's marketing.

Early on, just once, he took me with him. After shopping at the A&P, we went into Halstead's Hardware Store. They greeted him familiarly and he introduced me to everybody. There was a display of deerskin gloves. They asked me, Would you like a pair? No, thank you. No, that's all right, go ahead, take a pair—no charge. I chose one, trembling at this unveiling of the world's corruption, while Mr. Clark *laughed*.

MY AFTERNOONS WERE devoted to cleaning. One day I would "do" the West Wing downstairs, another day the upstairs, the Music Room another, the Rosens' bedroom and dressing rooms yet another. (A standing joke was how I left undisturbed on Mrs. Rosen's bedside table the hairbrush and bobbie pins that happened to be lying there when she died.)

An almost daily chore was washing windows and French doors; Mrs. Clark showed me how hot water, vinegar and newspaper make for a bright shine.

I cleaned as the Clarks taught me: dusted everything with cloth or feather duster (Mr. Sweeley lamented that Abercrombie & Fitch, the storied Manhattan outfitter of exotic expeditions, was phasing out its feather dusters), dry-mopped the wood and terrazzo floors, vacuumed rugs, scrubbed with Bon Ami. I did my best, took pride in the results, and it seemed easy.

All the while I looked at and studied the things that surrounded me. The Rosens had assembled an enormous collection of choice, rare things. Everything was old, the very lamps wired from Renaissance bronze candleholders. Nothing could have been more congenial to someone like me who finds time to be a kind of jelly that does not in fact flow.

I liked everything, but my favorites included the 15th-century Florentine ivory carving of a nude youth courting a girl in a tower, and the Henri II desk and chairs whose affinities to modern Scandinavian design astonished me, and the graceful lacquer chairs that sat in the sitting room until banished to the stair hall, replaced by blue-velvet Adam club chairs from the city house.

Also I admired the great Chinese eight-fold jade screen, a full-page color photograph of which appeared in the Burgundian Library's old set of the *Encyclopædia Brittanica*, and Canaletto's picture of Venice's *SS. Giovanni e Paolo* (never mind that it's now *school of*) is beautifully composed and colored, with an animated little grouping of people and marvelous sky. I heard Mrs. Stern, the Rosens' daughter, say that, standing in front of it during his mid-1950s stay, the Duke of Windsor had sighed, "I used to have 54 of these." (The Windsors slept in what we called the "Monkey Room," for its 18th-century Chinese jungle wallpaper.)

The Rosens' taste was very good, but didn't seem to extend past about 1820. I expect that both consciously rebelled against the Victoriana they were raised amidst, but from there their tastes went backwards, not forwards.

Even then I observed that the monetary value of the collection—which according to 1920s inventories cost the Rosens well over $1 million, back when (as Mr. Clark loved to repeat) "a dollar was a *dollar*"—would have grown more (today, immeasurably more) had they bought art of their own time. Possibly it's a shame they didn't forgo buying yet another period room and choose two or three Picassos instead. (Benjamin Seymour Guinness, Mr. Rosen's one-time partner at Ladenburg Thalmann, was a friend of Picasso's and his frequent host at his villa at Mougins, in the south of France, which the artist later bought, living there the last dozen years of his life.)

By contrast, the Rosens' tastes in music and fashion were decidedly up to date: Mrs. Rosen wore Fortuny, commissioned music from such modern composers as Bohuslav Martinů, and of course the Rosens' support of the Russian inventor Dr. Léon Theremin—his financial backing, her concertizing on the eponymous electronic instrument—placed them in the front lines of the avant garde.

I wish I knew more about the house's design and construction. Mr. Rosen previously had a summer place in Oyster Bay, Long Island—the house where Typhoid Mary had worked a fatal stint as cook for former owners—but in the 1920s bought the Bedford tract.

The Rosens were about to embark on building an enormous showplace when the 1929 Crash deflected their plans, whether because it straitened their means or made such conspicuous spending appear unseemly (though certainly building Caramoor gave work to many, including the extended family of Italian plasterers said to have moved in for a year).

Caramoor's architect of record is Christian Rosberg, though I always heard Mr. Rosen credited with every detail of its design; however, there hung in the front staircase an elevation of the Music Room rendered in blue chalk by C.P.H. Gilbert, architect of many storied New York country houses and city mansions. (The Cooper Hewitt Museum preserves Rosberg's drawing for a marvelous folly, never built, of an observatory for Caramoor.)

In any event, the house rises on the footprint of former stables. In my cottage was a mid-1930s aerial photograph showing a greenhouse where the Music Room now stands, with the dovecote in the courtyard's center. The stables conversion might explain the siting of the house on a lower slope than where many would choose to build.

AT 2:30 OR 3:00 O'CLOCK, when all was quiet and no one was about, I would find the plate Mrs. Clark left for me under a dampened towel in the back of her great range, and eat at the oilcloth-covered table in the help's dining room a few steps up from the kitchen.

Sandwiches — lots of BLTs and tuna salad or chicken salad, the bread toasted — were usual lunch fare, often with, on the side, tomatoes fried in breadcrumbs and Mrs. Clark's own herb garden's basil; sometimes veal cutlets or scrambled eggs and sausages, often excellent lentil or mulligatawny soup.

While eating I would greedily read some ancient Parke-Bernet or Anderson Art Gallery auction catalog, caches of which, dating back to 1900 or so and extending through Mr. Rosen's lifetime, lay in the sideboard there and in the low cabinets of the Burgundian Library. They fascinated me, especially those bearing penciled notations or prices or featuring items that had ended up at Caramoor.

Also I read miscellaneous fare from the stacked-up boxes of books — a 1930s account of the building of the Mt. Palomar telescope, a pre-war edition of John Gunther's *Inside Europe*.

Then it was back to work.

Early on, in addition to daily maintenance, I began a project of deep cleaning. Although its staff was only reduced to our skeleton crew after Mrs. Rosen died, the big house in some ways had long been neglected. The chandeliers, for instance, including the spectacular 18th-century Waterford chandelier in the pine-pilastered West Wing reception room, were dusty and dim. I undertook to brighten them, raising a stepladder and wiping the crystal droplets with newspaper doused in hot water and vinegar until they sparkled.

I did the same with all the Waterford candelabra—carried them to the kitchen, took them apart, cleaned each droplet on every strand and reassembled them. Even the Lenox and Haviland china had acquired stubborn scum from long daily use; over time I scrubbed it clean.

My project had two gratifying successes on the courtyard's summer porch. The fireplace hood looked to be plain stucco, but I guessed at the existence of a painted motif, and brought it to light one afternoon by lifting off 40 years of grime with wet sponges.

Also, learning from Mr. Clark that the marble-dolphin fountain beside the door was never used because no one any longer remembered how to turn it on, my younger brother helped me locate the cellar valves that controlled it, and thereafter it plashed pleasantly during Festival meals and receptions.

At one point I set out to clear the accumulation of junk in the storage rooms beneath the dining room and kitchen. That project upset Mr. Clark, by nature something of a pack rat. One day as we both grabbed at a pile of jealously preserved *used* floor-polishing pads, he mistook my movement and put up his dukes. Of course he was drunk, and things did improve.

Miss D'Arcy oversaw the donation of salvageable items from the cellar to a local thrift shop, including (regrettably, in retrospect) steamer trunks and the Rosens' son's crampons. What we deemed trash Ronnie Clark burned as usual in a clearing behind his house. Afterwards he sent one of Ray Mulligan's sons to ask me please not to throw out any more shotgun shells.

My deep-cleaning project hit an ignominious speed bump: Over time I scrubbed and waxed to shiny whiteness the dingy marble bases of the dozen wrought-iron standing lamps E.F.

Caldwell created for the Music Room, its anterooms and the dining room. Mr. Sweeley was horrified: "They had a finish on them!" He required me thereafter to ask his permission before undertaking such tasks.

I appreciated being left to work so largely on my own initiative. Fortunately I never broke anything, except one day I was dusting a porcelain bowl in the reception room when a wooden ring that lay inside its rim sprang out and fractured on the floor. I ran to get Mr. Bailey. He followed me back looking stern, then was incredulous that I'd bothered.

Occasionally my routine was disrupted. One day I was seconded to help move chairs and banquettes for a photographer, and to help his assistant haul a sheet back and forth behind them while the shutter was open for backgrounds of infinite depth. The assistant told me that, seeing the Ferdinand-and-Isabella chair in the Burgundian Library, he'd oh-so-carefully lowered himself into it—something I never did. (He also recommended a book that he said proved Jesus to have been a space alien.)

Mr. Clark's domain was the pantry and dining room, Mrs. Clark's the kitchen; the rest of the house was mine, save that on Saturdays when Mr. Sweeley *et al.* were away Mr. Clark and I polished the Music Room floor together. Plugging in the electric waxer, moving furniture as needed and throwing down chunks of Minwax, we went over the teak floorboards.

Then I would head off to change the beds in the East Wing, finding in the upstairs linen closet percale sheets in pink, yellow, green, blue and violet monogrammed—like the towels—*LBR*. Mrs. Clark did laundry for the big house and ironed the sheets (Mrs. Rosen, she told me, had required fresh ones daily). Mr. Clark never failed to suggest that I short-sheet the beds: "Give 'em the *treatment* instead of a *treat*."

Beds changed, I would settle down in the office for a long session reading. First I perused any issues Mr. Sweeley might have left lying about of *After Dark,* a magazine featuring moody, shadowy photographs of nude men, but mostly I read Mr. Rosen's business correspondence, carbon copies of which were bound in volumes. His letters vividly conveyed the excitement of plundering Europe for his collection during summertime trips after World War I and how frightening the Depression felt even to someone at the top of Wall Street. The background thus gleaned came in useful when I was writing *My Mad Russian,* my fictional treatment of the Rosens' relations with Dr. Theremin.

I'd actually heard of Theremin before I got to Caramoor, from Steve Drews, a family friend who co-founded the electronic music group *Mother Mallard.* For all that the *Times'* music critic Harold C. Schonberg — an occasional Caramoor dinner guest — had come across Dr. Theremin in the flesh in Russia in 1967, the story Mr. Sweeley passed on to me — as told him by Mrs. Rosen — was that one day in the 1930s Theremin vanished, no one (including his American wife, the black dancer Lavinia Williams) knew why or how, but the suspicion was that Stalin's agents had kidnapped him from where he lived next door to the Rosens' on West 54th Street and taken him home to be shot.

During the week, I'd knock off shortly after 4:00 p.m. to have a Coke and some of the Chips Ahoy cookies always to be found in the pantry drawer, and chat with Mr. Clark while he prepared the cocktail tray. At 4:30 my workday ended with turning down beds and asking Mr. Sweeley if anything more was wanted; nothing ever was.

Off I went, then, to take a long walk, my daily practice and delight since I was twelve years old.

OFTEN I WOULD leash up Mrs. Rosen's two enormous, friendly, aging Afghan Hounds — Towzer and Bruno? — in their kennel across the drive from the garage and take them over the grounds.

Mrs. Clark's aged mother, Mrs. Coyle, who lived with her daughter, tended to waylay us from her perch on a bench on the flagstone walk past the tennis court (lined by arbors whose tart grapes Vito pressed into wine for years; "Pretty good wine, too," Mr. Clark said).

Half the time I would stop to talk, although once Mrs. Coyle got going it was as hard to get away from her as from her daughter. Irish-born, she'd been in service herself (never hearing mention of Mrs. Clark's father, I came to suspect the *Mrs.* was assumed) and was full of sweet, dire warnings: Don't let them do this to you, don't let them do that. (When I left for college, she kindly pressed $40 into my palm.)

But half the time I would take advantage of Mrs. Coyle's poor eyesight to sneak round with the dogs into the Cedar Walk, going on to the walled garden that, with its medieval-style mount, survived from the old Hoyt estate; the Clarks said the Old Man liked to read there in its sheltered corner (I preferred reading at the tennis pavilion or on the steps down to the Venetian Theater lawn). The Rosens had embellished the garden with a bronze Paul Manship sundial and the pink marble "Juliet" gate from Verona.

Then we'd go down the half-mile-long driveway past banks of rhododendrons to the modest main gates, before returning to the big house.

One day Mr. Clark reported that he'd taken the dogs to the vet and had them put down, and not to say anything to his wife; he told her the vet had diagnosed terminal illnesses. She was upset. I don't know why he did it, as she loved them and took entire care of them, heaping up kibble for "the little buggers" (as she called pets and children) in a glazed brown bowl and in cold weather bringing them in from their doghouse to the warm cellar.

Other times I'd walk the famous Bedford bridle paths that wended through hundreds of acres of woods, more than 100 of which were Caramoor's. I don't recall ever taking the dogs on them; it might have been forbidden from the chance of coming upon horses, though I seldom saw any. The paths began beside the stucco barn whose chateau-style upstairs apartment was occupied during the Festival by Julius Rudel, its music director.

Generally I first walked past Mrs. Christina Rainsford's neighboring house, *Ethandune*, built by her late architect husband, Kerr Rainsford, and climbed her fire-lookout-style tower atop Mt. Aspetong. It brought one from beneath the forest canopy to a sudden sense of Long Island Sound and Hudson River Valley. Someone told me monarch butterflies emigrated past single-file, but I never witnessed such a spectacle.

Kerr Rainsford's father had been Rector of the Rosens' New York church, St. George's on Stuyvesant Square, back when J.P. Morgan was a parishioner and Mr. Rosen an usher. Mrs. Rainsford, author of several volumes of nature poetry, was a close friend of Mrs. Rosen's, according to the Clarks. I served her at garden parties, and remember seeing her handsome grandsons emerge from the woods to attend Festival rehearsals.

Eventually I'd climb down and walk on, getting glimpses of massive old places before turning back.

In winter snowmobiles sometimes screamed down the bridle paths, and for all I know had a right to; but the yowling was unbearable. At least once I ordered them off the paths beyond Ronnie Clark's house.

Occasionally, however, a different stinking racket would invade them in the form of a VW Bug with its body cut away. It belonged to Jeremy Willis, a classmate of Chris's and George's who appeared in *Lord of the Flies,* a movie I loved; Chris did an imitation of his one line: *"Henry."*

As he passed with a friendly wave, I'd give him my best scowl. His English parents rented a Caramoor carriage house, which like the Mulligan cottage and a barn nearby survived from the old Fahnestock estate. Mr. Clark told me that in the 1920s a bull had killed a man in that barn.

I LOVED LIVING in the chauffeur's cottage. It was one of two stucco houses making up a walled compound connected to the big house by the pergola extending out from its formal front door. An archway separated the cottages. The courtyard featured a car shed and garage with red-tile roofs (the garage was rented to a collector who stored a 1950s Lincoln there) and, tucked away in the corner, a clothes-drying area; wonderful to find oneself trapped between fresh sheets.

The cottage had four rooms and a screen porch: a kitchen whose Jacobean-revival sideboard, highboy, table and chairs were mates to sets at the Clarks' and the big house's help's dining room; a living room entered through French doors, and two bedrooms off a hallway, each with a sink. The smaller had a casement looking towards the big house and a sash window under the archway. I slept in the larger, one of whose casements overlooked the fenced meadow once used for horses, the other the asphalt dance floor and the dovecote. There was fine woodwork throughout. The bathroom was tiled in little blue-and-white squares and had a vertical stained-glass window and a magnificent tub, where I enjoyed many a long hot soak with issues of *Harper's* and *The New Yorker*.

A hallway door opened to a staircase. In the cellar were a washing machine, a furnace I learned to bleed to keep the pipes from banging, and an areaway to the courtyard. Upstairs were five bedrooms and a bathroom used in season by Festival electricians, with a door to a wisteria-wreathed outside staircase.

I seldom had reason to go up there, and whenever I did seemed to find a dead bat in a sink. Once I put my head through the trap door, hoping to find treasures in the attic; it was empty.

The living room, which looked into the courtyard through sash windows over the areaway, had a beautiful rug of yellow wool, cut down from one made for the city house shortly before Mrs. Rosen died. There was an antique glass-fronted bookcase and compact 1930s easy chairs, a couch, wrought-iron E.F. Caldwell lamps with parchment shades, and a wonderful six-sided 16th-century Italian walnut table, part of a set I found pictured in the Bardini Collection catalog. This was one of the big reading eras of my life; I would read for hours with my feet thrust out of a chair, steadily knocking that sturdy little table back and forth.

One day Mr. Sweeley and Mr. Bailey were in the Ping-Pong Room (the game room behind the West Wing family room) going through things lately brought from the city house. Among them was an enormous, explicit drawing of a female nude. I asked Mr. Sweeley if I might hang it in my cottage; he deferred (forever) a decision, but offered to let me hang an oil by Mr. Rosen's artist brother Ernest T. Rosen (who married Marie-Anne Carolus-Duran Feydeau, daughter of the portraitist Carolus-Duran and former wife of the playwright Georges Feydeau), depicting a characteristically gauzy woman, which I did.

Ernest Rosen's pictures have a look of their own but, despite the fact that France acquired one for the Luxembourg Museum, I wasn't particularly a fan.

Mr. Sweeley gave me permission to borrow books from the big house, and I took full advantage (though also using the Katonah Public Library). The Burgundian Library was one source; also, the Music Room's Spanish alcove, the sitting room, and the West Wing upstairs. I read Gibbon's *The Decline and Fall of the Roman Empire*, and Carlyle's *The French Revolution* and biography of Frederick the Great (with Carlyle's indignant declaration that to inquire into whether his subject loved men would be like a dog sniffing another's hindquarters).

Also I read *Seventy Summers*, the autobiography of Mrs. Rosen's uncle Poultney Bigelow, a journalist best known for his friendship from childhood with Kaiser Wilhelm, as well as coffee-table books galore about palaces, country houses and gardens, a volume Walter Lippman inscribed to "my friend Walter Rosen," a novel autographed by Hilaire Belloc, and Mr. Rosen's own slender 1933 volume, *The Handling of the War Debts* (his letter on the subject that year to the New York *Times* noted vividly that "the depression still eats its way into the heart of the world").

I keenly enjoyed Winston Churchill's biography of the first Duke of Marlborough, too. Churchill was a cousin of Mrs. Rosen's stepfather, the Hon. Lionel Guest, son of the first Viscount Wimborne, the steel magnate married to Churchill's aunt, but I know nothing of any relations between Churchill and the Rosens. *Wikipedia* notes that Ladenburg Thalmann, Mr. Rosen's firm, supplied the British with currencies that funded numerous covert projects during World War II.

The Clarks told me that Mr. Rosen's aunt perished in the Holocaust; certainly his sister Jeanne Magre, widow of French writer Maurice Magre, died at Auschwitz. Was that the closest the Holocaust came to Churchill personally?

Curiously, Hitler sought to exploit this same step-cousinship, in 1936 inviting Mrs. Rosen's brother, Maj. John Bigelow Dodge of the British Army, to Berchtesgaden, and giving him at the Berghof a private message to convey to Churchill. "I am a winner, and God looks favorably on winners," Hitler told Dodge, in proposing that Britain join him in an alliance against Russia (Dodge's "Digest," in his stepson Charles A. Sherman III's *Exciting Stories of My Personal Brushes with Greatness: Memoirs of Another Time*, records this "Extraordinary Conversation," pp. 127-130).

Major Dodge was wounded fighting in World War I's Gallipoli campaign, and happened to choose the site for his friend Rupert Brooke's grave there. In World War II, he won the nickname "The Artful Dodger" for his serial escapes from German prisoner-of-war camps; Steve McQueen's character in *The Great Escape* is said to be based partly on Maj. Dodge.

EARLY ON MR. SWEELEY kindly gave me Mrs. Rosen's old Columbia portable phonograph (a larger one of similar vintage remained in the sitting room). It had a fine tone, and on it I used to play my Beatles records, Beethoven piano concertos and string quartets, Bach's *B Minor Mass*, Handel, Mozart, Incredible String Band, Tim Buckley, Nina Simone, Laura Nyro, Bessie Smith, plus Rolling Stones albums borrowed from George Clark.

One day Mr. Sweeley expressed concern at hearing music

coming from my cottage the previous evening. As I recall, I'd put on a jazz compilation, opened the casements and wandered the lawns to Bill Evans' *Peace Piece*; but it might have been *Sympathy for the Devil*.

Governor Nelson Rockefeller visited Caramoor one Sunday in September 1970, landing in a helicopter at the John Jay Homestead a mile away and driving over in a motorcade. At the front door to greet him were Mr. Sweeley, Miss D'Arcy, Mr. Bailey, myself and some of the Governor's people, including a nice lady who made it her project that I meet him.

He arrived, strode past me with a sidelong glance *("Someone I should meet? I think not")*, and was borne down the West Wing remarking how his brother David had so often been there. The lady came up to me: "Did you meet him?" "Yes, thanks."

The Governor proceeded to the Venetian Theater, where before an invited audience he lauded his grandfather Senator Aldrich for making possible collections like the Rosens' by removing import duties on art and antiques. The next day's *Times* reported the speech as a pledge to open his family place at Pocantico Hills to the public; whatever the press release might have said, that was not the speech he gave.

The David Rockefellers indeed had been frequent visitors to Caramoor—the Clarks quite liked Peggy Rockefeller, who they said was cross-eyed—but only from David Rockefeller's autobiography did I learn that his roommate at Harvard was Walter Bigelow Rosen.

EVERY SPRING CARAMOOR gave a garden party. I distinctly remember my first, on a lovely Saturday late in May. Caterers dropped off boxes of caviar and *petits fours*, and

Mrs. Clark made stacks of Mrs. Rosen's favorite cucumber sandwiches — she had a trick that prevented their causing gas, she said — and vast quantities of delicious punch made from oranges, grapefruit, strawberries and other fruit, and liberally spiked with bourbon.

We put two bowls out on a table on the dance floor (later garden parties were held in the Spanish Courtyard), and kept them filled all afternoon. One punchbowl was officially teetotal, but Mr. Clark thought it great fun to spike both. He alerted me to the reliable phenomenon that a party's sound level explodes five minutes after liquor is served.

The guests included some of Mrs. Rosen's Pell and Bigelow cousins, Agnes DeMille and her husband (he ran the Sol Hurok organization, where Mr. Sweeley had worked), Audrey Michaels (who handled Caramoor's public relations) and a distinguished and discontented-looking neighbor, Mrs. Fosburgh — one of the famous Cushing sisters, Mr. Clark told me. Helen Clay Frick was a no-show, but Anne Bigelow Stern, the Rosens' daughter, was there with her sons John Scholz, an architect, and Walter Scholz, a short, plump, theatrical soul carrying a fancy walking stick and talking about his collection of them.

Walter Scholz spent much of the afternoon visiting with the Clarks, who in some sort were parent-figures. He'd gone to Yale, and originally wished to live at Caramoor and commute to New Haven in his Porsche; the Clarks told me they'd quietly put the kibosh on that scheme with Mrs. Rosen. Later that year Walter produced Kurt Vonnegut's play *Happy Birthday, Wanda June* Off-Broadway. He died in the late 1980s, his obit bravely stating the cause to be AIDS.

During the party a flamboyant Englishwoman and her escort came into the pantry. She told us her father, Sir Oswald Birley, had painted Mrs. Rosen's portrait, and that she'd made an extended 1940s visit to the city house.

Mr. Clark brought her reminiscences up short by remembering her—remembering taking her breakfast tray to the upper bedroom with twin Elizabethan beds. Exactly what might have transpired was left to our imaginations, but he made this unblushing woman blush. (My 1990 one-act play *The Garden Party* was based on this incident; with the Internet's dawning, I discovered her to be Maxime de la Falaise, a famous character in her own right.)

UNLIKE HIS WIFE, Mr. Clark had not instantly warmed to me, but it didn't take too long. I discovered what held good my whole working life, that doing a bit more than one's share eases relations with colleagues. But not only did I lighten his load, I listened to his stories.

For, like his wife, although possibly unbeknownst to her, Mr. Clark was a talker. He had a predilection for telling over and over (and over again) a limited and hoary repertoire of dirty jokes ("Well, how'd you *think* I rang the bell?" asks the man with four bandaged limbs at the brothel door; the horseman who manages—after others have failed—to pick up a greased nude girl explains, "Well, have you ever gone bowling?").

He also liked the one about the psychiatrist who, greeted with, "Good morning," broods, "Now, I wonder what he meant by that?"

Robert Lee Clark was born and raised in Clarksville, Tennessee, descended from George Rogers Clark, and a cousin, to boot, of Robert E. Lee's. Unfortunately, he personified the Southern racist; I first heard the word *jigaboo* from him, and when Marian Anderson came to dine, he asked me, "Get a load of her smell?" George Shirley one afternoon came into the pantry to find some ice, and Mr. Clark chased him off as if he were an intruder. He was a strong supporter of George Wallace, whom I despised; we had a lot of noisy arguments.

In the 1930s Mr. Clark served with the Army in the Panama Canal Zone; he gave me two pencil sketches he did there while in the hospital with malaria. On mustering out, he became Vincent Astor's chauffeur — unfortunately, I know no more than that bare fact. During the War he was working as a bank guard in Manhattan when his doctor advised a move to the countryside; hence, Caramoor, though he and his wife first worked some months at the city house, Mrs. Clark as Mrs. Rosen's lady's maid.

Mr. Clark was a perceptive, if acerbic, observer of people, and shared his wife's sense of the drama of their lives. When I arrived they had been at Caramoor for 26 years, and though they still resented the ancient snubs of other staff — European and unwelcoming, even outright hostile — their tenure now featured a satisfying narrative arc that took them from being despised outsider newcomers to insider sole survivors.

But those European staff members had their own troubles. So afraid of Mr. Rosen was the butler of that time (Horace?) that, when laying out his clothes in the wonderful barrel-vaulted dressing room while the Old Man was in his morning bath, he didn't dare move except when he heard splashing.

Also Horace would take the opportunity to peruse the coded notebook Mr. Rosen kept in his pocket, looking for investment tips, and in fact invested according to his interpretation of what he found, with the result that he lost all his money. (Though Mr. Sweeley referred to Mr. Rosen's dressing room as his *bedroom,* the Clarks were adamant that Mr. Rosen always slept in the Pope's Bed with his wife.)

The later butler, Freddie, was a Swiss with dyed hair whom William once saw, Mrs. Clark told me, loitering with a longing expression on the worst part of 42nd Street. Ernest, a longtime houseman, was German and before the War joined, along with other staff, the German American Bund that supported Hitler; Mr. Clark claimed that fact enabled Mr. Rosen to employ them at low wages ever afterwards.

The Clarks' own relationship had been a struggle, too. Mr. Clark intimated that he knew many women before his marriage, and settled down with the one only with difficulty. They agreed that his 40s, especially, had been all about sex; Mrs. Clark proclaimed many times she "wouldn't go through *that* again."

But they had achieved peace and mutual devotion, and won out at Caramoor, too. They credited Mrs. Rosen for standing by them: "She liked *us*," they would say — liked their down-home roughness and lack of pretentiousness, and Mrs. Clark's plain cooking. "The Old Lady was very good to us," they repeated time and again.

The Old Man was another matter. The Clarks never much cared for him. Though he was generous in giving Mr. Clark and Ronnie the use of his third-base box at Yankee Stadium, it rankled that he forbade staff to walk on Caramoor's grounds (after his death Mrs. Rosen lifted the ban); fortunately there was room for a swing set in the yard of the caretaker's cottage, which the Clarks occupied from the start.

Mr. Clark said if Mr. Rosen took a cab home from Broad Street to West 54th and found nothing small enough in his pocket, he'd dart through traffic at peril of life and limb to get change for a quarter from the Dorset Hotel doorman, then give the cabbie a dime tip.

Once Mr. Clark happened to walk into the Rosens' bedroom while they were going at it on the Pope's Bed. With utter composure Mr. Rosen looked over his shoulder and said, in his deep voice, "Yes, Robert?"

Another time he opened the door to Mrs. Rosen's dressing room to find Mr. Rosen showing her his erection.

"She was interested, too. He said 'Yes, Robert?'" Separating his thumb and forefinger, not widely, Mr. Clark added, "He only had about this much."

Mr. Rosen died in the Pope's Bed — a gilded confection of spiral columns made for Pope Urban VIII, and worthy of Bernini himself — after suffering a stroke in the Burgundian Library a few days earlier. Mr. Clark helped carry him to bed, Mr. Rosen garbledly asking (Mr. Clark insisted), *"Wherzahellimywallet?"*

The Clarks never much liked the Rosens' daughter, either. They keenly resented how in earlier years, whenever she saw either of them in Katonah, Mrs. Stern would cross the street rather than greet them.

Certainly Mrs. Stern was adept at ignoring me. I met her weeks after I started when she and her husband, New York Philharmonic principal cellist Carl Stern, came out in a Cadillac limousine to discuss house-museum matters over lunch. Mr. Stern was a large, friendly man of presence; his prostate cancer was advanced and he died not long afterwards.

Mrs. Stern's first husband — as the Clarks couldn't keep their faces straight in telling me — had also been a cellist. János Scholz, a teacher of Yo-Yo Ma's, during their marriage started the famous collection of Renaissance drawings he later donated to the Pierpont Morgan Library. The Clarks, scandalized that his favorite weekend wear was a pair of cutoff jeans with the pockets cut out, said he'd been compulsively unfaithful.

In similar vein, when Felice Harriman Francis, the

daughter of Mr. Rosen's brother Felix T. Rosen (a partner at Hayden, Stone) visited one day, Mr. Clark told me that as a young woman she was known for always carrying a condom in her purse.

Soon after the Clarks moved to Caramoor, their infant child died. Mrs. Clark bitterly recalled Mr. Rosen's trying to comfort her by telling her how much harder it is to lose a grown child. (The Clarks said that, on being notified of his son's death, Mr. Rosen sat down at the Music Room piano and played for hours.)

According to Mr. Clark, Mrs. Rosen's sole affair during her widowhood was with a Commandant of West Point in the 1950s.

Early on I took my parents and younger brother through the house and introduced them to the Clarks, who were charmed when Daddy thanked them for all they were doing for me.

UNFORTUNATELY, MR. CLARK was never quite sober. He kept a glass of Seagram's Seven going all day long, parking it on the pantry windowsill.

Preparing the cocktail tray, he would crack open a fresh fifth of Jack Daniel's, pour himself and Mr. Sweeley stiff drinks (and offer me one, too, which I generally, but not always, declined), top off the bottle at the tap, pour Miss D'Arcy's cranberry juice and Mr. Bailey's soft drink, fill a bowl with Fritos, add napkins, shoulder into his black jacket, carry the tray to the sitting room, come back, shoulder out of the jacket and take his drink over to his cottage, the ice rattling as he worked his way under the Music Room.

This was part of oldest Caramoor tradition. Mr. Clark

assured me that although Mr. Rosen always marked his bottles, that never prevented their being got at and topped off at the tap up to his mark.

He'd soon return to repeat the process, except staying to set the glass-topped table while his wife cooked, then announcing dinner, serving the plates she prepared and retrieving the tray from the sitting room.

After dinner Mr. Sweeley *et al.* retired to the sitting room to watch the color TV with a fire blazing. Often while watching his programs Mr. Sweeley would wax and polish some bronze object, leaving it for me to take back in the morning.

When Mr. Clark brought him a nightcap, he would remind Mr. Sweeley that he was activating the alarm. "Thank you, Robert," Mr. Sweeley would doubtless say. The announcement effectively restricted him to the East Wing for the rest of the evening; Mr. Bailey undertook to replenish his glass thereafter, evading the alarm's electric eyes and floor traps by taking a circuitous route to the pantry.

Mr. Clark, meanwhile, after pouring himself another drink and partially topping off the bottle, retired to his cottage.

But despite his statement, he would not, in fact, arm the alarm. Doing so — at the keypad behind the pantry — launched a countdown that gave him scant time to get to the far side of the Music Room and through the door to his cottage before all hell broke loose and the police arrived, and he was not a man interested in moving briskly, especially as the evening wore on.

At intervals, then, without risk of tripping the alarm, he would return to the pantry for refreshers. He must have discontinued topping off the bottle before the sour mash came to look like weak tea. In any event, by evening's end, between him and Mr. Sweeley, it was empty — as Mr. Clark put it, another "dead soldier."

Despite the furtiveness, I doubt there was much in the nightly routine not known to everybody — except, as developed later, about the alarm.

When Mr. Sweeley was not in residence, the alarm was kept armed. If I went over, I had to punch in the code within so many seconds of opening the door. It regularly malfunctioned: We'd know it had silently alerted the police by a cruiser's arrival; fortunately, they were cheerful about it. Sometimes it went off audibly, a bell screaming from the West Wing roof.

THE CLARKS THREW a party my first summer, and it was there that I drank hard liquor for the first time. A fellow guest named Percy, whom Mr. Clark knew from the American Legion, spontaneously offered me a job with his tree-trimming company; six months later Percy fell from a limb to his death. Among the guests were members of Mrs. Clark's women's club, the backbone of her social life; on club luncheon days, she'd fix Caramoor's lunch sandwiches right after breakfast, her hair tightly permed and mascara memorable.

At some point memory ceases — I blacked out for the only time in my life thus far, waking up next morning on the floor of my bedroom beside a puddle of vomit.

I was told Ronnie Clark had walked me home, and that the whole way I called and crooned to the wife of the young family that briefly rented the cottage across the archway from mine. Embarrassed, I rang her bell and apologized; she laughed and said she thought it funny. (Probably it was fortunate my first experience drinking was thus disastrous.)

Those neighbors acquired a puppy, which sat barking plaintively in the archway, the noise reverberating past endurance. "Dogs bark," my neighbor informed me when I complained. "Cats meow."

That was a reference to the two kittens a friend of Mother's pressed on me. The timid one ran off early on, when I made a scene about his soiling the rug. The other I formally passed on to my successor, a friend of my younger brother's. I keenly regret not doing better for them; it took too many years for me to learn how one must keep faith with one's animals.

After those neighbors moved out, a widowed Hurok colleague of Mr. Sweeley's moved in and went to work in the office. There were bumps—Mrs. Clark rebelled at having "another pair of feet shoved under my table!" and I'm afraid I jibed at cleaning her cottage weekly—but we got past them, and she even took me to the Bedford Playhouse to see *Butch Cassidy and the Sundance Kid* and *The Prime of Miss Jean Brodie*.

She stayed only a short time, however. She might have found too little to do, or been put off by Caramoor's very gay ménage. (Sometimes when I told people—at the Bedford Hills book store, for instance—where I worked the response was a knowing exchange of glances, noses wrinkled.)

One summer night Ronnie Clark and his wife Peggy Taylor swept me in their convertible along with young Mulligans and Taylors to the Mahopac drive-in to see *The Adventurers*. Perfect!

Peggy Taylor, a big and big-hearted woman, lived with her husband in the substantial stucco house past the Venetian Theater with a goat tethered in the yard. Mrs. Rosen had wanted Peggy and Ronnie to work in the city house, but he didn't like being indoors (though one winter he'd Minwaxed the big house's every interior door); hence, his job as superintendent, at which he worked hard.

Peggy's two brothers worked summers with Ronnie, as did sometimes their one-armed uncle. The brothers were just younger than I, with Afros blond and brunette, respectively, and an aversion to wearing shirts. Mr. Clark later told me the younger died in the late '70s of a drug overdose.

Even as Caramoor became more of a year-round operation, annual rhythms persisted. In the fall a crew boarded up the summer porch with Plexiglass panels stored in my garage. Winter was very quiet; some weeks Mr. Sweeley *et al.* stayed in town instead of coming out for the usual three or four days.

And it was spring when the winter wrappings were removed from Malvina Hoffman's bronze busts of Mr. Rosen and his son in their courtyard corner niches, and Ronnie brought the pickup truck into the Spanish Courtyard for Vito to oversee unloading the tubbed orange trees fresh from their winter sojourn off his greenhouse. Also, restorers came out to fill and smooth the outdoor sculptures and balustrades.

After school let out for the summer, one of Ray Mulligan's sons swept the Spanish Courtyard every morning.

THE MUSIC FESTIVAL in late June and July brought bonuses—a stipend of $20 per concert. (I was hired at $40 a week; two raises took that to $70, ample pay for essentially a part-time job with perks including housing and Blue Cross.)

The bonuses were generous but hard-earned money. Performers and musicians packed the summer porch for buffet meals: scrambled eggs, sausage, bacon, fruit, toast, English muffins and Entenmann's coffee cake for breakfast; soup, salad and sandwiches for lunch and dinner, loads of coffee all day long.

I helped serve and clean up from early to late. Artists—and sometimes their boyfriends—bunked upstairs in the West

Wing, in the ground-floor suite across the archway from the sitting room, and in the cottage next to mine, and I cleaned, made beds, scrubbed bathrooms. Frequent guests included Andrea Velis, Frank Corsaro and Tito Capobianco.

Rosalind McCag, a sweet local widow, volunteered in the office at Festival season. She used to urge me to come over and meet her garage apartment's young tenant, Loudon Wainwright III; she thought we'd hit it off, but of course I was too shy. So weary did Mrs. McCag get on concert days of giving out the same information over and over that she took to answering the phone with, "This is a recording. Tonight's performance . . ." George Sharp, Rosen Foundation Chairman, called one morning. "Goddamn it!" he barked at her "recording," and five minutes later roared up in his Mercedes, to her vast amusement.

Mr. Sweeley fell ill every year at Festival time. I remember his hemorrhaging on the toilet one morning while Mr. Bailey called an ambulance. He was in the hospital a week that year, as most years.

I didn't fare entirely well during the Festival myself, having an upset stomach most concert days (Mrs. Clark pressed ginger ale on me). Spanish Courtyard concerts were the worst, for they brought crowds swarming around the big house and cottages. People constantly tried the doors, sometimes actually managing to step inside the big house and taking it badly when asked to leave. The Clarks told me one Festival day they'd gone home to find a family picnicking at their dining-room table.

Once the New York Pro Musica, disregarding my warning, broke into the Burgundian Library, and its members were taking turns sitting in the Ferdinand-and-Isabella chair when I fetched Mr. Sweeley. Furious, he declared they would not be back.

At Spanish Courtyard concerts I served as doorman for the performers. In my first season, when Rudolf Firkušný, waiting out an ovation, admired the Music Room ceiling, I accidentally misinformed him it was Spanish (its central carved walnut section in fact comes from a palazzo in Lecce, Italy, the outer sections being painted plaster casts of it).

After the Guarneri Quartet played I passed a woman's note to its heartthrob violinist. For the use of Peggy Wood and Cyril Ritchard I placed a pitcher of ice water onstage, and for the monks' eerie singing entrance (and exit) in *Curlew River* I opened the summer-porch door on cue in the dark; it was Caramoor's privilege to give several Benjamin Britten operas their North American premieres.

For Venetian Theater performances Miss D'Arcy and Mr. Bailey manned a ticket booth beside Malvina Hoffman's Horse Head gates, while Ronnie Clark, George Clark and various Mulligans and Taylors directed cars into rows on the big lawn. Afterwards, 30 or 40 invited guests would attend a Spanish Courtyard reception — elegant affairs, save for the one Mr. Clark dampened by drunkenly shooting Champagne corks over people's heads.

Rehearsals could be memorably lovely. One evening I wandered the Cedar Walk with Mother and my younger brother as Julius Rudel conducted *Eine Kleine Nachtmusik*. On another, having invited family friends to the dress rehearsal of Purcell's *Dido and Aeneas*, I was mortified when Maureen Forester "marked," no sound issuing from her open mouth.

But her actual performance was memorable, as were Andrea Velis's in Monteverdi's *Combattimento di Tancredi e Clarinda* and Maralin Niska's and George Shirley's in Mozart's *Idomeneo*, whose ballet dancers swabbed the stage with Coca-Cola for a better grip. Astounding productions; so deliciously aristocratic to stage opera in the backyard!

Mrs. Rosen in 1957 commissioned the visionary architect Frederick Kiesler to build a theater around the classical colonnade long set up on the Lawn of Columns. (Mr. Sweeley likely knew him from their mutual involvement with the Juilliard School.)

The Venetian Theater is one of the very few Kiesler designs actually constructed, though his plans may not have been carried out completely. His vibrant autobiography *Inside the Endless House* (I read the Burgundian Library's copy) devotes a section — "Final Proportions," pp. 88-93 — to what he calls a "somewhat crucial incident," a "tour de farce" that makes for a funny but cutting vignette.

For, having approved his plans for the theater, "Mrs. Wright" changes her mind and decides she wants the structure's width cut by one foot. So as to demonstrate the necessity of the change, she whisks Kiesler out in her "dream Cadillac" to inspect the site:

> It reminded me of the limousine arrivals at a duel in
> the bois, seen so often in French films.

There Kiesler manages to persuade "Mrs. Wright" that his plans' proportions are correct, even as he registers the fact that she does not intend to follow his blueprints for converting the lawn to a tri-level tiled plaza surrounded by a covered arcade with tiers of stadium seating for inclement weather.

But the next morning, her "managing director" — not named, but clearly Mr. Sweeley — having stayed up until 3 a.m. discussing the matter with "Mrs. Wright," shows up at Kiesler's studio "in a whiff of urgency" to press again for the reduction in width:

He spoke directly to the drawing board (with its blueprints of the theater on it) as if hypnotized by it and without once turning toward me . . . Beads of sweat appeared on his forehead. I became concerned at his concern . . . Evidently it was not the foot. It was the anguish of not granting a wish important to the lady of the theater.

Obligingly, Kiesler forthwith cuts *three* feet from the Venetian Theater's width, and notes ruefully:

We architects and designers should take a course in diplomacy at an early stage of our professional game.

THE HOUSE MUSEUM first opened, in a small way, soon after the 1970 Festival. Bronzed-metal and Plexiglass barriers were installed at the West Wing doorways and rubber mats laid through the Music Room and hedged with velvet ropes. Stanchions bore descriptions of rooms and furnishings written by A. Hyatt Mayor. He began a downgrading of objects that apparently continues—the Cellinis became *school of,* the Canaletto *school of,* the Cranach *school of.*

Studying each room from the visitors' vantage point, I arranged such things as lamp cords and call-button wires to be minimally intrusive, and—probably not wisely—replaced dim bulbs with brighter ones. Also, I cleaned out the hearths, removing kindling and newspaper in some cases decades old and laying the shapeliest new logs I could find. When tours were scheduled—at first, just a few groups of not more than four on Saturdays; later, on Fridays as well—it was my job to light the house—rather an undertaking.

Miss D'Arcy was the original tour guide. I think she surprised herself by enjoying it. She greeted visitors at the gate, brought them into the Spanish Courtyard, checked their names off her list and collected the fees.

They entered the house at the courtyard's southwest corner, if need be hanging up coats in the cloakroom and using the guest suite's bathroom. Then she brought them past the front door and the West Wing's downstairs rooms, through the Music Room (everybody gasped), across to anteroom, powder room and dining room, and into the courtyard again. The Rosens' bedroom was not on the tour, though always asked after; people were also curious about the pantry and kitchen.

One day Miss D'Arcy showed Dame Judith Anderson through the house (Mrs. Clark and I were great fans of her Mrs. Danvers in *Rebecca*), and another time Mr. Sweeley guided Adolf Loewi, the Venice (later, Beverly Hills) dealer who sold so many things to the Rosens—a tottering old man murmuring pleasure at once again seeing his rooms and objects.

In 1971 the local Junior League rallied round to lead tours under Miss D'Arcy's aegis, and Mr. Bailey started to give tours, too. Soon, so did I.

I enjoyed showing people through the house and the incentive it gave me to study the new materials, as well as the original inventories and auction catalogs. It all bore fruit. I was a loopily enthusiastic success, my only difficulty paring my tour to a manageable hour's length.

The first time someone thanked me with a handshake transferring a folded $5 bill, I gave it back. But I learned fast, and soon was netting $10 or $15 on Saturday afternoons. The visitors were mainly groups of ladies or older couples, a remarkable proportion of the men offering wartime reminiscences of rescuing art stolen by the Nazis – I heard four or five such tales, which I wish I'd taken note of.

I liked to eavesdrop on the competition from the pantry, or from the cellar steps, or from the foyer between the Burgundian Library and *La Loggia* bedroom (a Theremin was stored in that foyer until Mr. Sweeley donated it to the Katonah Public Library). The Junior League ladies were hopeless. Miss D'Arcy was inaccurate, too, but winningly enthusiastic in employing the grandeur around her to glorify her friend Mrs. Rosen and – by reflection – herself.

Miss D'Arcy's describing herself as Mrs. Rosen's friend made the Clarks apoplectic: *Not* a friend, they insisted, more a *companion*. Nor was she a salaried employee, but as an interior decorator she earned commissions on items ordered for the house, from new cushions for the 28 dining-room chairs to the 1,400 rolls of toilet paper that arrived one day.

She was a small woman, always in black and perhaps already past 70. Mrs. Clark said she'd told her about being briefly married to a cruel man, and she told me she had an apartment at 53rd and Lex. And there ends my knowledge of her.

An anxious and uncomfortable person, given to gobbling Empirin, Miss D'Arcy was at Caramoor, I gathered, on the thin security of her history with Mrs. Rosen and on Mr. Sweeley's sufferance. But she was good to me, apt to slip me $5 bills folded into minute squares, saying, "You're *marvelous*." Mr. Clark mocked her unrelentingly; one day he imitated her ungainly gait as she headed up the East Wing from breakfast that morning farting at every step.

The Clarks did respect Mr. Sweeley, however. A native of Idaho, he'd earned degrees from the Juilliard School before going to work for Sol Hurok, whence Mrs. Rosen poached him for her Festival. That his father was a famous college football player, later a lawyer and judge, I had no idea. He used to play (and play well) the grand piano on the Music Room stage; *Don Giovanni*, he told me, contains the best music ever written.

Mr. Sweeley's lover, Mr. Hornung—they shared an apartment in Manhattan and, according to the Clarks, a house in northwest Connecticut—visited Caramoor only once in my time. As directed, I made up the bed in Mr. Rosen's dressing room for him, but the next morning reported to the half-scandalized Clarks, "No one slept in that bed."

The night of his visit marked the low point of my tenure. Shortly after I went to bed Mr. Clark woke me up with a phone call to tell me Mr. Sweeley wished to see me at the Rudels', but to come by the big house first. I pulled on my clothes and found Mrs. Clark waiting with an armload of sheets and pillowcases, her expression reading, *"You're in trouble now!"*

Mr. Sweeley was almost speechless with anger—the Rudels were expected at any moment, but I'd not made up their beds. In the next room Mr. Hornung remarked, "He's in a tizzy, all right."

I apologized, made the beds and all was well. The lapse was mine, though I may not have known the protocol for an off-season visit; but having been specially tasked to clean the place, should have had the wit to think about beds.

EVERY MONTH OR two Mr. Sweeley gave a dinner party for some half dozen guests. It was my helping serve at them that enabled me, in consultation with the Clarks, to style myself not merely *houseman* but *underbutler*.

I enjoyed these evenings. I put on black pants, white shirt, Freddie's old black jacket, a skinny black tie and shoes bought on Mr. Clark's recommendation, made of a black matte mesh with rubber soles (he assured me they were more comfortable than patent leather, and that no one would notice the difference).

Also, I put on a stern mien.

A tour being always part of the guests' evening, I'd go over early and light the house. Cocktails and after-dinner drinks were served in the Music Room, at the center circle of Louis XIII needlepoint armchairs.

Once a young guest beat me there and, mistaking me for a fellow diner, nervously introduced himself. I shook his hand, introduced myself, stepped over a rope and began turning on lamps. Mr. Clark said that whenever the Rosens spent an evening in the Music Room, they stationed a houseman with a phonograph in the musicians gallery to play records.

Only twice did we feed dinner guests at the smaller table: the composer Hans Werner Henze once, another time Mrs. Fritz Reiner, who complained about receiving no royalties for use of her husband's recording of *Thus Sprach Zarathustra* in *2001: A Space Odyssey*.

Everybody else got the full treatment at the main table, and Mr. Clark set a beautiful table indeed. Atop a Renaissance silk runner he arranged a floral centerpiece flanked by purple 18th-century Waterford salt cellars and candelabra. The cover plates were red-and-gold 18th-century Chinese exportware, and there were ranks of crystal and silver (which I helped polish). The room glittered from the ancient mirrors at the ceiling to the blue-and-silver 18th-century Chinese wallpaper (supposedly left over from Horace Walpole's Strawberry Hill), Giles Grendy's spectacular suite of *chinoiserie* chairs, lighted vitrines of coral, jade and rock-crystal carvings, the gilt bureau made for Frederick the Great and the E.F. Caldwell wedding-cake chandelier with tiers of yellowing silk shades.

Though it was not antique, I admired the table, too, with its gorgeous surface of tortoiseshell lacquer.

Mrs. Clark had two dinner-party entrees, leg of lamb (despite its being particularly "heavy") and roast beef. With both, soup — generally consommé from a can, if somewhat juiced up, or her own excellent lentil — and salad, roast potatoes, vegetables and a selection of ice creams: The good, plain cooking she proudly laid claim to.

Except for the butter and the soup, which we placed on the table ourselves, Mr. Clark and I carried serving dishes around for guests to help themselves, whether to salad, dressing, rolls, meat, gravy, horseradish, potatoes, vegetables, walnut sauce or chocolate syrup, every course signaled by Mr. Sweeley's ringing a bronze handbell that never failed to remind me of Mass. Accidents were few, generally limited to a lettuce leaf floating unremarked to the floor.

Mr. Clark made the textured butterballs beforehand, wielding a pair of paddles, then storing them in ice water.

Before dessert, he cleared the tabletop of crumbs, while I brought round the fingerbowls, a slice of lemon floating in each (after Mrs. Rosen died, Mr. Clark proposed doing away with fingerbowls, but Mr. Sweeley overruled him).

Guests included Mrs. Rosen's friend Marian Anderson and her husband; Martin Mayer; Alan Rich; Harold C. Schonberg; Carll Tucker III, and old friends and Girdle Ridge Road neighbors Paul G. Hoffman and his wife, Anna M. Rosenberg (Mr. Clark was especially respectful towards her, the former Assistant Secretary of Defense), as well as numerous "friends of Caramoor," *i.e.*, donors.

The Clarks told me that the grandest dinner party the Rosens ever gave took place in 1946, in honor of the

Headquarters Commission charged with finding a site for the United Nations. It recommended establishing a Vatican City-like enclave over more than 6,000 acres of Westchester and Fairfield Counties starting just south of Caramoor; in the event, such ad hoc groups as the Greenwich People's Committee (probably less Marxist-Leninist than it sounds) beat back the idea.

Although Mr. Sweeley occasionally grumbled that Julius Rudel had delusions of grandeur, he and his wife and sometimes their children dined on many occasions. Once Mr. Sweeley drunkenly announced to the table that he wished he had a son like me; I replying that would be all right with me, a Rudel daughter piped up, "What's going on here?"

Before one dinner party a terrible thunderstorm passed overhead; delicious, from inside the house. It was then only 40 years old but seemed ancient, certainly to me, and creaked impressively in all weathers; no wonder that the maids, as Mr. Clark claimed, had thought it haunted. (The Old Man's early-morning tours in his nightshirt, coffee cup in hand, scared them, too, he said.)

During my first dinner party Mr. Sweeley edged round the portholed swinging door to inform the ceiling that we could be heard at table; thereafter we kept our laughter and carrying on down to more subdued levels.

An odd point of tension was that we persisted in washing up by hand, despite Mr. Sweeley's (at William's urging) buying a portable dishwasher; but it was my preference as well as Mr. Clark's to wash by hand, although there was a great deal to wash. Mr. Sweeley would sometimes hang from the door to ask sadly why we weren't using his dishwasher.

And I got leftovers! At the end of the evening, Mrs. Clark would wrap a platter in aluminum foil, and I'd happily carry it home and feast with the kitties.

IN 1971 I got contact lenses and a driver's license, and bought (for $600) what proved a reliable 1966 VW Bug with 60,000 miles. The Clarks assured me I was entitled to a weekly tank of gas, which I felt better about after Mr. Bailey one day saw me filling up at the garage pump and said nothing.

With a car I could do everything I needed to: shop at the Katonah A&P ($20 bought two big paper sacks of groceries), or on Bedford Road at Caldor or the Bedford Barn, swing by the new McDonald's or see movies at the Bedford Playhouse ($1 on Monday), get to the library and bank, take my younger brother to our swimming hole in Brewster. Having a car expanded the solitary, if pleasing, nature of my life, but also made me feel I needed more money.

Soon I started working weekend nights as a security guard at the Hammond Museum in North Salem. Mr. Clark put me on to it—he'd worked that shift as a Pinkerton for several years (and also briefly guarded Seven Springs, the nearby Eugene Meyer estate, now Donald Trump's). When a new firm took over the Pinkerton's contract, he joined it and suggested that I do, too.

The crucial thing was to get there on time so as to relieve the guard on duty. I failed only once, the night of a Music Room reception for the Junior League that included the showing (by a projectionist who'd met Alfred Stieglitz) of a filmed 1950s TV interview with Mrs. Rosen. Riveting! Such posture, poise, enunciation in a high, mid-Atlantic, upper-class voice!

The affair went late, but the Clarks took over the dishwashing and off I dashed, probably hearing en route *American Pie* and *Maggie May,* radio hits of the day.

The Hammond Museum was a modest concrete-block structure atop a hill, featuring, at the times I saw it, a dramatically dark and foggy view, usually with a donkey braying nearby. It seemed mainly a museum of Miss Natalie Hays Hammond's tourist souvenirs; I don't recall seeing her own paintings.

She was a sweet, vague old lady, of interest to me because I knew that her father, John Hays Hammond, had been a spectacular personality of the 19th Century, Cecil Rhodes' $1 million-a-year mining engineer and a friend of Mark Twain's. Miss Hammond lived in a neighboring concrete-block Colonial with her cousin Miss Taylor, a handsome and commanding woman who on visits to Caramoor over the years incited Mr. Clark's lust; no less for his thinking her a Lesbian.

BY AUGUST 1971 I felt I should make more serious plans for my future. One Sunday I went up to Mr. Sweeley as he and Mr. Bailey sunbathed in the courtyard beside the 16th-century marble wellhead lately installed as a fountain (supplanting the birdbath that had long since replaced the dovecote) and gave my notice. "I'm not surprised," he said bitterly.

My job went to my younger brother, already working as a gardener for Ronnie Clark and living in an annex to Vito's cottage. Moving back to my parents', I enrolled in a BOCES architectural drafting course and took on a full-time night shift at the Hammond Museum.

The duties were hardly onerous — an hourly tour of building and grounds, an early a.m. refilling of the Japanese Garden's pond — but the hours proved brutal, and for all that it paid $2.50 an hour and gave me ample time to read, that

November I chucked both job and course to become a dining-room usher at Colonial Williamsburg's Williamsburg Inn, living in an employee dormitory. After an antic and enjoyable holiday season in Virginia, I realized it was another wrong turn and, kindly welcomed back to Caramoor, moved back into the chauffeur's cottage.

But first I spent my Christmas earnings on six weeks in Europe. Caramoor influenced that trip, sending me to Italy first. Flying Icelandic Airlines to Luxembourg (round trip: $168), I took an overnight train for Venice, where, at Mr. Sweeley's suggestion, I saw the Tintorettos at the Scuola di San Rocco, and at the Palazzo Rezzonico found doors painted by Tiepolo that were companions to those in Caramoor's dining room. Florence, Rome (I was amused to find a snack bar on the roof of St. Peter's), Paris; then two weeks in London, where the City cobbler who resoled my shoes remarked that, given the nails coming up into my feet, I was doing my penance on this earth. Another of Mr. Sweeley's suggestions took me through the Wallace Collection, and I saw Laurence Olivier in *Long Day's Journey into Night*.

I beat my postcards home; not having heard from me, Mrs. Clark concluded that, just as she expected, I'd been murdered.

In the summer of 1972 I took six weeks off — my younger brother again standing in for me — and made a 12,000-mile driving tour around the country, managing to work in a visit to San Simeon, having seen Biltmore the year before.

One evening Mr. Sweeley asked my brother to bring up a box from the front cellar. It contained 19th-century correspondence, and my brother said Mr. Sweeley and Miss D'Arcy spent the evening glancing at letters and tossing them into the fire while watching TV.

When my brother married in 1975, Mr. Sweeley graciously permitted the ceremony to take place on the Cedar Walk beside the statues and the reception at the tennis pavilion, where he and Miss D'Arcy came by to bestow their good wishes.

THE ROSENS' CITY house was sold around the time I started at Caramoor, and much furniture and many objects from it brought out and crammed into the big house—into the help's quarters over the garage (five bedrooms, two bathrooms, dining room), Freddie's room and the Ping-Pong Room—as well as into the barn beneath the Rudels'.

In 1972 much of the influx was sent to auction, and a new wing to house the rest begun to Mott B. Schmidt's design. I still think a better solution would have been to build across the hall from the downstairs West Wing rooms (so featureless is the West Wing's exterior that at my first sight of it I'd asked Chris, "Where's the house?") or converting the help's quarters, but Mr. Schmidt preferred to break up the house's pretty front with a new block.

Some nice rooms were thus lost: The cloakroom with Lalique sconces a few steps up from the front door; next to it, Freddie's room and bathroom; the guest suite; an exterior entrance and a staircase to the family room. Spiral stairs displaced the Ping-Pong Room; carpenters worked on them for months, with Mr. Schmidt coming out most afternoons to oversee progress.

The new restrooms were in use by visitors before I left, but the new wing's interiors, including several period rooms, were installed later. The new roof tiles were garishly red compared to the weathered old ones; Mr. Schmidt suggested daubing them with honey to promote their patination, but that seems not to have been done.

ONE NIGHT TOWARDS the end of my time there Caramoor was burglarized. I discovered the theft while lighting the house for a 10:00 o'clock tour the next morning. Coming sleepily from the West Wing into the Music Room, I saw that the Cranach—a princess peering deliciously past a velvet curtain—was gone from its place to the left of the Spanish alcove. The Cellini bronzes were gone, too, the male nude from beneath the Cranach, the horse from below the charming Guardi of a boy holding a string tied to a bird on the alcove's right side.

Though there was always the possibility that Mr. Sweeley had taken the bronzes to polish, that wouldn't explain the Cranach. Then I noticed a casement window open behind the draperies in the eastern bay and a broken pane; putting out my head, I found myself looking down our tallest ladder, which usually rested on the ground beside the Music Room's cellar.

I ran to Mr. Bailey, he called the police, and we all stood about regarding the open window while Mr. Clark, to my discomfiture, repeated, "Had to be a *young* man to get through there."

The police talked to all of us. Press showed up, too; the White Plains *Times-Dispatch* quoted anonymous me saying, "I understand the police want to question me?" (Next day's *Times'* front-page story referred to an unnamed "young caretaker" discovering the theft.)

Then the FBI took over. Two agents arrived and spoke to Mr. Sweeley and Mr. Clark. Afterwards, filling his pipe in the pantry, Mr. Clark told me to be sure when they interviewed me to confirm that the alarm had been armed the night before. But—I objected—it never is when Mr. Sweeley's in the house.

No, Mr. Clark agreed, but *say* so.

The FBI men—one very young—duly sat me down in the sitting room and asked for my account of discovering the burglary. I gave it, and they asked if the alarm had been on overnight, and I said no, it hadn't. (Sorry, Mr. Clark! Priggish of me? I suppose; when I mentioned the incident to my father 45 years later, he said, "I hope you didn't contradict Mr. Clark.")

In any case, everything was eventually recovered, although the last time I spoke to him Mr. Sweeley told me the Cranach had suffered damage.

My conscience in fact was not entirely clear, because my younger brother and I used to challenge each other: If you were going to burglarize Caramoor, how would you do it? I remember pretending to scheme one afternoon as, looking for leaks, we clambered over the Music Room roof (glimpsing that day—through a trapdoor in the musicians gallery ceiling?— the attic with its mighty steel girders). I've always wondered whether the burglars might not have taken Miss D'Arcy's tour; she always waxed most eloquent about precisely the things they stole.

The denouement proved controversial. Some months later, the Westchester County District Attorney announced the return of the stolen items, crediting two men, both with extensive burglary rap sheets—a pair seemingly straight out of the pages of Donald E. Westlake—for overseeing return of the loot in exchange for immunity from prosecution.

Adding to the controversy was that the deal immunized the same pair against prosecution for an unrelated burglary in Rye, from which, however, not all the items stolen were recovered. The burglars claimed to have robbed Caramoor on the orders of an unnamed patron who died before taking the loot off their hands.

A couple years later the same two men entered into another agreement with prosecutors, returning several Thomas Eakins masterpieces stolen from the Greenwich estate of Joseph Hirshhorn in exchange, once again, for immunity.

But perhaps karma exists: Years later, one thief's application for a license to run a White Plains boarding house was turned down because of his rap sheet.

GEORGE CLARK KILLED himself in the spring of 1974 by going into the big house's garage one night and starting the cars. It had space for five—a sixth space was fenced off for the generator—and the car keys dangled from a board behind the pantry. My dad wrote me in Siena, Italy, to tell me about it; there must have been a story in the *Patent Trader*.

His parents soon retired and moved with Mrs. Coyle upstate to a house near Sherburne, next door to the farmhouse Ronnie Clark had been renovating for years, and Mr. Clark stopped drinking. At some point, too, Ronnie Clark moved upstate to farm full-time.

In 2014 I saw Billy Wilder's *Sabrina* for the first time since watching it with George one evening at the chauffeur's cottage, and was dismayed to find that Audrey Hepburn's character attempts suicide by starting the cars in a mansion's garage (fortunately, Humphrey Bogart discovers her in time).

The last time I saw George Clark was for lunch at a Katonah café in January 1974 before I left for a year in Italy. He radiated pain, wincing as he looked out from a face carved of large features, surveying me wonderingly, lost, unreadable and unreachable.

That same day I swung by the big house to say hello, was

greeted by Mr. Sweeley, Miss D'Arcy and Mr. Bailey in friendly fashion, and with them watched President Nixon give a press conference in blinding California sunshine.

I also shared a great new idea with them: That Caramoor should host a jazz festival. How they laughed, Mr. Sweeley with his great booming, seldom-heard laugh—laughed and laughed! Gratifying to see that somebody had the same idea and how well established jazz is today at Caramoor.

I visited the Clarks in their new home in the summer of 1976, when Mrs. Coyle was still alive and Mrs. Clark's cats banished, at her husband's insistence, to a shed. On New Year's Day 1980 Mrs. Clark died unexpectedly of a heart attack, and at Mr. Clark's request I visited for a week. I think I last spoke to him in about 1984.

The last time I spoke to Mr. Sweeley was in 1976, on Katonah Avenue. From half a block away I saw him and shouted, *"Mr. Sweeley! Mr. Sweeley!"* Stopping as if shot in the back, he turned around, and I recall him as being distinctly cool.

But my final sight of him came years later in New York, on an afternoon in 1992 or so as my gay running club— Frontrunners—gathered in Central Park at West 72nd Street for its Wednesday evening run. In my peripheral vision I saw Mr. Sweeley walk past weeping. I knew he had an apartment on Central Park West, so didn't exactly take him to be an hallucination, but neither did I greet him.

I wish I had, or got in touch with him later; I owe Mr. Sweeley a great deal, which he deserved to hear me acknowledge. I hope he never regretted hiring me. He was only ever good to me. But I did think his continuing to live in the big house à la Mrs. Rosen, waited on hand and foot, rather farcical.

Also I wish I'd managed to be a better friend to George

Clark, and kept up better with his father; what would it have cost me? And I still lament the end of my friendship with Chris Benda, who I gather at some point transitioned to female. But what a teen-aged underbutler can never know is the substratum of grief and regret on which this world revolves.

SOON AFTER MY move to Caramoor the big house began to infuse itself into my dreams, and it has never left off doing so. Mr. Clark said he dreamed of the house, too. Though long hallways and sometimes specific rooms figure in them, my dreams mostly take place in spaces behind, below or over the Music Room — in spaces that in fact don't exist.

While I worked there, I was jealous of Caramoor's size and grandeur — wanted it to be overwhelmingly palatial, and was sorry to find San Simeon and Biltmore both so much more so. But Caramoor wasn't built for size or display for its own sake — rather, to house a family and a beloved, rather motley collection of architectural elements, furniture, objects and art, and in its eccentricity it manages to express the personalities that built it, including the ingenious puzzle-solving faculty that fits disparate elements into a more or less harmonious whole.

My last visit came in 1989, when I brought a vanload of college students, customers of the student-group business I was running that year. I didn't announce myself or ask after anyone, and encountered no one I knew. A lady whom I didn't recognize (but who I now think might have been Mrs. Gifford, a sweet friend of Mrs. Rosen's (*wanna-be* friend, according to the Clarks)) sat us down in the Music Room and in an exotic accent proceeded to tell us "a love story — the love story of

Walter and Lucie Rosen, and how they came to build Caramoor," and someone else showed us through the house.

This visit reconciled me to letting go my wish for grandeur—helped me realize at last that Caramoor in fact stands in scale with the Rosens' intentions and needs—in its way is *perfect*.

At the end of 1972, just turned 20, having gotten my GED and rejecting Mr. Sweeley's kind suggestion that I keep my job while commuting to NYU for an art history degree, I left to enter the University of Colorado. Although I realized there might be a future for me at Caramoor if I wanted it, slow as I was to mature, instinct told me I'd already absorbed what it had to offer.

But it's my great good fortune that my time at Caramoor has proved to be a moveable feast.

www.ingramcontent.com/pod-product-compliance
Lightning Source LLC
Chambersburg PA
CBHW050243110726
47898CB00007B/2263